SF: AUTHORS' CHOICE 4

SF:

AUTHORS' CHOICE 4

edited by HARRY HARRISON

G. P. Putnam's Sons, New York

CONTENTS

INTRODUCTION

In the first *Authors' Choice* volume, Theodore R. Cogswell wrote this comment:

> The only memory I have of writing any of my stories is that what took place seemed to me to be an inevitable process. . . . Writing is seduction. And I've never quite decided who is doing what and to whom.

He went on in greater detail to assure the friendly reader that it was impossible to tell anything about a story that was not already there in the story itself. Yet in this same anthology Philip José Farmer wrote a description of the background and preparation for writing his story that was three-quarters as long as the story he was writing about.

In case you are beginning to get the feeling that authors are an individualistic, withdrawn, outgoing, quiet, noisy, unthinking, intellectualizing bunch of people—why you are completely right. You have to be an individualist to be a writer as these comments prove over and over again. The name of the game we are trying to play here is insight; we are attempting to pin down some factor or factors in the act of creation that will add new dimensions to the stories themselves. The authors have been asked to contribute a story they feel particularly fond of, not necessarily their favorite story but one upon which they look with a feeling of some warmth. They were particularly encouraged to uncover stories they felt should have been anthologized and that have been overlooked by the dim-witted editors. Once these stories were selected each author then had complete freedom to say just what he wanted about it including, as in the case of Mr. Cogswell, the observation that the whole thing is a foolish and impossible task.

This series started in a small way. The first volume was filled with stories by writers whom I knew and respected, whom I wanted to pin down to some description of the creative process. The results were so satisfying that other volumes followed. There are enough good and professional authors in the field of science fiction to fill far more than that single book, and while I cannot claim to have captured every one of them, I have managed to run a large percentage to earth. There is no particular sequence to the volumes other than that I have tried, in each of them, to balance new authors against old practitioners in order to give a more complete spectrum of the writing being done in science fiction today. In this present anthology we have the celebrated Arthur C. Clarke balanced against the rising star of James Tiptree, Jr. Though balance is an unfair word. They are both laborers in our particular stainless steel vineyard. It was E. M. Forster who, while writing on the art of the novel, visualized all of the novelists of history as writing away at the same time in the reading room of the British Museum. Certainly it is a valid image, since books are shelved together and read at the same time no matter what their age. The same is true of science fiction. H. G. Wells was a nineteenth-century author, yet I recently saw one of his novels in the drugstore nestled against a short story collection of Brian W. Aldiss. I don't think either of them suffered from the association and the proximity.

So while the novelists scribble away in the British Museum, the science fiction writers are also hard at work—but where? Perhaps in the cabin of some great spaceship with the stars of interstellar space shining through the portholes like those familiar holes in a blanket. I have tiptoed around this cabin and disturbed a few of those hard at work here and have asked them to take a look at their labors and to tell us about it.

Here is what they said.

HARRY HARRISON

SF: AUTHORS' CHOICE 4

OLD HUNDREDTH

Brian W. Aldiss

The whole human cavalcade is slowly on its way to the future, numbers swelling as it goes. Year by dusty year, the cavalcade grows noisier, while the innocent creatures dwelling in its track have more and more cause to be anxious about its depredations.

Where is it going? How long has it got to reach its unknown goal? And those who reach the goal—what relationship will they bear to those who set out blindly so many generations before?

These profound questions await answer. As yet, we can hardly understand them, even when they are applied to our own individual lives. But a writer may be allowed to sketch some sort of tentative answer now and again.

I have no religious faith. Unfortunately, I have a profoundly religious sense of life, and can't break the habit. Even when I was a child, I found myself viewing what went on about me sub specie aeternitatis. This may sound like a case of alienation, but the fact is that nowadays—it would be unfair to speak up for that silent and long-vanished child—I enjoy a strong sense of being part of the flows and tides of Earth.

In our generation, we are accustomed to thinking of Earth as a kind of spaceship which uses the sun as power-source while recycling all its abundant but not infinite resources. The stuff of which we are made, and the natural world about us, is a recombination of the stuff of which the early amoebae in the primordial ocean, the lowly plants which first covered the land, the slow dinosaurs, the men of the Stone Age, the Angles, Saxons, and

Jutes, and Uncle Tom Cobbleigh and all were made. Everything that once existed now exists. From this it follows that we also will inevitably be ground down to provide the basic ingredients for new recipes of life throughout the remaining millions of years of Earth's history. And all our science and technology, on which we place such great store, is not going to alter the situation.

A sense of this large harmony is what I tried to impart in "Old Hundredth," using a veritable old harmony at the centre of the story to give body to my intention. Or so I tell you, reader, now, some dozen years after I wrote it. I'm speaking now in a critical cool; at the time, in creative heat, things may have looked a little different.

As the critic Edmund Crispin has observed, I have a special feeling for the autumnal, and "Old Hundredth" is, in his words, "a dream of the last long autumn of Earth" (I think American readers would agree that the word "fall" would be misleading here). Much else that Crispin says about the story is too flattering to be quoted; but I may add that it was one that gave me pleasure even before he favoured it with his commendation, perhaps because I came somewhere near to achieving what I was attempting.

Although I was trying to make everything old and dusty and— we need a word for Bygone-in-the-future—I was aiming at joy, rather in the way that C. S. Lewis gets joy into his novel Out of the Silent Planet, *and in a strange fashion joy does still move like a serpent through the paragraphs—for me at least, rereading it before sending off a copy to Editor Harrison for the latest volume in his series.*

To be more prosaic about the subject. The title originally had a double meaning. Ted Carnell wrote to me in 1960 asking for a special contribution to the centennial number of New Worlds *which he edited. I wanted to write an especially appropriate something, and the title "Old Hundredth" immediately came bubbling to the surface and would not go away.*

Good old Ted! Nobody else could have performed his mam-

moth task of making bricks with so little straw as he did for so long. He had every reason to celebrate his long haul to Number 100. No other British magazine lived so long. He paid on acceptance, too, and I got a check for ten pounds sterling on May 25, 1960. The story was anthologized in that year's Best SF, edited by Judy Merril (remember Judy Merril?), when it earned rather more than ten pounds. Since then, it has been reprinted half-a-dozen or so times.

It's just an animal story. But in the background you can hear the murmur of the human cavalcade.

—Brian W. Aldiss

The road climbed dustily down between trees as symmetrical as umbrellas. Its length was punctuated at one point by a musi-column standing on the sandy verge. From a distance, the column was only a faint stain in the air. As sentient creatures neared it, their psyches activated it, it drew on their vitalities, and then it could be heard as well as seen. Their presence made it flower into pleasant noise, instrumental or chant.

All this region was called Ghinomon, for nobody lived here any more, not even the odd hermit Impure. It was given over to grass and the weight of time. Only a few wild goats activated the musi-column nowadays, or a scampering vole wrung a brief chord from it in passing.

When old Dandi Lashadusa came riding down that dusty road

on her baluchitherium, the column began to intone. It was just an indigo trace on the air, hardly visible, for it represented only a bonded pattern of music locked into the fabric of that particular area of space. It was also a transubstantio-spatial shrine, the eternal part of a being that had dematerialized itself into music.

The baluchitherium whinnied, lowered its head, and sneezed onto the gritty road.

"Gently, Lass," Dandi told her mare, savouring the growth of the chords that increased in volume as she approached. Her long nose twitched with pleasure as if she could feel the melody along her olfactory nerves.

Obediently, the baluchitherium slowed, turning aside to crop fern, although it kept an eye on the indigo stain. It liked things to have being or not to have being; these half-and-half objects disturbed it, though they could not impair its immense appetite.

Dandi climbed down her ladder onto the ground, glad to feel the ancient dust under her feet. She smoothed her hair and stretched as she listened to the music.

She spoke aloud to her mentor, half the world away, but he was not listening. His mind closed to her thoughts, he muttered an obscure exposition that darkened what it sought to clarify.

". . . useless to deny that it is well-nigh impossible to improve anything, however faulty, that has so much tradition behind it. And the origins of your bit of metricism are indeed embedded in such a fearful antiquity that we must needs—"

"Tush, Mentor, come out of your black box and forget your hatred of my 'metricism' a moment," Dandi Lashadusa said, cutting her thought into his. "Listen to the bit of 'metricism' I've found here, look at where I have come to, let your argument rest."

She turned her eyes about, scanning the tawny rocks near at hand, the brown line of the road, the distant black and white magnificence of ancient Oldorajo's town, doing this all for him, tiresome old fellow. Her mentor was blind, never left his cell in Peterbroe to go farther than the sandy courtyard, hadn't physically left that green cathedral pile for over a century. Woman-like, she thought he needed change. Soul, how he rambled on! Even now, he was managing to ignore her and refute her.

". . . for consider, Lashadusa woman, nobody can be found to father it. Nobody wrought or thought it, phrases of it merely *came* together. Even the old nations of men could not own it. None of them knew who composed it. An element here from a Spanish pavan, an influence there of a French psalm tune, a flavour here of early English carol, a savour there of late German chorals. Nor are the faults of your bit of metricism confined to bastardy. . . ."

"Stay in your black box then, if you won't see or listen," Dandi said. She could not get into his mind; it was the Mentor's privilege to lodge in her mind, and in the minds of those few other wards he had, scattered round Earth. Only the mentors had the power of being in another's mind—which made them rather tiring on occasions like this, they would not get out of it. For over seventy years, Dandi's mentor had been persuading her to die into a dirge of his choosing (and composing). Let her die, yes, let her transubstantio-spatialize herself a thousand times! His quarrel was not with her decision but her taste, which he considered execrable.

Leaving the baluchitherium to crop, Dandi walked away from the musicolumn towards a hillock. Still fed by her steed's psyche, the column continued to play. Its music was of a simplicity, with a dominant-tonic recurrent bass part suggesting pessimism. To Dandi, a savant in musicolumnology, it yielded other data. She could tell to within a few years when its founder had died and also what kind of a creature, generally speaking, he had been.

Climbing the hillock, Dandi looked about. To the south where the road led were low hills, lilac in the poor light. There lay her home. At last she was returning, after wanderings covering half a century and most of the globe.

Apart from the blind beauty of Oldorajo's town lying to the west, there was only one landmark she recognized. That was the

Involute. It seemed to hang iridal above the ground a few leagues on; just to look on it made her feel she must at once get nearer.

Before summoning the baluchitherium, Dandi listened once more to the sounds of the musicolumn, making sure she had them fixed in her head. The pity was her old fool wise man would not share it. She could still feel his sulks floating like sediment through his mind.

"Are you listening now, Mentor?"

"Eh? An interesting point is that back in 1556 by the old pre-Involutary calendar your same little tune may be discovered lurking in Knox's Anglo-Genevan Psalter, where it espoused the cause of the third psalm——"

"You dreary old fish! Wake yourself! How can you criticize my intended way of dying when you have such a fustian way of living?"

This time he heard her words. So close did he seem that his peevish pinching at the bridge of his snuffy old nose tickled hers too.

"What are you doing *now*, Dandi?" he inquired.

"If you had been listening, you'd know. Here's where I am, on the last Ghinomon plain before Crotheria and home." She swept the landscape again and he took it in, drank it almost greedily. Many mentors went blind early in life shut in their monastic underwater dens; their most effective visions were conducted through the eyes of their wards.

His view of what she saw enriched hers. He knew the history, the myth behind this forsaken land. He could stock the tired old landscape with pageantry, delighting her and surprising her. Back and forward he went, flicking her pictures; the Youdicans, the Lombards, the Ex-Europa Emissary, the Grites, the Risorgimento, the Involuters—and catch-words, costumes, customs, courtesans, pelted briefly through Dandi Lashadusa's mind. Ah, she thought admiringly, who could truly live without these priestly, beastly, erudite, erratic mentors?

"Erratic?" he inquired, snatching at her lick of thought. "A thousand years I live, for all that time to absent myself from the world, to eat mashed fish here with my brothers, learning history, studying *rapport,* sleeping with my bones on stones—a humble being, a being in a million, a mentor in a myriad, and your standards of judgment are so mundane you find no stronger label for me than erratic? Fie, Lashadusa, bother me no more for fifty years!"

The words nattered and squeaked in her head as if she spoke herself. She felt his old chops work phantom-like in hers, and half in anger half in laughter called aloud, "I'll be dead by then!"

He snicked back hot and holy to reply, "And another thing about your footloose swan song—in Marot and Beza's Genevan Psalter of 1551, Old Time, it was musical midwife to the one hundred and thirty-fourth psalm. Like you, it never seemed to settle!" Then he was gone.

"Pooh!" Dandi said. She whistled Lass.

Obediently the great rhino-like creature, eighteen feet high at the shoulder, ambled over. The musicolumn died as the mare left it, faded, sank to a whisper, silenced: only the purple stain remained, noiseless, in the lonely air. Lass reached Dandi. Lowering its great Oligocene head, it nuzzled its mistress's hand. She climbed the ladder on to that ridged plateau of back.

They made contentedly towards the Involute, lulled by the simple and intricate feeling of being alive.

Night was settling in now, steady as snow. Hidden behind banks of mist, the sun prepared to set. But Venus was high, a gallant half-crescent four times as big as the Moon had been before the Moon, spiralling farther and farther from Earth, had shaken off its parent's clutch to go dance round the sun, a second Mercury. Even by that time Venus had been moved by gravito-traction into Earth's orbit, so that the two sister worlds circled each other as they circled the sun.

The stamp of that great event still lay everywhere, its tokens not only in the crescent in the sky. For Venus put a strange spell on the hearts of man, and a more penetrating displacement in his genes. Even when its atmosphere was transformed into a muffled breathability, it remained an alien world; against logic, its opportunities, its possibilities, were its own. It shaped men, just as Earth had shaped them. On Venus, men bred themselves anew.

And they bred the so-called Impures. They bred new plants, new fruits, new creatures—original ones, and duplications of creatures not seen on Earth for aeons past. From one line of these familiar strangers Dandi's baluchitherium was descended. So, for that matter, was Dandi.

The huge creature came now to the Involute, or as near as it cared to get. Again it began to crop at thistles, thrusting its nose through dewy spiders' webs and ground mist.

"Like you, I'm a vegetarian," Dandi said, climbing down to the ground. A grove of low fruit trees grew nearby; she reached up into the branches, gathered and ate, before turning to inspect the Involute. Already her spine tingled at the nearness of it; awe, loathing and love made a part-pleasant sensation near her heart.

The Involute was not beautiful. True, its colours changed with the changing light, yet the colours were fish-cold, for they belonged to another universe. Though they reacted to dusk and dawn, Earth had no stronger power over them. They pricked the eyes. Perhaps too they were painful because they were the last signs of materialist man. Even Lass moved uneasily before that ill-defined lattice, the upper limits of which were lost in thickening gloom.

"Don't fear," Dandi said. "There's an explanation for this, old girl." She added sadly, "There's an explanation for everything, if we can find it."

She could feel all the personalities in the Involute. It was a frozen screen of personality. All over the old planet the structures stood, to shed their awe on those who were left behind. They were the essence of man. They were man—all that remained of him.

When the first flint, the first shell, was shaped into a weapon, that action shaped man. As he moulded and complicated his tools, so they moulded and complicated him. He became the first scientific animal. And at last, via information theory and great computers, he gained knowledge of all his parts. He formed the Laws of Integration, which reveal all beings as part of a pattern and show them their part in the pattern. There is only the pattern, the pattern is all the universe, creator and created. For the first time, it became possible to duplicate that pattern artificially; the transubstantio-spatializers were built.

All mankind left their strange hobbies on Earth and Venus and projected themselves into the pattern. Their entire personalities were merged with the texture of space itself. Through science, they reached immortality.

It was a one-way passage.

They did not return. Each Involute carried thousands or even millions of people. There they were, not dead, not living. How they exulted or wept in their transubstantiation, nobody left could say. Only this could be said: man had gone, and a great emptiness was fallen over the Earth.

"Your thoughts are heavy, Dandi Lashadusa. Get you home." Her mentor was back in her mind. She caught the feeling of his moving round and round in his coral-formed cell.

"I must think of man," she said.

"Your thoughts mean nothing, do nothing."

"Man created us; I want to consider him in peace."

"He only shaped a stream of life that was always entirely out of his control. Forget him. Get on to your mare and ride home."

"Mentor—"

"Get home, woman. Moping does not become you. I want to hear no more of your swan song, for I've given you my final word on that. Use a theme of your own, not of man's. I've said it a million times and I say it again."

"I wasn't going to mention my music. I was only going to tell you that . . ."

"What then?" His thought was querulous. She felt his powerful tail tremble, disturbing the quiet water of his cell.

"I don't know. . . ."

"Get home then."

"I'm lonely."

He shot her a picture from another of his wards before leaving her. Dandi had seen this ward before in similar dreamlike glimpses. It was a huge mole creature, still boring underground as it had been for the last twenty years. Occasionally it crawled through vast caves; once it swam in a subterranean lake; most of the while it just bored through rock. Its motivations were obscure to Dandi, although her mentor referred to it as "a geologer." Doubtless if the mole was vouchsafed occasional glimpses of Dandi and her musicolumnology, it would find her as baffling. At least the mentor's point was made: loneliness was psychological, not statistical.

Why, a million personalities glittered almost before her eyes!

She mounted the great baluchitherium mare and headed for home. Time and old monuments made glum company.

Twilight now, with just one streak of antique gold left in the sky, Venus sweetly bright, and stars peppering the purple. A fine night for being alive on, particularly with one's last bedtime close at hand.

And yes, for all her mentor said, she was going to turn into that old little piece derived from one of the tunes in the 1540 *Souter Liedekens*, that splendid source of Netherlands folk music. For a moment, Dandi Lashadusa chuckled almost as eruditely as her mentor. The sixteenth-century Old Time, with the virtual death of plainsong and virtual birth of the violin, was most interesting to her. Ah, the richness of facts, the texture of man's brief history! Pure joy! Then she remembered herself.

After all, she was only a megatherium, a sloth as big as an elephant, whose kind had been extinct for millions of years until man reconstituted a few of them in the Venusian experiments. Her modifications in the way of fingers and enlarged brain gave her no real qualifications to think up to man's level.

Early next morning, they arrived at the ramparts of the town Crotheria where Dandi lived. The ubiquitous goats thronged about them, some no bigger than hedgehogs, some almost as big as hippos—what madness in his last days provoked man to so many variations on one undistinguished caprine theme?—as Lass and her mistress moved up the last slope and under the archway.

It was good to be back, to push among the trails fringed with bracken, among the palms, oaks, and treeferns. Almost all the town was deeply green and private from the sun, curtained by swathes of Spanish moss. Here and there were houses—caves, pits, crude piles of boulders or even genuine man-type buildings, grand in ruin. Dandi climbed down, walking ahead of her mount, her long hair curling in pleasure. The air was cool with the coo of doves or the occasional bleat of a merino.

As she explored familiar ways, though, disappointment overcame her. Her friends were all away, even the dreamy bison whose wallow lay at the corner of the street in which Dandi lived. Only pure animals were here, rooting happily and mindlessly in the lanes, beggars who owned the Earth. The Impures—descendants of the Venusian experimental stock—were all absent from Crotheria.

That was understandable. For obvious reasons, man had increased the abilities of herbivores rather than carnivores. After the Involution, with man gone, these Impures had taken to his towns as they took to his ways, as far as this was possible to their natures. Both Dandi and Lass, and many of the others, consumed massive amounts of vegetable matter every day. Gradually a wider and wider circle of desolation grew about each town (the greenery in the town itself was sacrosanct), forcing a semi-nomadic life on to its vegetarian inhabitants.

This thinning in its turn led to a decline in the birth rate. The travellers grew fewer, the towns greener and emptier; in time they had become little oases of forest studding the grassless plains.

"Rest here, Lass," Dandi said at last, pausing by a bank of brightly flowering cycads. "I'm going into my house."

A giant beech grew before the stone façade of her home, so close that it was hard to determine whether it did not help support the ancient building. A crumbling balcony jutted from the first floor. Reaching up, Dandi seized the balustrade and hauled herself on to the balcony.

This was her normal way of entering her home, for the ground floor was taken over by goats and hogs, just as the second floor had been appropriated by doves and parakeets. Trampling over the greenery self-sown on the balcony, she moved into the front room. Dandi smiled. Here were her old things, the broken furniture on which she liked to sleep, the vision screens on which nothing could be seen, the heavy manuscript books in which, guided by her know-all mentor, she wrote down the outpourings of the musicolumns she had visited all over the world.

She ambled through to the next room.

She paused, her peace of mind suddenly shattered by danger.

A brown bear stood there. One of its heavy hands was clenched over the hilt of a knife.

"I am no vulgar thief," it said, curling its thick black lips over the syllables. "I am an archaeologer. If this is your place, you must grant me permission to remove the man things. Obviously you have no idea of the worth of some of the equipment here. We bears require it. We must have it."

It came towards her, panting doggy fashion with its jaws open. From under bristling eyebrows gleamed the lust to kill.

Dandi was frightened. Peaceful by nature, she feared the bears above all creatures for their fierceness and their ability to organize. The bears were few: they were the only creatures to show signs of wishing to emulate man's old aggressiveness.

She knew what the bears did. They hurled themselves through

the Involutes to increase their power; by penetrating those patterns, they nourished their psychic drive, so the Mentor said. It was forbidden. They were transgressors. They were killers.

"Mentor!" she screamed.

The bear hesitated. As far as he was concerned, the hulking creature before him was merely an obstacle in the way of progress, something to be thrust aside without hate. Killing would be pleasant but irrelevant; more important items remained to be done. Much of the equipment housed here could be used in the rebuilding of the world, the world of which bears had such high haphazard dreams. Holding the knife threateningly, he moved forward.

The Mentor was in Dandi's head, answering her cry, seeing through her eyes, though he had no sight of his own. He scanned the bear and took over her mind instantly, knifing himself into place like a guillotine.

No longer was he a blind old dolphin lurking in one cell of a cathedral pile of coral under tropical seas, a theologer, an inculcator of wisdom into feebler-minded beings. He was a killer more savage than the bear, keen to kill anything that might covet the vacant throne once held by men. The mere thought of men could send this mentor into shark-like fury at times.

Caught up in his fury, Dandi found herself advancing. For all the bear's strength, she could vanquish it. In the open, where she could have brought her heavy tail into action, it would have been an easy matter. Here, her weighty forearms must come into play. She felt them lift to her mentor's command as he planned for her to clout the bear to death.

The bear stepped back, awed by an opponent twice its size, suddenly unsure.

She advanced.

"No! Stop!" Dandi cried.

Instead of fighting the bear, she fought her mentor, hating his hate. Her mind twisted, her dim mind full of that steely fishy one, as she blocked his resolution.

"I'm for peace!" she cried.

"Then kill the bear!"

"I'm for peace, not killing!"

She rocked back and forth. When she staggered into a wall, it shook; dust spread in the old room. The Mentor's fury was terrible to feel.

"Get out quickly!" Dandi called to the bear.

Hesitating, it stared at her. Then it turned and made for the window. For a moment it hung with its shaggy shabby hindquarters in the room. Momentarily she saw it for what it was, an old animal in an old world, without direction. It jumped. It was gone. Goats blared confusion on its retreat.

"Bitch!" screamed the Mentor. Insane with frustration, he hurled Dandi against the doorway with all the force of his mind.

Wood cracked and splintered. The lintel came crashing down. Brick and stone shifted, grumbled, fell. Powdered filth billowed up. With a great roar, one wall collapsed. Dandi struggled to get free. Her house was tumbling about her. It had never been intended to carry so much weight, so many centuries.

She reached the balcony and jumped clumsily to safety, just as the building avalanched in on itself, sending a great cloud of plaster and powdered mortar into the overhanging trees.

For a horribly long while the world was full of dust, goat bleats, and panic-stricken parakeets.

Heavily astride her baluchitherium once more, Dandi Lashadusa headed back to the empty region called Ghinomon. She fought her bitterness, trying to urge herself towards resignation.

All she had was destroyed—not that she set store by possessions: that was a man trait. Much more terrible was the knowledge that her mentor had left her forever; she had transgressed too badly to be forgiven this time.

Suddenly she was lonely for his persnickety voice in her head, for the wisdom he fed her, for the scraps of dead knowledge he tossed her—yes, even for the love he gave her. She had never seen him, never could: yet no two beings could have been more intimate.

She missed too those other wards of his she would glimpse no more: the mole creature tunnelling in Earth's depths, the seal family that barked with laughter on a desolate coast, a senile gorilla that endlessly collected and classified spiders, an aurochs —seen only once, but then unforgettably—that lived with smaller creatures in an Arctic city it had helped build in the ice.

She was excommunicated.

Well, it was time for her to change, to disintegrate, to transubstantiate into a pattern not of flesh but music. That discipline at least the Mentor had taught and could not take away.

"This will do, Lass," she said.

Her gigantic mount stopped obediently. Lovingly she patted its neck. It was young; it would be free.

Following the dusty trail, she went ahead, alone. Somewhere far off one bird called. Coming to a mound of boulders, Dandi squatted among gorse, the points of which could not prick through her thick old coat.

Already her selected music poured through her head, already it seemed to loosen the chemical bonds of her being.

Why should she not choose an old human tune? She was an antiquarian. Things that were gone solaced her for things that were to come.

In her dim way, she had always stood out against her mentor's absolute hatred of men. The thing to hate was hatred. Men in their finer moments had risen above hate. Her death psalm was an instance of that—a multiple instance, for it had been fingered and changed over the ages, as the Mentor himself insisted, by men of a variety of races, all with their minds directed to worship rather than hate.

Locking herself into thought disciplines, Dandi began to dissolve. Man had needed machines to help him to do it, to fit into the Involutes. She was a lesser animal: she could unbutton herself into the humbler shape of a musicolumn. It was just a matter of *rearranging*—and without pain she formed into a pattern that was not a shaggy megatherium body . . . but an indigo column, hardly visible. . . .

Lass for a long while cropped thistle and cacti. Then she ambled forward to seek the hairy creature she fondly—and a little condescendingly—regarded as her equal. But of the sloth there was no sign.

Almost the only landmark was a faint violet-blue dye in the air. As the baluchitherium mare approached, a sweet old music grew in volume from the dye. It was a music almost as old as the landscape itself and certainly as much travelled, a tune once known to men as The Old Hundredth. And there were voices singing: "All creatures that on Earth do dwell. . . ."

FAIR

John Brunner

Every story has a story behind it, one way or another. . . . This one, "Fair," was written in 1955 and first appeared in the March, 1956, issue of New Worlds SF. *If a dedicated collector takes the trouble to go and consult his files of that magazine, he will discover that it was listed last on the contents page, and, what's more, under the name of "Keith Woodcott."*

And then, if he pursues the matter far enough to check the results of the readers' poll on that issue, which appeared a few months later, he will find that it's duly credited to Brunner after all.

What had happened was simply that the late E. J. Carnell, then editor of NWSF, had been worried about the "avant-garde" quality of the story and had felt it might alienate some of the readers who, by then, were coming to regard me as a writer worth following. Accordingly he had said he would publish it only if I would let him use the Woodcott name, previously employed on those occasions when I had more than one story in the same issue. (In Science Fantasy *17 I had three and briefly became "Trevor Staines" as well!)*

I was a trifle disgruntled because I felt, and still do feel, that it was a good piece of work. However, you can't afford to bite the hand that feeds you, and at that time the Nova magazines were virtually my only market, so I consented.

Somewhat to Ted's astonishment, the reaction from the readership was altogether very favorable, and when it came to pub-

lishing the votes sent in, he clean forgot about the pseudonym.

Now behind that story-behind-the-story there's another story. I had originally written the opening section, about 1,800 words of it, still earlier; I was in fact in my teens. But I couldn't maintain the pressure at which that first scene had come boiling out. It went just so far and stopped dead. I knew, though, that it was pretty damned good, so I didn't—fortunately—throw it away; I kept it lying around until the day arrived when I happened to glance at it again and said to myself, "Ah! That's how the rest of it ought to go!"

And it did, and it did. Eventually it was described by a contributor to the NWSF letter-column as "worthy of inclusion in an anthology of the best of anything"—heady words to a novice like me, pregnant with encouragement at a time when (as I've explained above) even very experienced editors were immensely reluctant to take on any story that smacked of being "difficult" or "experimental." In fact, there was nothing experimental about this one at all, except insofar as it represented a departure from the very plain type of narrative I'd used in most of my earlier work. A personal experiment, though, doesn't make a story experimental in the ordinary sense.

All of which leads one into an area which is perennially tempting to a writer of SF: that type of parallel-world speculation which revolves around the question, "How would my career have turned out if such-and-such a story had been accepted when I first wrote it, instead of years later?"

One thinks of Edmond Hamilton's What's It Like Out There? which he wrote in the thirties but which didn't see print until the fifties. One thinks, equally, of Philip José Farmer's gigantic award-winning novel which had the carpet pulled out from under it owing to a certain party's reputed dishonesty, and which has only recently surfaced in the guise of the "Riverworld" series. And so on.

In my own case, I wonder what would have happened to my career if The Squares of the City had been published the year I wrote it (1960) instead of five years later, and nine years later in Britain. And what would have happened if someone had published Manalive, *my novel about the CND movement, which my London agent said was at the time the best thing of mine he had read . . . but which was sat on from springtime to November by a famous left-wing publisher in the year before the last Aldermaston March, and which the Society of Authors did not get back for me until after its topicality had been destroyed forever.*

Well, life is full of little disappointments . . . and some not so little!

This, though, is the reverse of a disappointment. It's a real pleasure to be able to introduce "Fair" to the public all over again. For one thing, I'm proud of it. Normally, when a story that dates as far back as this one is scheduled for reprinting, I revise it completely; "Fair" I have been able to leave untouched. And for another thing I'm reminded whenever I think about it that despite the petty wrangling we've seen in recent years about the "right" and the "wrong" way to write SF, the readership can sometimes be a lot more open-minded than even a skilled editor imagines.

And that, essentially, is what the story's about: openmindedness. Here's to it—it's good stuff.

—John Brunner

"Roll up! Roll up!"

The words were English, and therefore human, but the vocal cords behind it were electrons strung out on a wire, the resonating chambers which gave it volume the vacuum in radio tubes, the throats which sent it blasting its message into the night multiple and gigantic.

"YOU'LL FIND IT HERE! WHATEVER IT IS!"

. . . Wrapped in a gaudy package three miles across and tied with a blood-red bow. The package is more important than the merchandise; wrap it right and the one-every-minute men (and women) will buy. And buy. And buy.

"DO YOU WANT ROMANCE?"

Maybe he was a genius, the man who got that shuddering, suggestive, leering note into that sterile mechanical uncomprehending roar. He was certainly a success.

"DO YOU WANT THRILLS?"

Add sub- and supersonics to taste; result, a rising of the hair on the back of the neck, a fearful but somehow pleasant tonic dose of adrenalin through the system. Knowing how it's done makes no difference. It reminds the maiden lady of the night she was *sure* there was a man following her—but she doesn't come here, does she? We can forget about her. It reminded Jevons of the sensation of hanging in space produced by turning over on top of a loop—fifty, a hundred thousand feet above the earth, at a thousand, fifteen hundred miles an hour.

"DO YOU WANT AMUSEMENT?"

Some people are amused by odd things, the monstrous tone seemed to imply, faking a conniving, understanding innuendo which it could never have possessed, a tolerance of human foibles which it did not know except as figures in an accounting bank. There was a hint of a belly laugh; Jevons thought wildly of Moloch, and his brazen stomach filled with fire.

"WELL? COME AND GET IT!"

But there was one thing they didn't offer, something you weren't supposed to want because there wasn't any of it to speak of. Peace and quiet.

"SEE THE COLOSSAL—WATCH THE TREMENDOUS— COME TO THE GIGANTIC—"

Have you nothing but superlatives in your vocabulary? Jevons found the mechanical voice setting up a conversation in his mind; he was talking to the overtones, verbally duelling with an intelligence that wasn't there. And, in a way, he was answered.

"THIS IS THE BIGGEST! THIS IS THE BEST!"

Lights! Sound! (No camera—this is *here* and *now* and *real*.) ACTION! Okay, boys, roll 'em! Where? Why the hell should I care? In the hay, maybe. After all, it's up to you. Who are *you*? Why the hell should I care? I'm a machine. But for the sake of argument with yourself, you might be Alec Jevons, ex-test pilot, ex-serviceman, ex-child and ex-husband, ex-this and ex-that, ex-practically everything. Even approaching the ultimate—almost an ex-*man*. But I started out with an advantage. I was *never* human. I don't know what I'm missing.

"—shillings please. That will be five shillings please. That will be five shil—"

This is *here* and *now*—remember that. It isn't at home and it isn't five thousand miles away, and home is where the heart is except that hearts haven't got anything to do with it and you know what people are like five thousand miles away—*don't you*? You're supposed to; after all, you've been told often enough. Be a good boy and say *ugh*.

The turnstile clicked, and as if it had been the cradle switch of a phone sounding, the undercurrent dialogue in Jevons's head went with it. The brass-lunged giant had served its purpose; he was inside. Once he was in, the giant became aware of him as a symbol in a computer memory bank, a member statistic in a profit and loss account. But he no longer heard its voice.

Overhead, the rolling way; he could hear it rumble a basso ostinato to the twiddling discordant flashy runs in the right hand which the soprano, alto and tenor cries of the concession-holders flung at random into the night. They offered to scare him out of his wits, to shock him and/or delight him; they offered to let him prove himself—various things. Kind of them, thought Jevons sourly. To let you pay for admission, pay them as well, and then get you to do the work.

He walked forward blindly into the swirl and whirl of the Fair, down one of the mile-long arteries which bore the lifeblood of the machines towards its multiple hearts. The lifeblood was money; the people were incidental, ornery, hard to cope with. Money obeyed the rules of statistical distribution, and what you gained upon the roundabouts you lost upon the swings, in general, except when man—the wild factor—decided to be cussed and awkward. Then you changed the rules.

The crowd broke around him like polychrome waves against a granite rock, and that wasn't too bad as a metaphor except that the rock too was moving. It *was* grey as granite, compared to the humming-bird gaudiness of the flush-faced girls, the black-and-white starkness of the boys (implication: efficiency, masculinity, no nonsense). He walked straight ahead, which would have been impossible for most people; he attracted stares. For one thing, he was—not young. The other fairgoers were, for the most part. Youth is the hectic time. The remainder were recapturers of youth, busy failing to re-create more than an awareness that they could not stand the pace so well any more, never realising that if the young people they envied could have their elders' self-knowledge and so little false pride they too would have admitted that the pace was less than ecstatically bearable.

They stared for a moment. Then—somehow—they forgot to notice the wrinkles on his face, the grey hairs at his temples. Instead, they noticed his shoulders, and read purpose—incomprehensible, hence to be shunned, to be feared, to be hated—behind the watery blue eyes. He looked dangerous. Therefore he managed to walk a straight path through the Fair, which would have been to most men impossible and to all women unthinkable, what with the youths lounging at corners waiting for a woman to impress, snatch at, crush casually—if their ennui had reached extreme—and toss back as if she were an undersized fish into the running rolling stream carrying the life-blood of money to the organs of the Fair—the steam organs, electronic organs, pseudo-human organs like the throats of the shouting giant who roared out across the countryside to come and be merry, even if you didn't eat anything but salted nuts and popcorn and even if you drank nothing but a milk-shake (correction: soya-milk-shake; everything at the Fair was expensive, but not prohibitive, for that slowed down the lifeblood's trickle) for tomorrow we die, or if not tomorrow then the next day or the next.

I shouldn't be here, thought Jevons suddenly. This is a place for people who can't think and must do. I'm a person who can do but must think. Why did I come here, anyway? Looking for an answer? And if so, what's my question?

"Lonely, honey?"

Lord above, is she really so bad she has to solicit right here in the Fair? Guess she must be.

"Go to hell!"

And that's liable to be my answer, thought Jevons. If I ever find a question that makes even as much sense as hers.

He reached the base of a spiraling escalator, channeling a flow into the upper level of the Fair—the level of the rolling way which was an entertainment in itself, worth the entrance money alone, if one was young and agile and with fast reflexes. The outer strip girdled the Fair at five miles an hour, but the inmost one was doing fifty. Escalators—laid out flat, mostly. But you could be bumped if you stayed on more than once around the Fair; the spot on which you stood remembered your weight and incited you to patronise a concession instead of a service. The game was to stay on your feet at a fifty-mile lick after completing the circle.

Or so he'd heard. The Fair had been less elaborate in his young days. Watch it, Jevons! You're starting to admit your age. (And why not? Because if you remember that you've been around so long, you admit that you were responsible—this was your doing, this mechanical time-destroying hurlyburly, this feverish seeking after temporary nirvana. *This was your fault!*)

All right, admit your age in terms of time, but not in terms of senility. The spiral escalator wound its challenge at him, and he thrust aside a youth in black whose shoulder bulged with the shape of a gun. It had to be one of the modern plastic models, or the scanners at the gate would have taken it away. Almost too late Jevons flung an acid and unmeant apology towards the muzzle of the weapon where it had suddenly appeared in the boy's hand; the spiral had taken him out of sight and range before the whitening finger could close on the trigger, but he heard the scream from the disappointed girl, the gunman's companion: "Whyncha do it, huh? Whyncha? Ya think I wanna be alla time with a bassard who can be shoved aroun' like he was—"

The escalator's inverted peristalsis pushed him out like vomit from its yellow-lipped mouth, on to the upper level, and the Fair was all around him, swirling and breathing like angry water. The noise was redoubled. Across the way from him the crowd parted and the source of screaming, frenetic music was plain: a band of girls in minuscule costumes blasting through shiny brass horns, and one thundering out incessant rhythm on a kit of amplified drums. She was fat; she shook. In an ecstasy of concupiscence by proxy a fat old man on the next concession stared and shook between howling the attractions of his show.

The way scampered past him, a hundred feet broad, in sections. He had had reflexes good enough to put ten or twenty tons of airplane through impossible manoeuvres fifty feet from the ground—not long ago. As if in a dream he stepped forward, adjusting to the roll and flow of the way like a dancer allowing for a clumsy partner. Ahead, a girl was being bumped for completing her circuit; she rode the writhing spot on the way for ten seconds before it flung her rolling and screaming among the feet of a party of men on the forty-mile section. One of the men gave her a sharp kick, and they were past.

Staggering, the girl made for the edge, and an Uncle in the jester's uniform which made the patrolmen of the Fair a grim joke caught her arm.

"Whatcha mean tryin' ta ride the way when ya know it's for goin' someplace else not comin' backa where ya were?"

The girl was crying, rivers of tears spreading and splotching her heavy make-up. The Uncle turned to throw her off the way, and by that time Jevons had been carried out of sight.

And what's it to you anyway? he asked himself savagely, and immediately knew that the answer was in the thrill of the beat of the rollers beneath his feet, in the shudder and grind of the occasional worn, unoiled bearing which punctuated the smooth rhythm of the ride, taking him and sliding its suppleness into the bones of his body, saying do this and do this—

—and he was sidling across the way towards the fifty-mile strip as if he had been riding the way since he was a child, taking up and absorbing ten miles an hour more at every transition without a tremor or a stumble.

This is the spot, he thought, as he finally steadied on the central strip. Okay; now do your damnedest.

Around him the Fair whirled into a multi-coloured pool of sounds and smells. There weren't many people running the way tonight. A party of kids around ten or twelve fought on to the middle strip not too far from him, but soon caught sight of an attraction ahead and tumbled away again. Watching them, Jevons was immediately back at their age, remembering how he had come out to watch the construction of this first and greatest of the Fairs, which had been only an amusement park. The roller coaster had been bigger and better than any other; that had been the start of it. Now there were others—so many others. A million people a night in this Fair alone, the slogans claimed. A million people on the run from the uncomfortable reality of silence and thought, from the danger of tomorrow, from the waiting death poised above them in the sky—which, mercifully, you couldn't see inside the Fair because it was roofed against rain . . .

And now admit the blame, will you? His relaxing body let him get at the idea and worry it like a dog with a beloved bone, shooting agony through ancient and rotting teeth in the consciousness which was the only justification for the human race, and which these people were doing their level best to lose for the space of a hectic pleasure-filled night . . .

Where did it all start? You should know; you were there at the time. Prophesy after the event—go on! It *began* when the first mother comforted her frightened child with some distraction; it went on when men forgot to grow up, when the bogeyman of childhood became the real man over the sea, the bogeyman who waited all the time to drop H-bombs and nerve-gas on the silent, comfortable homes—from which, naturally, they fled.

Oh, war was coming. It had been coming for years and years, it had always been coming and always would be until it came and no one questioned the fact any longer. As sure as you're born to a heritage of fear, he told a child ahead of him silently, it's going to come. Because people have been told it will for so long they feel it's sort of—expected of them.

And then the end of the Fairs and the beginning of hell—and yet wasn't this already hell in some people's books, this eternity of disappointment, of seeking for something forever out of reach?

Escapism. Escape. Get away. *Run*—run the way at the Fair because you might get your fool self killed, and is life worth living anyway?

All over the country, a million people a night here, those who aren't lying awake and worrying into the darkness of their rooms, those without a future—they're diving into one everlasting present, they think, only it doesn't last, for dawn comes again and again, and the sun reminds you of the hydrogen bomb and rain reminds you of a nerve-gas spray (shout it! "Gas! Gas!" And would they bother, though they've been trained in passive defence and anti-gas and anti-radiation exercises, the boys and the girls in the two years they sacrifice on the altar of hate—would they take the trouble to run further and faster than they've run already, which is all the way from reality?)

Five and a half miles at fifty miles an hour and WHOOMP the floor began to shift under his feet. The bumps started small; they would grow if he did not heed their warning. He was too far away in time—the way had not even been built then—and he shifted automatically with the ease of a surfrider taking a wave.

Well, it began—his mind ran on—and that was all right for a while. It can't hurt to flee to imagination from an imaginary menace; it's losing the battle with something real that makes it so bad.

Shift; turn. No good. Try twisting. But the data reveal to the memory bank that the same weight, plus or minus alterations caused by different distribution of it, remains. A quarter-mile too far. Half a mile.

But they had lost that battle. And it was his fault—his and all the others' who should have seen it coming. Who could have taken their lives in their hands and refused to allow the slow growth of the hatred and the fear which now dominated (no, not his children—ex-husband, likewise ex-father) these youths and their girls, tarts before they were twenty, but lost and empty and without a future since they were ten.

Three-quarters of a mile too far, and the surface of the way tossing like the Atlantic in a gale, and the man riding it without more than a twitch, an exquisitely controlled adjustment of position.

"Hey, cobbers! Here's an old cabbage who can really do it! Come eye! Say, *lookit* that 'tique-o go, babe!"

A mile too far; and the unheard-of, the improbable, but not the impossible: the relays stretched further than the designers had allowed for, the switches closed, the circuits cooled, the floor relaxing into levelness, and the way swirling onwards and onwards, round and round, until it caught up with itself—but it was not a snake, it had no threat of total disappearance hanging over it. Not that way.

"Hey, fatha! Where'd ya learn ta ride the way like that? Man, I sure wish I coulda done that! Mister how come who the hell are say fatha could you use a girl lord above antique you gave me the screamin' WHAT'S THE BIG IDEA BUSTER?"

Out of the chattering acclamation of the boys and girls, the shout of an Uncle, his face thunderous with rage and as incongruous with his gaudy jester's dress as the automatic he wore at his hip instead of a fool's bauble. Jevons was suddenly back from railing at himself and his generation, and there was noise and tinsel reality about him again. One of the youths rounded on the Uncle.

"Go cart yourself, ya lousy interferin' crot," he said in a voice as sweet as honey. The Uncle wasn't looking at or listening to him; he was seeing the expression in Jevons's eyes—the look of a ghost compelled forever to haunt the scene of the murder for which he was damned. It was that, that only which suddenly closed his mouth, damped his jauntiness, lost him again across the flowing writhing track amid the yowls of the concessionaires.

But the girl who hung on the speaker's arm looked up with adoring eyes and told him how clever he was to have driven the Uncle away, and the boy, sharp to collect his advantage, was gone with her to seek the darkness of a corner where the only intruders would be other couples bent on the same errand. The remainder of the group clamoured at Jevons, praising him, making his mind squirm with the effusiveness of their hero-worship.

"Guess you old-timers can still show us a thing or two," said one of the girls—the one he had half-heard offering to ditch her boy for him—with reluctant affected candidness; begging, pleading to be shown a thing or two her boy was too young to have learned to do properly, and Jevons felt suddenly sick.

So he had beaten the machine, the brain of glass and germanium and copper which poured out the endless river of the way. *So what?* Take your praise and stick it—well, anyway. Show you a thing or two, sister? (Daughter, more like.) You wouldn't understand what I'd like to show you; you wouldn't want to. He rebuked himself for accepting their hollow plaudits even for a fraction of a second, and their cries rang like curses behind his head as he swam blindly back across the river of mankind towards the bank, the solidity, the beach of the concessions.

"COME AND—" they blasted at him. "DO YOU WANT TO—" they screamed at him.

All right. So we began by running away from the enemy who never showed his hand. That was twenty-thirty years ago. We hated him: first because of the things we were told he was going to do, then because of the things he hadn't done after all. What heroism is there—what medals are there to be won—what glamour is there in a war which has never been fought, in a war which when it is fought will be a hell with all the appurtenances—roasting flesh and slow torment for everyone?

Goddamned lousy stinking miserable son of a—foreigner . . .

"Sorry, Jevons. We can't use you any longer."

"*What?* Why?"

"Well, your mother—"

Okay, so she was naturalised. Laughing boy is half-foreign; would those kids have smothered him with praise if they had known? If he had addressed them in the tongue he had spoken fluently before he could mumble a word of English? Would the Uncle have retreated? Would his gun have stayed in its holster? Not on your sweet life.

"I'm sorry, Alec. But you can't expect me to go on. You haven't got a job and no prospect of finding another. I'm leaving you—that's flat!" ("And I'm going to sue for divorce because of nonsupport"—only she hadn't said that; then it was just in her mind.)

Would that longing-eyed girl have offered herself body and—well, whatever she kept under that thatch of dyed hair? Never. There would have been the horror waiting a few years ahead: "Sorry, Miss—"

What the hell would her name be, anyway? A good Anglo-Saxon one, probably. Say Smith. "No, Miss Smith. We find that five years ago you—uh—associated with a man whose antecedents were open to suspicion."

Clang! went the iron gate in his mind. Now, as yet, it was only the gateway to most jobs, all government posts, all privileges; perhaps by that time it would be the entrance to a prison.

Begin by hating the man across the sea. There's no reason for it—there doesn't have to be. If you don't need a reason for hating somebody, why stop there? Why not hate the man next door? It's just as valid.

There was a concession down there on his right which had a less garish, less noisy display than most, but it was big and the posters were subtle. He was drawn towards it, aimlessly, unthinkingly.

It was popular; as he came up, the doors opened and the crowd moved out, seeming replete, seeming subdued by what they had been through: no screaming, laughing, giggling . . . What did they have done to them in there? Have the guts scared out of them? That was the sort of thing they might call fun—to run, masochistically, from a world of fear to a world of fear.

He raised his head and read slowly down the wording of the nearest poster, and at the end of it he said to himself: well, this is it. This is the ultimate betrayal. This is THE END, and you, you brass-lunged giants, can shout it for the world to hear.

The poster said—and quite quietly, in restrained lettering (which was wrong: the end of the world should be announced in bold-face type and for preference on paper edged with mourning black)—it said: BE SOMEONE ELSE! WHO DO YOU WANT TO BE? A TEST PILOT/MOVIE STAR/BIG GAME HUNTER/DEEPSEA DIVER/GREAT LOVER ! ! ! ! ! !

The picture showed a dozen unlikely dancing girls performing for a handsome, grinning youth.

There was a man in a dark suit on a platform before the ticket-booth. He was an odd barker. He used no pitch (touch a barker's pitch and be defiled, put in Jevons's mind irrelevantly). He didn't have to. The posters were enough to keep the flow going.

This was what had been going to eliminate movies and TV, Jevons remembered, before the Fairs took away their trade by offering more and better entertainment wrapped in a giant economy-size package. He had heard about it. Total sensory iden-tification was what they called it. They used it for training intelligence agents, to find out who would break fastest under what kind of interrogation, to dress a man in another personality. Tot-sensid for short. *Tot* was German for "dead," so that meant the sense of your id was dead. Joke. Ha ha.

And here it was, fouling the comparatively clean air of the Fair. Here is the last word: we save you *all* the trouble. Get out of your body as well as your worries. Don't be yourself—you're a slob anyway. Be someone bigger and better and more successful, and when it's all over everybody will be one person, and we'll change his name to Adam and this is where we came in.

"Next house just starting, sir," said the barker who was less like a barker than any other concessionaire at the Fair. "Why don't you come in? I can assure you it's very popular, our show."

It would be, thought Jevons sourly. How to "get away from it all" without even taking the trouble to *go*. Yes, and why shouldn't he take a basinful? You've come to expiate your sin, haven't you? Your sin of omission? You're here to take part in the hell you've bequeathed to the younger generation; how can you stop now?

He nodded wearily. "Yes, I'm coming in."

The room held about a hundred couches, singles, and quiet ushers divided the customers, men on the right, women on the left. Jevons saw a man (?) begging an usher to let him (?) go where he (?) wanted, and red-painted fingernails flashed as he (?) tried to press money into the usher's hand. The usher looked sick, and Jevons felt sick; he dropped himself uncaring on a vacant couch and looked at the brain-box he was supposed to slide his head into. All done without mirrors; equally, without screens or cathode-ray tubes—with only the senses of the people taking part.

Then the lights went out and a voice from nowhere cried to the audience to press their heads into position and he did so and he was no longer Alec Jevons—

But he was back in the cockpit of a plane and it was a sweet piece of machinery at that. It had a surge of power when he opened the fuel feed which flattened him against his seat; he felt the familiar swell of the g-suit, pressing the blood away from his limbs as he hurled the plane into a tight turn.

The illusion was perfect, and it struck a chord deeper than he had known existed in him. Oh, to be back where I came from! he cried out, realising with a small part of his mind that he wasn't *really* here but content to lose that knowledge—

And yet that was running away, too. What had he liked about the high and lonely reaches of the air, up there with the daytime stars? Nobody else. No more milling yelling seething humanity.

And it was over, and he was sweating. So that was why he wanted to get back into a plane which no one would ever use in the war which was supposed to be coming, instead of being down here on solid ground trying to put right the effects of those same sins of omission he was running from.

The next one was equally perfect, and he was married. He was just married. But married according to some ceremony which was foreign (and the word came with a bang up to his consciousness) and he didn't care because it was the happiest day of his life and there was a splendidly pretty girl waiting for him when night fell, and she reached out to him in the doorway of their hut (*hut?*) with her teeth standing out brilliantly in her black face (BLACK ? ? ?) and he looked down in growing astonishment and found that his skin too was black and he didn't give a damn because the sensory effects were going all the way. All—the—way. All . . . the . . . way . . .

And the lights were on, and people rose slowly, satedly and worriedly from their couches, as if there was something wrong they couldn't quite place, and yet with quiet satisfaction, and there was a sudden tenderness in the way the youths went to meet their girls, girls they had quite probably never seen before they picked them up on the edge of the way tonight. He sat for a long time on his couch with his head in his hands, until an usher tapped his shoulder.

"Do you want to stay for the next house, sir? It's a complete change of programme, you know—but we have to insist on a separate payment for each performance—"

"Yes," said Jevons with sudden decision. "Yes, I'm staying." The money he paid out represented his supper for tonight, now that he was unemployed, but hell, he had put his finger on something and he wanted to make sure what it was.

Few other people had stayed. Few others who had been a test pilot—this evening—and an African bride or bridegroom, dived with him into the eerie green-blue wastes of a Pacific pearl-fishery and became a Malay dying slowly of an overtaxed heart and overtaxed lungs and ruptured eardrums and near-starvation. It was not pleasant, but it was *real.*

Afterwards he had just been married by a ritual he did not recognise but which he guessed might well be Jewish, and the girl he had married called him dearest in the flat-sounding syllables of Russian, which he understood in a peculiar double way: half through the brain-box, half because he knew quite well what she was saying anyway.

It was that which made him gasp, and which cleared his mind and brought him up fiercely from the couch with complete disregard for the fate of the brain-box he tore off and sent him to the nearest usher to demand who was in charge.

"In charge, sir? The man you'll find on the stand in front of the concession—he's the manager."

Jevons had gone before the usher had finished speaking, was clawing at the sleeve of the man on the stand—the barker who was not like a barker. "How did you think of this?" he demanded almost savagely, in fear lest this hope should be denied him.

The barker gave him a long slow thoughtful searching look and said, "You are a very intelligent man, Mr.—?"

"Jevons. Alec Jevons."

"How do you see it, then?"

"You're teaching these people about the men and women they hate because they think they're different. They come out realising that an African and a Russian—"

"And a German and a Chinese and a Malay—that's about as far as our range goes at the moment—"

"—have exactly the same feelings and emotions, pleasures and troubles as ourselves!" Jevons finished the sentence in a flushed rush, colour boiling to his face with excitement, pouring over his words.

"Very clever of you, Mr. Jevons," said the barker. "You are our first customer who has realised."

"But—the Russian sequence in particular—how did you get it past the censors—and the sex, too?"

"This is a government-sponsored concern, of course. Surely you didn't think Totsensid was a process a private firm could market? The sex, I admit, is a bait—but you noticed it is *not* the cheap kind you pick up at a Fair."

Jevons's heart was singing a silent paean of rejoicing; he chuckled, and the sound threatened to soar into hysterical laughter.

"We don't often get people here as—old—as you," the barker said. "It's tomorrow we're interested in, not today. We've spent too long making a mess of the world to put it right in a hurry, but we've made a beginning. The brotherhood of man is on the way, as we usually say. Yes, *both* sides of the Iron Curtain." He eyed Jevons's untidy clothes. "You could be one of those who helped it along, if you want. Need a job?"

Jevons had started to say yes, when he remembered. "A government concern? They wouldn't have me. My mother was naturalised—that's why I was thrown out of my last job."

"Don't be a fool," said the barker flatly. "What do you think we're trying to get rid of? Report tomorrow evening at seven, will you? I'll have it fixed by then. So long."

Back across the way, back down the spiral, back through the turnstile, back to a world in which there was a sort of hope after all, back to the reality in which there would *not* be hell, there would *not* be war, and the Fairs would vanish because life would be worth living instead of foreboding.

The turnstile clicked; the conversation began again, only this time Jevons was echoing instead of arguing with the brass-lunged giant.

"THIS IS THE BIGGEST!" shouted the giant. "THIS IS THE BEST!"

And in Jevons's heart a small voice loaned the machine the humanity it did not possess. "This *is* the biggest!" Jevons shouted happily to the world. "This *is* the best!"

THE FORGOTTEN ENEMY

Arthur C. Clarke

It is very seldom that I can remember either the writing or the genesis of a particular story; "The Forgotten Enemy" is one of the rare exceptions. The initial idea must have come in the winter of 1937 or '38, when I was living at 88 Gray's Inn Road, London, in a flat famous throughout science fiction fandom, which I shared with William F. Temple and Maurice K. Hanson. Here were produced innumerable amateur magazines, and here too were held the meetings of the fledgling British Interplanetary Society. The flat still exists: I drove past it only last month, wondering if the present inhabitants had any idea of its weird history; but the pub next door was neatly excised during the Blitz.

From my minuscule bedroom it was possible to see the dome of St. Paul's, looming over the city, and I remember looking at it one winter day when the snow was falling and saying to myself, "Suppose it just goes on snowing, and doesn't stop . . . ever. . . ." Of course, this was in the best traditions of the British Catastrophe School, founded by H. G. Wells and ably sustained by John Beynon Harris (John Wyndham), C. S. Youd (John Christopher), both frequent visitors to the flat—and Jim Ballard, who was too young to know about us in those days.

But I didn't sit down to write a novel of another Ice Age; in fact, I didn't sit down to write anything. Looking at my records, I am astonished to find that it was ten years before I wrote up the idea, on 21-22 February, 1948, while I was taking my degree at King's College. The story was first printed in the King's

College Review for December, 1948, which was rather appropriate since much of the action takes place in the University's Senate House, Bloomsbury. Despite this prior publication, I later sold it to Ted Carnell's New Worlds (Number 5). I note with interest that I got an advance of £2-0/0 and £1-7/0 later. Since then, it has done rather better.

It is probably obvious from this story that I do not like cold weather. So that is doubtless the reason why I am writing these notes at midwinter—about four hundred miles from the Equator.

—Arthur C. Clarke
Colombo, Ceylon

The thick furs thudded softly to the ground as Professor Millward jerked himself upright on the narrow bed. This time, he was sure, it had been no dream; the freezing air that rasped against his lungs still seemed to echo with the sound that had come crashing out of the night.

He gathered the furs around his shoulders and listened intently. All was quiet again: from the narrow windows on the western walls long shafts of moonlight played upon the endless rows of books, as they played upon the dead city beneath. The world was utterly still; even in the old days the city would have been silent on such a night, and it was doubly silent now.

With weary resolution Professor Millward shuffled out of bed, and doled a few lumps of coke into the glowing brazier. Then he made his way slowly towards the nearest window, pausing now and then to rest his hand lovingly on the volumes he had guarded all these years.

He shielded his eyes from the brilliant moonlight and peered out into the night. The sky was cloudless: the sound he had heard had not been thunder, whatever it might have been. It had come from the north, and even as he waited it came again.

Distance had softened it, distance and the bulk of the hills that lay beyond London. It did not race across the sky with the wantonness of thunder, but seemed to come from a single point far to the north. It was like no natural sound that he had ever heard, and for a moment he dared to hope again.

Only Man, he was sure, could have made such a sound. Perhaps the dream that had kept him here among these treasures of civilization for more than twenty years would soon be a dream no longer. Men were returning to England, blasting their way through the ice and snow with the weapons that science had given them before the coming of the Dust. It was strange that they should come by land, and from the north, but he thrust aside any thoughts that would quench the newly kindled flame of hope.

Three hundred feet below, the broken sea of snow-covered roofs lay bathed in the bitter moonlight. Miles away the tall stacks of Battersea Power Station glimmered like thin white ghosts against the night sky. Now that the dome of St. Paul's had collapsed beneath the weight of snow, they alone challenged his supremacy.

Professor Millward walked slowly back along the bookshelves, thinking over the plan that had formed in his mind. Twenty years ago he had watched the last helicopters climbing heavily out of Regent's Park, the rotors churning the ceaselessly falling snow. Even then, when the silence had closed around him, he could not bring himself to believe that the North had been abandoned forever. Yet already he had waited a whole generation, among the books to which he had dedicated his life.

In those early days he had sometimes heard, over the radio which was his only contact with the South, of the struggle to colonize the now-temperate lands of the Equator. He did not know the outcome of that far-off battle, fought with desperate skill in the dying jungles and across deserts that had already felt the first touch of snow. Perhaps it had failed; the radio had been silent now for fifteen years or more. Yet if men and machines were indeed returning from the north—of all directions—he might again be able to hear their voices as they spoke to one another and to the lands from which they had come.

Professor Millward left the University building perhaps a dozen times a year, and then only through sheer necessity. Over the past two decades he had collected everything he needed from the shops in the Bloomsbury area, for in the final exodus vast supplies of stocks had been left behind through lack of transport. In many ways, indeed, his life could be called luxurious: no professor of English literature had ever been clothed in such garments as those he had taken from an Oxford Street furrier's.

The sun was blazing from a cloudless sky as he shouldered his pack and unlocked the massive gates. Even ten years ago packs of starving dogs had hunted in this area, and though he had seen none for years he was still cautious and always carried a revolver when he went into the open.

The sunlight was so brilliant that the reflected glare hurt his eyes; but it was almost wholly lacking in heat. Although the belt of cosmic dust through which the Solar System was now passing had made little difference to the sun's brightness, it had robbed it of all strength. No one knew whether the world would swim out into the warmth again in ten or a thousand years, and civilization had fled southwards in search of lands where the word "summer" was not an empty mockery.

The latest drifts had packed hard, and Professor Millward had little difficulty in making the journey to Tottenham Court Road. Sometimes it had taken him hours of floundering through the snow, and one year he had been sealed in his great concrete watchtower for nine months.

He kept away from the houses with their dangerous burdens of snow and their Damoclean icicles, and went north until he came to the shop he was seeking. The words above the shattered windows were still bright: JENKINS & SONS. RADIO AND ELECTRICAL. TELEVISION A SPECIALITY.

Some snow had drifted through a broken section of roofing, but the little upstairs room had not altered since his last visit a dozen years ago. The all-wave radio still stood on the table, and empty tins scattered on the floor spoke mutely of the lonely hours he had spent here before all hope had died. He wondered if he must go through the same ordeal again.

Professor Millward brushed the snow from the copy of *The Amateur Radio Handbook for 1965*, which had taught him what little he knew about wireless. The test-meters and batteries were still lying in their half-remembered places, and to his relief some of the batteries still held their charge. He searched through the stock until he had built up the necessary power supplies, and checked the radio as well as he could. Then he was ready.

It was a pity that he could never send the manufacturers the testimonial they deserved. The faint 'hiss' from the speaker brought back memories of the B.B.C., of the nine o'clock news and symphony concerts, of all the things he had taken for granted in a world that was gone like a dream. With scarcely controlled impatience he ran across the wave-bands, but everywhere there was nothing save that omnipresent hiss. That was disappointing, but no more: he remembered that the real test would come at night. In the meantime he would forage among the surrounding shops for anything that might be useful.

It was dusk when he returned to the little room. A hundred miles above his head, tenuous and invisible, the Heaviside Layer would be expanding outwards toward the stars as the sun went down. So it had done every evening for millions of years, and for half a century only, Man had used it for his own purposes, to reflect around the world his messages of hate or peace, to echo with trivialities or to sound with music once called immortal.

Slowly, with infinite patience, Professor Millward began to traverse the shortwave bands that a generation ago had been a babel of shouting voices and stabbing morse. Even as he listened, the faint hope that he had dared to cherish began to fade within him. The city itself was no more silent than the once-crowded oceans of ether. Only the faint crackle of thunderstorms half the world away broke the intolerable stillness. Man had abandoned his latest conquest.

Soon after midnight the batteries faded out. Professor Millward did not have the heart to search for more, but curled up in his furs and fell into a troubled sleep. He got what consolation he could from the thought that if he had not proved his theory, he had not disproved it either.

The heatless sunlight was flooding the lonely white road when he began the homeward journey. He was very tired, for he had slept little, and his sleep had been broken by the recurring fantasy of rescue.

The silence was suddenly broken by the distant thunder that came rolling over the white roofs. It came—there could be no doubt now—from beyond the northern hills that had once been London's playground. From the buildings on either side little avalanches of snow went swishing out into the wide street; then the silence returned.

Professor Millward stood motionless, weighing, considering, analysing. The sound had been too long-drawn out to be an ordinary explosion—he was dreaming again—it was nothing less than the distant thunder of an atomic bomb, burning and blasting away the snow a million tons at a time. His hope revived, and the disappointments of the night began to fade.

That momentary pause almost cost him his life. Out of a side-street something huge and white moved suddenly into his field of vision. For a moment his mind refused to accept the reality of what he saw; then the paralysis left him and he fumbled desperately for his futile revolver. Padding toward him across the snow, swinging its head from side to side with a hypnotic, serpentine motion, was a huge polar bear.

He dropped his belongings and ran, floundering over the snow toward the nearest buildings. Providentially the Underground entrance was only fifty feet away. The steel grille was closed, but he remembered breaking the lock many years ago. The temptation to look back was almost intolerable, for he could hear nothing to tell how near his pursuer was. For one frightful moment the iron lattice resisted his numbed fingers. Then it yielded reluctantly and he forced his way through the narrow opening.

Out of his childhood there came a sudden incongruous memory of an albino ferret he had once seen weaving its body ceaselessly across the wire netting of its cage. There was the same reptile grace in the monstrous shape, almost twice as high as a man, that reared itself in baffled fury against the grille. The metal bowed but did not yield beneath the pressure; then the bear dropped to the ground, grunted softly, and padded away. It slashed once or twice at the fallen haversack, scattering a few tins of food into the snow, and vanished as silently as it had come.

A very shaken Professor Millward reached the University three hours later, after moving in short bounds from one refuge to the next. After all these years he was no longer alone in the city. He wondered if there were other visitors, and that same night he knew the answer. Just before dawn he heard, quite distinctly, the cry of a wolf from somewhere in the direction of Hyde Park.

By the end of the week he knew that the animals of the north were on the move. Once he saw a reindeer running southward, pursued by a pack of silent wolves, and sometimes in the night there were sounds of deadly conflict. He was amazed that so much life still existed in the white wilderness between London and the Pole. Now something was driving it southward, and the knowledge brought him a mounting excitement. He did not believe that these fierce survivors would flee from anything save Man.

The strain of waiting was beginning to affect Professor Mill-ward's mind, and for hours he would sit in the cold sunlight, his furs wrapped round him, dreaming of rescue and thinking of the way in which men might be returning to England. Perhaps an expedition had come from North America across the Atlantic ice. It might have been years upon its way. But why had it come so far north? His favourite theory was that the Atlantic ice-packs were not safe enough for heavy traffic farther to the south.

One thing, however, he could not explain to his satisfaction. There had been no air reconnaissance; it was hard to believe that the art of flight had been lost so soon.

Sometimes he would walk along the ranks of books, whisper-ing now and then to a well-loved volume. There were books here that he had not dared to open for years, they reminded him so poignantly of the past. But now, as the days grew longer and brighter, he would sometimes take down a volume of poetry and reread his old favourites. Then he would go to the tall windows and shout the magic words over the rooftops, as if they would break the spell that had gripped the world.

It was warmer now, as if the ghosts of lost summers had re-turned to haunt the land. For whole days the temperature rose above freezing, while in many places flowers were breaking through the snow. Whatever was approaching from the north was nearer, and several times a day that enigmatic roar would go thundering over the city, sending the snow sliding upon a thousand roofs.

There were strange, grinding undertones that Professor Mill-ward found baffling and even ominous. At times it was almost as if he were listening to the clash of mighty armies, and some-times a mad but dreadful thought came into his mind and would not be dismissed. Often he would wake in the night and imagine he heard the sound of mountains moving to the sea.

So the summer wore away, and as the sound of that distant battle drew steadily nearer Professor Millward was the prey of ever more violent alternating hopes and fears. Although he saw

no more wolves or bears—they seemed to have fled southward—
he did not risk leaving the safety of his fortress. Every morning
he would climb to the highest window of the tower and search
the northern horizon with fieldglasses. But all he ever saw was
the stubborn retreat of the snows above Hampstead, as they
fought their bitter rearguard action against the sun.

His vigil ended with the last days of the brief summer. The
grinding thunder in the night had been nearer than ever before,
but there was still nothing to hint at its real distance from the
city. Professor Millward felt no premonition as he climbed to the
narrow window and raised his binoculars to the northern sky.

As a watcher from the walls of some threatened fortress might
have seen the first sunlight glinting on the spears of an advancing
army, so in that moment Professor Millward knew the truth. The
air was crystal-clear, and the hills were sharp and brilliant against
the cold blue of the sky. They had lost almost all their snow.
Once he would have rejoiced, but it meant nothing now.

Overnight, the enemy he had forgotten had conquered the last
defences and was preparing for the final onslaught. As he saw
that deadly glitter along the crest of the doomed hills, Professor
Millward understood at last the sound he had heard advancing
for so many months. It was little wonder he had dreamed of
mountains on the march.

Out of the north, their ancient home, returning in triumph to
the lands they had once possessed, the glaciers had come again.

WARRIOR

Gordon R. Dickson

"Warrior" is one of the short stories that fits itself into the chinks of what has been called the Dorsai Stories, but really should be called the science fiction leg of the Childe Cycle, which has now been nearly fourteen years in writing and will probably take another ten years or so to finish.

The plan of the Childe Cycle as it was originally set up called for three historical novels, three contemporary novels spanning the twentieth century alone, and three science-fiction (future) novels. The whole group of novels was planned to cover roughly a thousand years, from the fourteenth century to the twenty-fourth century, and to advance a philosophical argument based on a science fictional story line—that is, the nine projected novels would chronicle, from the facts of a historical and contemporaneous base, an evolution in the basic nature of Man, which had its beginning in the fourteenth century, was in full stride—if unrecognized—in our own time, and becomes accomplished finally some five hundred years from now.

As you might expect, I have been trapped by the science fiction third of the Cycle. For one thing, it has turned out that it was not practical to get publishers to publish—at least when the first books of the Cycle were being written—science fiction novels that were the length of a good historical novel. It was necessary to break the basic three stories of the sf end of the Cycle down into smaller units. This, plus the addition of other material as the Cycle matured, changed the sf end at last from three novels to six, of which

four have now been published. They are, in order of publication,
Dorsail (*titled* The Genetic General *in the abbreviated Ace paperback version*); Necromancer; Soldier, Ask Not; *and* The
Tactics of Mistake.

*Two books remain. The last novel will almost certainly be
titled* Childe. *The next to the last as yet has no permanent title.*

*The first of the historical novels deals with the life of Sir John
de Hawkwood, fourteenth-century English condottiere (soldier
of fortune) who ended up captaining the forces of Florentian
League against the Milanese under Gian Galeazzo Visconti, toward the end of the fourteenth century.*

*The second historical is tentatively planned to deal with John
Milton—but not as a poet. It will look at the Cromwellian government in England through the eyes of Milton during and about
the period he made himself available as a pamphleteer to the
Republic.*

*The third will almost certainly center on Robert Browning, the
nineteenth-century English poet, even if it does not deal with him
directly.*

*The three twentieth-century novels are yet to be pinned down.
I have their pattern in mind, but it is too soon to talk about them,
even generally.*

*The sum total of all this is that the nine originally planned
novels, or their eventual equivalent, will add up to what is essentially one very long novel, with the same internal structure
that goes into a much shorter work. However, so much for plans
and their execution. What has emerged over the last dozen years
or so, in addition to these plans, is a fair scattering of shorter
stories, raised by the process of doing the larger pieces. "Warrior" was one such. "Kensie, Brother" is another.*

*There are more as yet untitled and unwritten. And as I find
time between the novels that are the true parts of the Cycle, I
will try to get some of these shorter stories done and published.
Meanwhile, for the information of those who are interested, I
should mention that there are a number of Graemes appearing*

in the books of the Cycle. First of these is Cletus Grahame, hero of The Tactics of Mistake, *who writes the military bible for the Dorsai mercenaries. Next, there is his great-grandson, Eachan Khan Graeme, nephew of that Kamal Graeme who was first among the Graemes to marry a girl from the Maran world. Eachan is also elder brother to James, who died at Donneswort, and father to Mor, who was tortured to death by William of Ceta—for which William paid at the hands of Eachan's younger son, Donal Graeme, who was something more even than a Dorsai, and whose story is written in the novel* Dorsai! *Eachan is also (though the secret is buried) of relation to Hal, who lives in the last two novels and brings the thousand years of evolutionary struggle to its determined end.*

—Lastly, Eachan Khan Graeme is older brother as well to the pair who were born after James; the strange twins, Kensie and Ian Graeme, of whom it was said that the first had twice any man's brightness and the second had no brightness at all but two men's shadow. But never were two brothers closer.

"Kensie, Brother" is the story of their parting.

—Gordon R. Dickson

The spaceliner coming in from New Earth and Freiland, worlds under the Sirian sun, was delayed in its landing by traffic at the spaceport in Long Island Sound. The two police lieutenants, waiting on the bare concrete beyond the shelter of the Terminal buildings, turned up the collars of their cloaks against the hissing sleet, in this unweatherproofed area. The sleet was turning into tiny hailstones that bit and stung all exposed areas of skin. The gray November sky poured them down without pause or mercy; the vast, reaching surface of concrete seemed to dance with their white multitudes.

"Here it comes now," said Tyburn, the Manhattan Complex police lieutenant, risking a glance up into the hailstorm. "Let me do the talking when we take him in."

"Fine by me," answered Breagan, the spaceport officer, "I'm only here to introduce you—and because it's my bailiwick. You can have Kenebuck, with his hood connections, and his millions. If it were up to me, I'd let the soldier get him."

"It's him," said Tyburn, "who's likely to get the soldier—and that's why I'm here. You ought to know that."

The great mass of the interstellar ship settled like a cautious mountain to the concrete two hundred yards off. It protruded a landing stair near its base like a metal leg, and the passengers began to disembark. The two policemen spotted their man immediately in the crowd.

"He's big," said Breagan, with the judicious appraisal of someone safely on the sidelines, as the two of them moved forward.

"They're all big, these professional military men off the Dorsai world," answered Tyburn a little irritably, shrugging his shoulders against the cold, under his cloak. "They breed themselves that way."

"I know they're big," said Breagan. "This one's bigger."

The first wave of passengers was rolling toward them now, their quarry among the mass. Tyburn and Breagan moved forward to meet him. When they got close they could see, even through the hissing sleet, every line of his dark, unchanging face looming above the lesser heights of the people around him, his military erectness molding the civilian clothes he wore until they might as well have been a uniform. Tyburn found himself staring fixedly at the tall figure as it came toward him. He had met such professional soldiers from the Dorsai before, and the stamp of their breeding had always been plain on them. But this man was somehow more so, even than the others Tyburn had seen. In some way he seemed to be the spirit of the Dorsai, incarnate.

He was one of twin brothers, Tyburn remembered now from the dossier back at his office. Ian and Kensie were their names, of the Graeme family at Foralie, on the Dorsai. And the report was that Kensie had two men's likability, while his brother Ian, now approaching Tyburn, had a double portion of grim shadow and solitary darkness.

Staring at the man coming toward him, Tyburn could believe the dossier now. For a moment, even, with the sleet and the cold taking possession of him, he found himself believing in the old saying that, if the born soldiers of the Dorsai ever cared to pull back to their own small, rocky world and challenge the rest of humanity, not all the thirteen other inhabited planets could stand against them. Once Tyburn had laughed at that idea. Now, watching Ian approach, he could not laugh. A man like this would live for different reasons from those of ordinary men—and die for different reasons.

Tyburn shook off the wild notion. The figure coming toward him, he reminded himself sharply, was a professional military man—nothing more.

Ian was almost to them now. The two policemen moved in through the crowd and intercepted him.

"Commandant Ian Graeme?" said Breagan. I'm Kaj Breagan of the spaceport police. This is Lieutenant Walter Tyburn of the Manhattan Complex Force. I wonder if you could give us a few minutes of your time?"

Ian Graeme nodded, almost indifferently. He turned and paced along with them, his longer stride making more leisurely work of their brisk walking, as they led him away from the route of the disembarking passengers and in through a blank metal door at one end of the Terminal, marked UNAUTHORIZED ENTRY PRO-HIBITED. Inside, they took an elevator tube up to the offices on the Terminal's top floor, and ended up in chairs around a desk in one of the offices.

All the way in, Ian had said nothing. He sat in his chair now with the same indifferent patience, gazing at Tyburn, behind the desk, and at Breagan, seated back against the wall at the desk's right side. Tyburn found himself staring back in fascination. Not at the granite face, but at the massive, powerful hands of the man, hanging idly between the chairarms that supported his forearms. Tyburn, with an effort, wrenched his gaze from those hands.

"Well, Commandant," he said, forcing himself at last to look up into the dark, unchanging features, "you're here on Earth for a visit, we understand."

"To see the next-of-kin of an officer of mine." Ian's voice, when he spoke at last, was almost mild compared to the rest of his appearance. It was a deep, calm voice, but lightless—like a voice that had long forgotten the need to be angry or threatening. Only . . . there was something sad about it, Tyburn thought.

"A James Kenebuck?" said Tyburn.

"That's right," answered the deep voice of Ian. "His younger brother, Brian Kenebuck, was on my staff in the recent campaign on Freiland. He died three months back."

"Do you," said Tyburn, "always visit your deceased officers' next of kin?"

"When possible. Usually, of course, they died in line of duty."

"I see," said Tyburn. The office chair in which he sat seemed hard and uncomfortable underneath him. He shifted slightly. "You don't happen to be armed, do you, Commandant?"

Ian did not even smile.

"No," he said.

"Of course, of course," said Tyburn, uncomfortable. "Not that it makes any difference." He was looking again, in spite of himself, at the two massive, relaxed hands opposite him. "Your . . . extremities by themselves are lethal weapons. We register professional karate and boxing experts here, you know—or did you know?"

Ian nodded.

"Yes," said Tyburn. He wet his lips, and then was furious with himself for doing so. *Damn my orders,* he thought suddenly and whitely, *I don't have to sit here making a fool of myself in front of this man, no matter how many connections and millions Kenebuck owns.*

"All right, look here, Commandant," he said, harshly, leaning forward. "We've had a communication from the Freiland-North Police about you. They suggest that you hold Kenebuck—James Kenebuck—responsible for his brother Brian's death."

Ian sat looking back at him without answering.

"Well," demanded Tyburn raggedly after a long moment, "do you?"

"Force-leader Brian Kenebuck," said Ian calmly, "led his Force, consisting of thirty-six men at the time, against orders farther than was wise into enemy perimeter. His Force was surrounded and badly shot up. Only he and four men returned to the lines. He was brought to trial in the field under the Mercenaries Code for deliberate mishandling of his troops under combat conditions. The four men who had returned with him testified against him. He was found guilty and I ordered him shot."

Ian stopped speaking. His voice had been perfectly even, but there was so much finality about the way he spoke that after he finished there was a pause in the room while Tyburn and Breagan stared at him as if they had both been tranced. Then the silence, echoing in Tyburn's ears, jolted him back to life.

"I don't see what all this has to do with James Kenebuck, then," said Tyburn. "Brian committed some . . . military crime, and was executed for it. You say you gave the order. If anyone's responsible for Brian Kenebuck's death, then, it seems to me it'd be you. Why connect it with someone who wasn't even there at the time, someone who was here on Earth all the while, James Kenebuck?"

"Brian," said Ian, "was his brother."

The emotionless statement was calm and coldly reasonable in the silent, brightly lit office. Tyburn found his open hands had shrunk themselves into fists on the desk top. He took a deep breath and began to speak in a flat, official tone.

"Commandant," he said, "I don't pretend to understand you. You're a man of the Dorsai, a product of one of the splinter cultures out among the stars. I'm just an old-fashioned Earthborn— But I'm a policeman in the Manhattan Complex and James Kenebuck is . . . well, he's a taxpayer in the Manhattan Complex."

He found he was talking without meeting Ian's eyes. He forced himself to look at them—they were dark, unmoving eyes.

"It's my duty to inform you," Tyburn went on, "that we've had intimations to the effect that you're to bring some retribution to James Kenebuck, because of Brian Kenebuck's death. These are only intimations, and as long as you don't break any laws here on Earth, you're free to go where you want and see whom you like. But this *is Earth, Commandant.*"

He paused, hoping that Ian would make some sound, some movement. But Ian only sat there, waiting.

"We don't have any Mercenaries Code here, Commandant," Tyburn went on harshly. "We haven't any feud-right, no *droit-de-main.* But we do have laws. Those laws say that though a man may be the worst murderer alive, until he's brought to book in our courts, under our process of laws, no one is allowed to harm a hair of his head. Now, I'm not here to argue whether this is the best way or not; just to tell you that that's the way things are." Tyburn stared fixedly into the dark eyes. "Now," he said, bluntly, "I know that if you're determined to try to kill Kenebuck without counting the cost, I can't prevent it."

He paused and waited again. But Ian still said nothing.

"I know," said Tyburn, "that you can walk up to him like any other citizen, and once you're within reach you can try to kill him with your bare hands before anyone can stop you. I can't stop you in that case. But what I can do is catch you afterwards, if you succeed, and see you convicted and executed for murder. And you *will* be caught and convicted, there's no doubt about it. You can't kill James Kenebuck the way someone like you would kill a man, and get away with it here on Earth—do you understand that, Commandant?"

"Yes," said Ian.

"All right," said Tyburn, letting out a deep breath. "Then you understand. You're a sane man and a Dorsai professional. From what I've been able to learn about the Dorsai, it's one of your military tenets that part of a man's duty to himself is not to throw his life away in a hopeless cause. And this cause of yours to bring Kenebuck to justice for his brother's death is hopeless."

He stopped. Ian straightened in a movement preliminary to getting up.

"Wait a second," said Tyburn.

He had come to the hard part of the interview. He had prepared his speech for this moment and rehearsed it over and over again, but now he found himself without faith that it would convince Ian.

"One more word," said Tyburn. "You're a man of camps and battlefields, a man of the military; and you must be used to thinking of yourself as a pretty effective individual. But here, on Earth, those special skills of yours are mostly illegal. And without them you're ineffective and helpless. Kenebuck, on the other hand, is just the opposite. He's got money—millions. And he's got connections, some of them nasty. And he was born and raised here in Manhattan Complex." Tyburn stared emphatically at the tall, dark man, willing him to understand. "Do you follow me? If you, for example, should suddenly turn up dead here, we just might not be able to bring Kenebuck to book for it. Where we absolutely could, and would bring you to book if the situation were reversed. Think about it."

He sat, still staring at Ian. But Ian's face showed no change, or sign that the message had gotten through to him.

"Thank you," Ian said. "If there's nothing more, I'll be going."

"There's nothing more," said Tyburn, defeated. He watched Ian leave. It was only when Ian was gone, and he turned back to Breagan that he recovered a little of his self-respect. For Breagan's face had paled.

Ian went down through the Terminal and took a cab into Manhattan Complex, to the John Adams Hotel. He registered for a room on the fourteenth floor of the transient section of that hotel and inquired about the location of James Kenebuck's suite in the resident section; then sent his card up to Kenebuck with a request to come by to see the millionaire. After that, he went on up to his own room, unpacked his luggage, which had already been delivered from the spaceport, and took out a small, sealed package. Just at that moment there was a soft chiming sound and his card was returned to him from a delivery slot in the room wall. It fell into the salver below the slot and he picked it up. The penciled note read: COME ON UP. K

He tucked the card and the package into a pocket and left his transient room. And Tyburn, who had followed him to the hotel, and who had been observing all of Ian's actions from the second of his arrival, through sensors placed in the walls and ceilings, half rose from his chair in the room of the empty suite directly above Kenebuck's, which had been quietly taken over as a police observation post. Then, helplessly, Tyburn swore and sat down again, to follow Ian's movements in the screen fed by the sensors. So far there was nothing the policeman could do legally —nothing but watch.

So he watched as Ian strode down the softly carpeted hallway to the elevator tube, rose in it to the eightieth floor and stepped out to face the heavy, transparent door sealing off the resident section of the hotel. He held up Kenebuck's card with its message to a concierge screen beside the door, and with a soft sigh of air the door slid back to let him through. He passed on in, found a second elevator tube, and took it up thirteen more stories. Black doors opened before him—and he stepped one step forward into a small foyer to find himself surrounded by three men.

They were big men—one, a lantern-jawed giant, was even bigger than Ian—and they were vicious. Tyburn, watching through the sensors in the foyer ceiling that had been secretly placed there by the police the day before, recognized all of them from his files. They were underworld muscle hired by Kenebuck at word of Ian's coming; all armed, and brutal, and hair-trigger—mad dogs of the lower city. After that first step into their midst, Ian stood still. And there followed a strange, unnatural cessation of movement in the room.

The three stood checked. They had been about to put their hands on Ian to search him for something, Tyburn saw, and probably to rough him up in the process. But something had stopped them, some abrupt change in the air around them. Tyburn, watching, felt the change as they did; but for a moment he felt it without understanding. Then understanding came to him.

The difference was in Ian, in the way he stood there. He was, saw Tyburn, simply . . . waiting. That same patient indifference Tyburn had seen upon him in the Terminal office was there again. In the split second of his single step into the room he had discovered the men, had measured them, and stopped. Now, he waited, in his turn, for one of them to make a move.

A sort of black lightning had entered the small foyer. It was abruptly obvious to the watching Tyburn, as to the three below, that the first of them to lay hands on Ian would be the first to find the hands of the Dorsai soldier upon him—and those hands were death.

For the first time in his life, Tyburn saw the personal power of the Dorsai fighting man, made plain without words. Ian needed no badge upon him, standing as he stood now, to warn that he was dangerous. The men about him were mad dogs, but, patently, Ian was a wolf. There was a difference with the three, which Tyburn now recognized for the first time. Dogs—even mad dogs—fight, and the losing dog, if he can, runs away. But no wolf runs. For a wolf wins every fight but one, and in that one he dies.

After a moment, when it was clear that none of the three would move, Ian stepped forward. He passed through them without even brushing against one of them to the inner door opposite, and opened it and went on through.

He stepped into a three-level living room stretching to a large, wide window, its glass rolled up, and black with the sleet-filled night. The living room was as large as a small suite in itself, and filled with people, men and women, richly dressed. They held cocktail glasses in their hands as they stood or sat, and talked. The atmosphere was heavy with the scents of alcohol and women's perfumes and cigarette smoke. It seemed that they paid no attention to his entrance, but their eyes followed him covertly once he had passed.

He walked forward through the crowd, picking his way to a figure before the dark window, the figure of a man almost as tall as himself, erect, athletic-looking with a handsome, sharp-cut face under whitish-blond hair that stared at Ian with a sort of incredulity as Ian approached.

"Graeme . . . ?" said this man, as Ian stopped before him. His voice in this moment of off-guardedness betrayed its two levels, the semihoodlum whine and harshness underneath, the polite accents above. "My boys . . . you didn't"—he stumbled—"leave anything with them when you were coming in?"

"No," said Ian. "You're James Kenebuck, of course. You look like your brother." Kenebuck stared at him.

"Just a minute," he said. He set his glass down, turned and went quickly through the crowd and into the foyer, shutting the door behind him. In the hush of the room there was heard, a short, unintelligible burst of sharp voices, then silence again. Kenebuck came back into the room, two spots of angry color high on his cheekbones. He came back to face Ian.

"Yes," he said, halting before Ian. "They were supposed to . . . tell me when you came in." He fell silent, evidently waiting for Ian to speak, but Ian merely stood, examining him, until the spots of color on Kenebuck's cheekbones flared again.

"Well?" he said, abruptly. "Well? You came here to see me about Brian, didn't you? What about Brian?" He added, before Ian could answer, in a tone suddenly brutal, "I know he was shot, so you don't have to tell me he showed all sorts of noble guts . . . refused a blindfold and that sort of—"

"No," said Ian. "He didn't die nobly."

Kenebuck's tall, muscled body jerked a little at the words, almost as if the bullets of an invisible firing squad had poured into it.

"Well . . . that's fine!" he laughed, angrily. "You come light-years to see me and then you tell me that! I thought you liked him—liked Brian."

"Liked him? No." Ian shook his head. Kenebuck stiffened, his face for a moment caught in a gape of bewilderment. "As a matter of fact," went on Ian, "he was a glory-hunter. That made him a poor soldier and a worse officer. I'd have transferred him out of my command if I'd had time before the campaign on Freiland started. Because of him, we lost the lives of thirty-two men in his Force that night."

"Oh." Kenebuck pulled himself together, and looked sourly at Ian. "Those thirty-two men. You've got them on your conscience, is that it?"

"No," said Ian. There was no emphasis on the word as he said it, but somehow to Tyburn's ears above, the brief short negative dismissed Kenebuck's question with an abruptness like contempt. The spots of color on Kenebuck's cheeks flamed.

"You didn't like Brian and your conscience doesn't bother you —what're you here for, then?" he snapped.

"My duty brings me," said Ian.

"Duty?" Kenebuck's face stilled, and went rigid.

Ian reached slowly into his pocket as if he were surrendering a weapon under the guns of an enemy and did not want his move misinterpreted. He brought out the package from his pocket.

"I brought you Brian's personal effects," he said. He turned and laid the package on a table beside Kenebuck. Kenebuck stared down at the package and the color over his cheekbones faded until his face was nearly as pale as his hair. Then slowly, hesitantly, as if he were approaching a booby-trap, he reached out and gingerly picked it up. He held it and turned to Ian, staring into Ian's eyes almost demandingly.

"It's in here?" said Kenebuck, in a voice barely above a whisper, and with a strange emphasis.

"Brian's effects," said Ian, watching him.

"Yes . . . sure. All right," said Kenebuck. He was plainly trying to pull himself together, but his voice was still almost whispering. "I guess . . . that settles it."

"That settles it," said Ian. Their eyes held together. "Goodby," said Ian. He turned and walked back through the silent crowd and out of the living room. The three muscle-men were no longer in the foyer. He took the elevator tube down and returned to his own hotel room.

Tyburn, who with a key to the service elevators, had not had to change tubes on the way down as Ian had, was waiting for him when Ian entered. Ian did not seem surprised to see Tyburn there, and only glanced casually at the policeman as he crossed to a decanter of Dorsai whisky that had since been delivered up to the room.

"That's that, then!" burst out Tyburn, in relief. "You got in to see him and he ended up letting you out. You can pack up and go now. It's over."

"No," said Ian. "Nothing's over yet." He poured a few inches of the pungent, dark whisky into a glass, and moved the decanter over another glass. "Drink?"

"I'm on duty," said Tyburn, sharply.

"There'll be a little wait," said Ian, calmly. He poured some whisky into the other glass, took up both glasses, and stepped across the room to hand one to Tyburn. Tyburn found himself holding it. Ian had stepped on to stand before the wall-high window. Outside, night had fallen, but—faintly seen in the lights from the city levels below—the sleet here above the weather shield still beat like small, dark ghosts against the transparency.

"Hang it, man, what more do you want?" burst out Tyburn. "Can't you see it's you I'm trying to protect—as well as Kenebuck? I don't want *anyone* killed! If you stay around here now, you're asking for it. I keep telling you, here in Manhattan Complex you're the helpless one, not Kenebuck. Do you think he hasn't made plans to take care of you?"

"Not until he's sure," said Ian, turning from the ghost-sleet, beating like lost souls against the window glass, trying to get in.

"Sure about what? Look, Commandant," said Tyburn, trying to speak calmly, "half an hour after we heard from the Freiland-North Police about you, Kenebuck called my office to ask for police protection." He broke off, angrily. "Don't look at me like that! How do I know how he found out you were coming? I tell you he's rich, and he's got connections! But the point is, the police protection he's got is just a screen—an excuse—for whatever he's got planned for you on his own. You saw those hoods in the foyer!"

"Yes," said Ian unemotionally.

"Well, think about it!" Tyburn glared at him. "Look, I don't hold any brief for James Kenebuck! All right—let me tell you about him! We knew he'd been trying to get rid of his brother since Brian was ten—but blast it, Commandant, Brian was no angel, either."

"I know," said Ian, seating himself in a chair opposite Tyburn.

"All right, you know! I'll tell you, anyway!" said Tyburn. "Their grandfather was a local kingpin—he was in every racket on the eastern seaboard. He was one of the mob, with millions he didn't dare count because of where they'd come from. In their father's time, those millions started to be fed into legitimate business. The third generation, James and Brian, didn't inherit anything that wasn't legitimate. Hell, we couldn't even make a jaywalking ticket stick against one of them, if we'd ever wanted to. James was twenty and Brian ten when their father died, and when he died the last bit of tattle-tale gray went out of the family linen. But they kept their hoodlum connections, Commandant!"

Ian sat, glass in hand, watching Tyburn almost curiously.

"Don't you get it?" snapped Tyburn. "I tell you that, on paper, in law, Kenebuck's twenty-four carat gilt-edge. But his family was hoodlum, he was raised like a hoodlum, and he thinks like a hood! He didn't want his young brother Brian around to share the crown prince position with him—so he set out to get rid of him. He couldn't just have him killed, so he set out to cut him down, show him up, break his spirit, until Brian took one chance too many trying to match up to his older brother, and killed himself off."

Ian slowly nodded.

"All right!" said Tyburn. "So Kenebuck finally succeeded. He chased Brian until the kid ran off and became a professional soldier—something Kenebuck wouldn't leave his wine, women, and song long enough to shine at. And he can shine at most things he really wants to shine at, Commandant. Under that hood attitude and all those millions he's got a good mind and a good body that he's made a hobby out of training. But, all right. So now it turns out Brian was still no good, and he took some soldiers along when he finally got around to doing what Kenebuck wanted, and getting himself killed. All right! But what can you do about it? What can anyone do about it, with all the connections, and all the money and all the law on Kenebuck's side of it? And, why should you think about doing something about it, anyway?"

"It's my duty," said Ian. He had swallowed half the whisky in his glass, absently, and now he turned the glass thoughtfully around, watching the brown liquor swirl under the forces of momentum and gravity. He looked up at Tyburn. "You know that, Lieutenant."

"Duty! Is duty that important?" demanded Tyburn. Ian gazed at him, then looked away, at the ghost-sleet beating vainly against the glass of the window that held it back in the outer dark.

"Nothing's more important than duty," said Ian, half to himself, his voice thoughtful and remote. "Mercenary troops have the right to care and protection from their own officers. When they don't get it, they're entitled to justice, so that the same thing is discouraged from happening again. That justice is a duty."

Tyburn blinked, and unexpectedly a wall seemed to go down in his mind.

"Justice for those thirty-two dead soldiers of Brian's!" he said, suddenly understanding. "That's what brought you here!"

"Yes." Ian nodded, and lifted his glass almost as if to the sleet-ghosts to drink the rest of his whisky.

"But," said Tyburn, staring at him, "you're trying to bring a civilian to justice. And Kenebuck has you outgunned and out-maneuvered—"

The chiming of the communicator screen in one corner of the room interrupted him. Ian put down his empty glass, went over to the screen and depressed a stud. His wide shoulders and back hid the screen from Tyburn, but Tyburn heard his voice.

"Yes?"

The voice of James Kenebuck sounded in the hotel room.

"Graeme—listen!"

There was a pause.

"I'm listening," said Ian, calmly.

"I'm alone now," said the voice of Kenebuck. It was tight and harsh. "My guests have gone home. I was just looking through that package of Brian's things. . . ." He stopped speaking and the sentence seemed to Tyburn to dangle unfinished in the air of the room. Ian let it dangle for a long moment.

"Yes?" he said, finally.

"Maybe I was a little hasty . . ." said Kenebuck. But the tone of his voice did not match the words. The tone was savage. "Why don't you come up, now that I'm alone, and we'll . . . talk about Brian, after all?"

"I'll be up," said Ian.

He snapped off the screen and turned around.

"Wait!" said Tyburn, starting up out of his chair. "You can't go up there!"

"Can't?" Ian looked at him. "I've been invited, Lieutenant."

The words were like a damp towel slapping Tyburn in the face, waking him up.

"That's right. . . ." He stared at Ian. "Why? Why'd he invite you back?"

"He's had time," said Ian, "to be alone. And to look at that package of Brian's."

"But—" Tyburn scowled. "There was nothing important in that package. A watch, a wallet, a passport, some other papers . . . Customs gave us a list. There wasn't anything unusual there."

"Yes," said Ian. "And that's why he wants to see me again."

"But what does he want?"

"He wants me," said Ian. He met the puzzlement of Tyburn's gaze. "He was always jealous of Brian," Ian explained, almost gently. "He was afraid Brian would grow up to outdo him in things. That's why he tried to break Brian, even to kill him. But now Brian's come back to face him."

"Brian . . . ?"

"In me," said Ian. He turned toward the hotel door.

Tyburn watched him turn, then suddenly, like a man coming out of a daze, he took three hurried strides after him as Ian opened the door.

"Wait!" snapped Tyburn. "He won't be alone up there! He'll have hoods covering you through the walls. He'll definitely have traps set for you—"

Easily, Ian lifted the policeman's grip from his arm.

"I know," he said. And went.

Tyburn was left in the open doorway staring after him. As Ian stepped into the elevator tube, the policeman moved. He ran for the service elevator that would take him back to the police observation post above the sensors in the ceiling of Kenebuck's living room.

When Ian stepped into the foyer the second time, it was empty. He went to the door to the living room of Kenebuck's suite, found it ajar, and stepped through it. Within, the room was empty, with glasses and overflowing ashtrays still on the tables; the lights had been lowered. Kenebuck rose from a chair with its back to the far, large window at the end of the room. Ian walked toward him and stopped when they were little more than an arm's length apart.

Kenebuck stood for a second staring at him, the skin of his face tight. Then he made a short almost angry gesture with his right hand. The gesture gave away the fact that he had been drinking.

"Sit down!" he said. Ian took a comfortable chair and Kenebuck sat down in the one from which he had just risen. "Drink?" said Kenebuck. There was a decanter and glasses on the table beside and between them. Ian shook his head. Kenebuck poured part of a glass for himself.

"That package of Brian's things," he said, abruptly, the whites of his eyes glinting as he glanced up under his lids at Ian, "there was just personal stuff. Nothing else in it!"

"What else did you expect would be in it?" asked Ian, calmly.

Kenebuck's hands clenched suddenly on the glass. He stared at Ian, and then burst out into a laugh that rang a little wildly against the emptiness of the large room.

"No, no—" said Kenebuck, loudly. "I'm asking the questions, Graeme. I'll ask them! What made you come all the way here to see me, anyway?"

"My duty," said Ian.

"Duty? Duty to whom—Brian?" Kenebuck looked as if he would laugh again, then thought better of it. There was the white, wild flash of his eyes again. "What was something like Brian to you? You said you didn't even like him."

"That was beside the point," said Ian, quietly. "He was one of my officers."

"One of your officers! He was my brother! That's more than being one of your officers!"

"Not," answered Ian in the same voice, "where justice is concerned."

"Justice?" Kenebuck laughed. "Justice for Brian? Is that it?"

"And for thirty-two enlisted men."

"Oh—" Kenebuck snorted laughingly. "Thirty-two men . . . those thirty-two men!" He shook his head. "I never knew your thirty-two men, Graeme, so you can't blame me for them. That was Brian's fault; him and his idea—what was the charge they tried him on? Oh, yes, that he and his thirty-two or thirty-six men could raid enemy headquarters and come back with the enemy commandant. Come back . . . covered with glory." Kenebuck laughed again. "But it didn't work. Not my fault."

"Brian did it," said Ian, "to show you. You were what made him do it."

"Me? Could I help it if he never could match up to me?" Kenebuck stared down at his glass and took a quick swallow from it, then went back to cuddling it in his hands. He smiled a little to himself. "Never could even *catch* up to me." He looked whitely across at Ian. "I'm just a better man, Graeme. You better remember that."

Ian said nothing. Kenebuck continued to stare at him, and slowly Kenebuck's face grew more savage.

"Don't believe me, do you?" said Kenebuck, softly. "You better believe me. I'm not Brian, and I'm not bothered by Dorsais. You're here, and I'm facing you—alone."

"Alone?" said Ian. For the first time Tyburn, above the ceiling over the heads of the two men, listening and watching through hidden sensors, thought he heard a hint of emotion—contempt—in Ian's voice. Or had he imagined it?

"Alone—well!" James Kenebuck laughed again, but a little cautiously. "I'm a civilized man, not a hick frontiersman. But I don't have to be a fool. Yes, I've got men covering you from behind the walls of the room here. I'd be stupid not to. And I've got this. . . ." He whistled, and something about the size of a small dog, but made of smooth, black metal, slipped out from behind a sofa nearby and slid on an aircushion over the carpeting to their feet.

Ian looked down. It was a sort of satchel with an orifice in the top from which two metallic tentacles protruded slightly.

Ian nodded slightly.

"A medical mech," he said.

"Yes," said Kenebuck, "cued to respond to the heartbeats of anyone in the room with it. So you see, it wouldn't do you any good, even if you somehow knew where all my guards were and beat them to the draw. Even if you killed me, this could get to me in time to keep it from being permanent. So, I'm unkillable. Give up!" He laughed and kicked at the mech. "Get back," he said to it. It slid back behind the sofa.

"So you see . . ." he said. "Just sensible precautions. There's no trick to it. You're a military man—and what's that mean? Superior strength. Superior tactics. That's all. So I outpower your strength, outnumber you, make your tactics useless—and what are you? Nothing." He put his glass carefully aside on the table with the decanter. "But I'm not Brian. I'm not afraid of you. I could do without these things if I wanted to."

Ian sat watching him. On the floor above, Tyburn had stiffened.

"Could you?" asked Ian.

Kenebuck stared at him. The white face of the millionaire contorted. Blood surged up into it, darkening it. His eyes flashed whitely.

"What're you trying to do—test me?" he shouted suddenly. He jumped to his feet and stood over Ian, waving his arms furiously. It was, recognized Tyburn overhead, the calculated, self-induced hysterical rage of the hoodlum world. But how would Ian Graeme below know that? Suddenly Kenebuck was screaming. "You want to try me out? You think I won't face you? You think I'll back down like that brother of mine, that—" He broke into a flood of obscenity in which the name of Brian was freely mixed. Abruptly, he whirled about to the walls of the room, yelling at them. "Get out of there! All right, out! Do you hear me? All of you! Out—"

Panels slid back, bookcases swung aside and four men stepped into the room. Three were those who had been in the foyer earlier when Ian had entered for the first time. The other was of the same type.

"Out!" screamed Kenebuck at them. "Everybody out. Outside, and lock the door behind you. I'll show this Dorsai, this—" Almost foaming at the mouth, he lapsed into obscenity again.

Overhead, above the ceiling, Tyburn found himself gripping the edge of the table below the observation screen so hard his fingers ached.

"It's a trick!" he muttered between his teeth to the unhearing Ian. "He planned it this way! Can't you see that?"

"Graeme armed?" inquired the police sensor technician at Tyburn's right. Tyburn jerked his head around momentarily to stare at the technician.

"No," said Tyburn. "Why?"

"Kenebuck is." The technician reached over and tapped the screen, just below the left shoulder of Kenebuck's jacket image. "Slug-thrower."

Tyburn made a fist of his aching right fingers and softly pounded the table before the screen in frustration.

"All right!" Kenebuck was shouting below, turning back to the still-seated form of Ian, and spreading his arms wide. "Now's your chance. Jump me! The door's locked. You think there's anyone else near to help me? Look!" He turned and took five steps to the wide, knee-high to ceiling window behind him, punched the control button and watched as it swung wide. A few of the whirling sleet-ghosts outside drove from out of ninety stories of vacancy into the opening—and fell dead in little drops of moisture on the windowsill as the automatic weather shield behind the glass blocked them out.

He stalked back to Ian, who had neither moved nor changed expression through all this. Slowly, Kenebuck sank back down into his chair, his back to the night, the blocked-out cold, and the sleet.

"What's the matter?" he asked, slowly, acidly. "You don't do anything? Maybe *you* don't have the nerve, Graeme?"

"We were talking about Brian," said Ian.

"Yes, Brian . . ." Kenebuck said, quite slowly. "He had a big head. He wanted to be like me, but no matter how he tried—how I tried to help him—he couldn't make it." He stared at Ian. "That's just the way he decided to go into enemy lines when there wasn't a chance in the world. That's the way he was—a loser."

"With help," said Ian.

"What? What's that you're saying?" Kenebuck jerked upright in his chair.

"You helped him lose." Ian's voice was matter of fact. "From the time he was a young boy, you built him up to want to be like you—to take long chances and win. Only your chances were always safe bets, and his were as unsafe as you could make them."

Kenebuck drew in an audible, hissing breath.

"You've got a big mouth, Graeme!" he said, in a low, slow voice.

"You wanted," said Ian, almost conversationally, "to have him kill himself off. But he never quite did. And each time he came back for more, because he had it stuck into his mind, carved into his mind, that he wanted to impress you—even though by the time he was grown, he saw what you were up to. He knew, but he still wanted to make you admit that he wasn't a loser. You'd twisted him that way while he was growing up, and that was the way he grew."

"Go on," hissed Kenebuck. "Go on, big mouth."

"So, he went off-Earth and became a professional soldier," went on Ian, steadily and calmly, "not because he was drafted like someone from Newton, or a born professional from the Dorsai, or hungry like one of the ex-miners from Coby, but to show you you were wrong about him. He found one place where you couldn't compete with him, and he must have started writing back to you to tell you about it—half rubbing it in, half asking for the pat on the back you never gave him."

Kenebuck sat in the chair and breathed. His eyes were all one glitter.

"But you didn't answer his letters," said Ian. "I suppose you thought that'd finally make him desperate enough to do something fatal. But he didn't. Instead he succeeded. He went up through the ranks. Finally, he got his commission and made Force-Leader, and you began to be worried. It wouldn't be long, if he kept on going up, before he'd be above the field officer grades, and out of most of the actual fighting."

Kenebuck sat perfectly still, leaning forward a little. He looked almost as if he were praying, or putting all the force of his mind to willing that Ian finish what he had started to say.

"And so," said Ian, "on his twenty-third birthday—which was the day before the night on which he led his men against orders into the enemy area—you saw that he got this birthday card. . . ." He reached into a side pocket of his civilian jacket and took out a white, folded card that showed signs of having been savagely crumpled but was now smoothed out again. Ian opened it and laid it beside the decanter on the table between their chairs, the sketch and legend facing Kenebuck. Kenebuck's eyes dropped to look at it.

The sketch was a crude outline of a rabbit, with a combat rifle and battle helmet discarded at its feet, engaged in painting a broad yellow stripe down the center of its own back. Underneath this picture was printed in block letters the question, "WHY FIGHT IT?"

Kenebuck's face slowly rose from the sketch to face Ian, and the millionaire's mouth stretched at the corners, and went on stretching into a ghastly version of a smile.

"Was that all . . . ?" whispered Kenebuck.

"Not all," said Ian. "Along with it, glued to the paper by the rabbit, there was this. . . ."

He reached almost casually into his pocket.

"No, you don't!" screamed Kenebuck, triumphantly. Suddenly he was on his feet, jumping behind his chair, backing away toward the darkness of the window behind him. He reached into his jacket and his hand came out holding the slug-thrower, which cracked loudly in the room. Ian had not moved, and his body jerked to the heavy impact of the slug.

Suddenly, Ian had come to life. After being hammered by a slug, the shock of which should have immobilized an ordinary man, he was out of the chair on his feet and moving forward. Kenebuck screamed again—this time with pure terror—and began to back away, firing as he went.

"Die, you—! Die!" he screamed. But the towering Dorsai figure came on. Twice it was hit and spun clear around by the heavy slugs, but like a football fullback shaking off the assaults of tacklers it plunged on, with great strides narrowing the distance between it and the retreating Kenebuck.

Still screaming, Kenebuck came up with the back of his knees against the low sill of the open window. For a second his face distorted itself out of all human shape in a grimace of its terror. He looked, to right and to left, but there was no place left to run. He had been pulling the trigger of his slug-thrower all this time, but now the firing pin clicked at last upon an empty chamber. Gibbering, he threw the weapon at Ian, and it flew wide of the driving figure of the Dorsai, now almost upon him, great hands outstretched.

Kenebuck jerked his head away from what was rushing toward him. Then, with a howl like a beaten dog, he turned and flung himself through the window before those hands could touch him, into ninety-odd stories of unsupported space. And his howl carried away down into silence.

Ian halted. For a second he stood before the window, his right hand still clenched about whatever it was he had pulled from his pocket. Then, like a toppling tree, he fell.

As Tyburn and the technician with him finished burning through the ceiling above and came dropping through the charred opening into the room, they almost landed on the small object that had come rolling from Ian's now-lax hand. An object that was really two objects glued together—a small paintbrush and a transparent tube of glaringly yellow paint.

"I hope you realize, though," said Tyburn, two weeks later on an icy, bright December day as he and the recovered Ian stood just inside the Terminal waiting for the boarding signal from the spaceliner about to take off for the Sirian worlds, "what a chance you took with Kenebuck. It was just luck it worked out for you the way it did."

"No," said Ian. He was as apparently emotionless as ever; a little more gaunt from his stay in the Manhattan hospital, but he had mended with the swiftness of his Dorsai constitution. "There was no luck. It all happened the way I planned it."

Tyburn gazed in astonishment.

"Why," he said, "if Kenebuck hadn't had to send his hoods out of the room to make it seem necessary for him to shoot you himself when you put your hand into your pocket that second time . . . or if you hadn't had the card in the first place—" He broke off, suddenly thoughtful. "You mean . . . ?" He stared at Ian. "Having the card, you planned to have Kenebuck get you alone . . . ?"

"It was a form of personal combat," said Ian. "And personal combat is my business. You assumed that Kenebuck was strongly entrenched, facing my attack. But it was the other way around."

"But you had to come to him. . . ."

"I had to appear to come to him," said Ian, almost coldly, "otherwise he wouldn't have believed that he had to kill me—before I killed him. By his decision to kill me, he put himself in the attacking position."

"But he had all the advantages!" said Tyburn, his head whirling. "You had to fight on his ground, here where he was strong—"

"No," said Ian. "You're confusing the attack position with the defensive one. By coming here, I put Kenebuck in the position of finding out whether I actually had the birthday card and the knowledge of why Brian had gone against orders into enemy territory that night. Kenebuck planned to have his men in the foyer shake me down for the card—but they lost their nerve."

"I remember," murmured Tyburn.

"Then, when I handed him the package, he was sure the card was in it. But it wasn't," went on Ian. "He saw his only choice was to give me a situation where I might feel it was safe to admit having the card and the knowledge. He had to know about that, because Brian had called his bluff by going out and risking his neck after getting the card. The fact Brian was tried and executed later made no difference to Kenebuck. That was a matter of law—something apart from hoodlum guts, or lack of guts. If no one knew that Brian was braver than his older brother, that was all right; but if I knew, he could only save face under his own standards by killing me."

"He almost did," said Tyburn. "Any one of those slugs—"

"There was the medical mech," said Ian, calmly. "A man like Kenebuck would be bound to have something like that around to play safe—just as he would be bound to set an amateur's trap." The boarding horn of the spaceliner sounded. Ian picked up his luggage bag. "Good-by," he said, offering his hand to Tyburn.

"Good-by," he muttered. "So you were just going along with Kenebuck's trap, all of it. I can't believe it. . . ." He released Ian's hand and watched as the big man swung around and took the first two strides away toward the bulk of the ship shining in the winter sunlight. Then, suddenly, the numbness broke clear from Tyburn's mind. He ran after Ian and caught at his arm. Ian stopped and swung half around, frowning slightly.

"I can't believe it!" cried Tyburn. "You mean you went up there, *knowing* Kenebuck was going to pump you full of slugs

and maybe kill you—all just to square things for thirty-two enlisted soldiers under the command of a man you didn't even like?
I don't believe it—you can't be that cold-blooded! I don't care
how much of a man of the military you are!"

Ian looked down at him. And it seemed to Tyburn that the
Dorsai face had gone away from him, somehow as remote and
stony as a face carved high up on some icy mountaintop.

"But I'm not just a man of the military," Ian said. "That was
the mistake Kenebuck made, too. That was why he thought that
stripped of military elements, I'd be easy to kill."

Tyburn, looking at him, felt a chill run down his spine as cold
as wind off a glacier.

"Then, in heaven's name," cried Tyburn, "what are you?"

Ian looked from his far distance down into Tyburn's eyes and
the sadness rang as clear in his voice finally, as iron-shod heels
on barren rock.

"I am a man of war," said Ian, softly.

With that, he turned and went on, and Tyburn saw him black
against the winter-bright sky, looming over all the other depart-
ing passengers, on his way to board the spaceship.

ET IN ARCADIA EGO

Thomas M. Disch

*I very much wanted to be, and very much wasn't, a prodigy.
Half the people I know wrote and, worse, published their first
stories or poems or even novels before they'd turned twenty, but
I didn't get a story into print till I was twenty-two, and that one
wasn't a winner. How gratifying to be able to plunk down your
literary maidenhead and say to the ages, Voilà! But not for me.*

*This story is the opposite of such precosities: It's what I wasn't
able to write when I was seventeen. I know because I tried. The
first—ur—version of it may even go back before I had my own
typewriter (October, 1957, an Olivetti Lettera 22) but it wasn't
till the summer of 1960 (I was twenty, and this was my last
chance to be a boy wonder) that I presented a final draft of it,
in lieu of a term paper, to Maurice Baudin, Jr., with whom I was
taking an evening course, "The Novella," at NYU. Entitled: "The
Chthonian Smell." I'm afraid that about summed it up. The rock-
etship Archangel lands on the planet Chthonia; the four over-
civilized crew members discover a race of noble savages, human
in all respects but one, which is revealed in the last, leaden
paragraph.*

And yet (I always thought), and yet. . . .

*Bad as I knew that story to be (and I never sent it to a maga-
zine—never) I sensed the seed in it of something that would
have been worth doing, if I'd done it.*

*During the next ten years I went on to write a great deal of
science fiction, but never again did I attempt that theme which*

more than any other defines sf—the exploration of another world, the encounter with alien forms of life. I prided myself that I understood what such tales were about better than anyone who was actually writing them. Indeed, the chief obstacle in the way of my creating my own avatar was that I had so many and such various theories. First, such stories were about sex. (What stories aren't?) Then, about the emergence of the United States as an imperial power. Then, though less necessarily, about man's relationship to machines and to himself considered as a machine; related to this theme was the curious lack of affect that usually seemed to obtain between the crew members on these expeditions. If I couldn't write the story that I glimpsed through all this theoretical foliage, I was content that no one else had been able to either. For some reason, most fiction, in proportion as it advances toward the farther reaches of space and time, grows lackluster and olive drab. Perhaps it's only that against backgrounds so exotic the pulpy tissue that constitutes 80 percent of most sf becomes, more noticeably, lifeless. It does not grate nearly so much when Perry Mason sits down to a steak dinner for a chapter as when the same dinner is served on Aldebaran V in the year 2500. Even at a meal of hydroponic glop the table settings don't change; some few new words are introduced, but the syntax is immutable.

As, of course, it must be—to a degree. The demand for a totally transformed environment, pushed to its limit, would require a writer to invent a new language for each story he writes. But the sense of such a shift having taken place can be suggested, and when it is, the result is that touch of strange that is the raison d'etre for sf.

A roundabout way of self-congratulation: for with "Et in Arcadia Ego" I felt that for the first time I had laid hold of the very essence of what I understood science fiction to be, that I had found, as never before, my voice.

Indeed, with just the first four paragraphs I knew I had it: a prose that slides by quarter-notes and leaps by octaves; lyric *outbursts leading to deadly banalities; details dwelt upon at inexplicable length and whole masses of exposition disposed of in a shrug; and always this feeling of the whole thing not quite balancing, of the narrator being perfectly mad and at the same time completely ordinary.*

Not that, for having found this voice, the story was then any easier to write. (Only two other stories have taken me longer to bring to completion—"The Roaches" and "Emancipation.") I began "Et in Arcadia Ego" in January of 1969 while living in Milford, Pennsylvania, resumed it that spring in New York, and finished it late in the fall.

The actual moment of its conception I remember with unusual vividness. I used frequently to walk about the wooded hills just outside Milford. Some years before real estate developers had thought to subdivide these woods into lots, and as a result, an incongruous, wide gravel road wound about through the pines and hemlocks. Various pieces of road equipment had been abandoned along this road, and these machineries were gradually becoming part of the landscape. During one day-long hike one of these rusting machines captured me and held me the way a painting can when you're ripe for it. The result was this story and, more directly and immediately, a short poem called "The Caterpillar"[1]:

> *I want to confess*
> *a sneaking fondness for it—*
> *as:*
>
> > *in spring*
>
> *With blossoms*
> *poking through its treads*
> *& trying so hard*
> *to be rectangular*
> > *then*

[1] First published in *Ronald Reagan: the Magazine of Poetry.* Copyright 1970.

in summer, shedding
skins of paint, less noticeable
amid the bother
of things growing
(it seems peculiar, but it does not
seem more than that):

Fall,
    & its rust
is scarcely discordant
with the then
level of taste.

It is at its best
in winter:
        alone
in all these woods
it is unmoved
by the snow.

The obvious link between this and the story that follows is the machine on the altar of the temple, that shrine to death hidden (like the "Wolf") at the center of the Arcadian world. The title itself, familiar as it is, conceals a similar ambivalence. As an inscription on a tomb or monument in various paintings of pastoral scenes (notably Poussin's), it may refer either, elegiacally, to some shepherd lad ("I too [have lived] in Arcady") or to Death itself ("I too [exist] in Arcady"). For me, in the woods that day, the rusted, snow-covered machine seemed to bear that same inscription, with a peculiar modern difference.

"A pastoral!" I thought. "That's what all those stories always are—pastorals!" By the end of that evening I had those first four paragraphs written as they stand now and all the principal elements of the plot noted down.

Violà.

—*Thomas M. Disch*

It is hard to understand why dawn lands on these hills, exciting the chains of carbon with quanta of light, or why, when we step beyond a particular line traced across the marble pavement of the courtyard of π, we have been forced to reappraise certain temporal relationships. It is enough, perhaps, that we should rely upon our captain, Captain Garst Flame, who does not hesitate to resolve dilemmas of this nature with ruthless rationality—even, at times, like Alexander, with an Ax.

There are four continents, roughly equal in area, grouped in opposing pairs two to each hemisphere, so that a simple W traced upon the mercator projection would adequately describe our first hasty itinerary, ticklings of the fingers that would soon so firmly *enclose*.

The planet moves in an eccentric orbit about RR, a highly irregular variable in the Telescope. A primitive theocracy governs the Arcadians, whose diet consists largely of herbal salads, milk and dairy products, and a savoury spiced meat resembling our mutton.

Even at noon the light of RR is tinged with blue, just as his eyes are always blue: genius is not too strong a word for Captain Flame, of whose tragic fate this is the unique record. To him the indigenes present the firstlings of their flocks; him we of the crew (Oo Ling, the lovely Micronesian biochemist; Yank, our impetuous freckle-nosed navigator; Fleur, who took her double doctorate in Cultanthrop and Partfizz; myself, geologist and official Chronicaster to the Expedition) thrice have raised to the nomenclature of *Palus Nebularum*.

The central massif of the White Mountains describes a broad "U" above which the sister cities of Hapax and Legomenon form a gigantic umlaut of arcane beauty. Fleur has recorded and analyzed the structure of the Temple. Her breakdown shows that the centers of curvature, marked by the double circles of the three interfaces of the interpenetrating hemispheres, lie *in a straight line*, the same that has been traced upon the marble that paves the courtyard of π. From this it can be proven that the

Arcadian mathematics, so primitive in other respects, is based upon a shrewd understanding of the physical properties of soap bubbles. We have spent many hours in the commonroom discussing the implications of Fleur's discovery. Oo Ling, who is contracted to my bed, questions Fleur's recommendations of clemency, which I am inclined to support, provisionally. How I love to look into the depths of those ianthine eyes, two vernal flowers floating on a skin of cream, to touch the oily quiff that clings, like iron bonded to aluminum, to that noble brow. Oo Ling, I desire you, pressing my fist into my genitals as I pronounce your name, Oo Ling!

But I fear the imminence of our dissent. Your voice will be with Yank's, mine with Fleur's, and the decision will rest with Captain Flame, who has remained through all these bull-sessions, impassive, serene, showing to us a smile that mocks every attempt at interpretation.

Captain Flame, it is with tears that I record the tragedy of your fate.

I am extending my orological investigations, assisted by the indigenes Miliboeus and Tityus, sons of the Abba Damon, who holds the staff of π. Miliboeus, as the elder, wears a kirtle of heavy mortling dyed the color of fine glauconite; the younger Tityus, uninitiate to the Arcadian mysteries, dresses in simple dun fluff fastened with leather thongs. My own suit on these field trips is a tough corporal unit of flesh-patterned polyisoprene, which can be activated to simulate any sacral movements, such as walking, running, skipping, etc. This, we have learned, is a useful subterfuge, in view of the Arcadian predilection for natural forms.

On the eleventh trimester of our Conquest, Miliboeus said: "Death sings to us, Abba."

And Tityus: "Just as the clouds struggle toward their disappearance, alas, our hearts contest with our minds."

I replied, in the Arcadian tongue: "Brothers, I do not understand. The sun is at solstice. Your blood courses through your veins swiftly as water spills down the mountainside. Youth you possess, wisdom you shall inherit, and poetry—"

Tityus interrupted my peroration, slapping an insect that crawled in the fluff of his thigh. He showed me the smear on the palm of his hand. "It is thus," he said sadly.

"And thus," said Miliboeus, licking the smear from his brother's hand.

Astonished, I reached the captain at once by telstar and narrated this incident to him, while the enlarged image of his hand wandered thoughtfully among the swollen Greek letters of the primary unit. Captain Flame spends all his uncoordinated moments on the bridge now, breathing its metamorphic air, sealing from us all channels except the red and yellow bands. Dammed, our love swells. Moths beat white wings against the protective shell of glass. Images that betoken our more animal nature, which we share, in a sense, with the Arcadians, and I have seen, in the captain's blood, and heard, in his screams, the cost of transcendence.

"I expected this," he said, at red, my narration having terminated.

"I did not expect this," I said. "I did not know that you expected this."

Oo Ling joined our communication: "I expected this too—for these reasons: first, they have kept us in ignorance of their mysteries; second, we are not allowed within the Temple; third, their daily speech is filled with imprecise denotations."

"I object," I replied. "Firstly, it cannot be the mysteries that Miliboeus fears, for he is initiate. Secondly, all primitive cultures observe similar taboos. Thirdly, the inexactness of their speech is characteristic of its emergence from the Rhematic age. I maintain that they are naïve, merely."

"That is probable," the captain said, "and it is this very probability that led me to experience anxiety. Naïveté can be more counterproductive than active deception and, if intransigent, is an argument for genocide."

"Do you feel a large degree of anxiety?" I asked.

"I had felt only a small degree of anxiety, but this message has caused it to enlarge, and it is still enlarging now." He bipped the image of a swelling iridescent sphere.

Oo Ling descended gracefully to the yellow band. "Have you had sex today, Garst?"

"No, nor yesterday."

"Maybe you're just feeling horny. Why don't I come to your bed?"

"Good idea. Are you free now?"

"Yes. I'll finish with these proteins later. I need a good lay myself." Oo Ling blanked off our link.

"With your permission, Captain, I'd like to observe."

"As you please," he replied, with circumspection in the image of his eyes, *bleu d'azur, bleu celeste.* The wall irised open and the floor drove him towards the bed, which puckered to receive that splendid torso, those limbs tensed with an heroic lust. I moved in for a close-up of his loins, then followed the rippling, golden flesh slowly upward, as Cellini's finger might have caressed fauld, breastplate, and gorget of his own molding. I tightened my shot to a single staring disc of *bleu d'azur,* in which I saw, as in a mirror, the image of Oo Ling. Oo Ling, I desire you, pressing my fist, then and now, into my genitals as I pronounce your name, as your image falls and rises on the image of our doomed captain, Garst Flame.

When you come, I come with you, and we are together there, the three of us, and then, sighing, I must break the link, and I find myself sitting, half-disengaged from my unit of polyisoprene, with the two youths, Miliboeus and Tityus, staring at my happiness and pride.

They show me specimens of the rocks they have been collecting, while, at a distance, a lamb bleats with a lamb's naïve anxiety and the lurid sunset shifts from peach to mauve to indigo, a phenomenon as puzzling to me, as arcane, as beautiful, as the expression on his lips when he is not smiling.

This happened on Day Theta/11th trimester of our Conquest of Arcadia, according to the sequence described.

Now, as an eagle will swoop down upon an incautious hare, the strong talons shredding her pink flesh, so dawn's light pounces on the geanticlinal welts of the White Mountains. Yank has noted in his report the presence of certain new faculae on the surface of RR, heralding perhaps some cosmic disease. Light seems uniform, yet is thronged with data: coded histories of all future events dance in its waves like the motes that people the sunbeams, sunbeams that awaken the sheep in their fold, whose glad conclamation then wakes the tardy shepherds Miliboeus and Tityus, as in the age of Dickens and Pope the sound of songbirds might have awakened a poor London chimneysweep, the victim of economic oppressions. The image of their brotherly kisses flickers on the screen of the commonroom, and the image of the morning sunlight, the bleating of the flock.

I lean across the trough to let my fingers graze the down of your hand and trace the curve (a lituus) of your silken quiff. I whisper in your ear: "And who is *my* brother?"

Shall I interpret your laugh? Shall I admit that your smile is an auspex to be ranked with sunspots and birdsong, with deformations of the liver, the pancreas, and the intestines? You are as solemn as a sarabande by Lully, as arousing as Brahms' "Lullaby." When I regard your sexual organ, engorged with blood, I lose all sense of kinship patterns, of teamwork, of philosophy.

And your reply: "Oo Ling?"

And my echo: "I cannot tell you all that I am feeling."

Fleur pokes a finger in my ribs. "You two lovebirds have got to break it up. We've got our work cut out for us today."

Obediently we return our attention to the screen:

The shepherds wake, and walk towards their death, as a young man of good family, in the heyday of the Industrial Revolution,

might have ascended the Jungfrau to enjoy one of its many celebrated views. The random motions of individual sheep become,
in aggregate, a progress as direct as the path of an arrow.

Simultaneously, at the temple, the Abba Damon unlocks, with
a cadeuceus-shaped key, the gilded doors. The opposing helices
of the two serpents are of complementary shades, blue and
orange. The key is so shaped and so colored that the slightest
motion seems to set the two snakes writhing.

Unseen, except by our miniature cameras, the twin serpents
writhe in the lock; the doors swing open, and Damon leads forth
the celebrants. The procession follows him in single file along
the line retraced that same morning upon the marble pavements
with the blood of Miliboeus and Tityus. Above the Abba's head
sways his crozier of office, decorated with brand-new orange and
blue Celanese acetate ribbons, the gift of Oo Ling, who, watching this solemn, scary moment with me in the commonroom, cups
my breasts in his hands, naming, as they flash past on an ancillary
screen, the names of the amino acids composing the phenyla-
lanine chain: "Voline, Aspartic acid, Glutaric acid, Voline . . ."
(And so on.) Just as once, twenty or thirty years ago (though
this seems probable enough, I *remember* nothing of the sort), a
much shorter Oo Ling might have recited that same litany at my
maternal knee.

More affecting, however, than Oo Ling's prattle is the fuss that
Yank is making over the community's coffee pot. Will Fleur have
cream, he wants to know. Will I take sugar? Of course I will! And
thank you very much.

The cameras float up the mountainside in the wake of the flock,
documenting the thousand flowers crushed beneath the feet of
lamb and ewe, tup and yearling: anemones, bluebells, cinerarias
and daisies; lush eglantine and pale forsythia; gentians; haw-
thorns, irises, and April's bright-hued jonquils; and many other
kinds of flowers as well, all of them crushed by innumerable
sheep. Sometimes, however, Miliboeus would stoop to pluck one
of the more enticing blooms, then knit its stem into one of the

garlands, bucolic and complex, with which he'd crowned himself and his kid brother.

"Well, there's coffee for everyone," Yank said, with a little sigh of accomplishment.

"But I see five cups," I pointed out, "and there are only four of us."

"Yes, Mary's right," Fleur said. "Captain Flame is missing!"

It didn't take us long to discover our leader's whereabouts, once the dials were properly adjusted. For he too was on that mountainside, halfway between the two young victims and the procession of priests, who were, already, opening the vault in the hillside—how had it escaped our detection all this time?—from which, with the terrible inevitability of nuclear fission, the Wolf emerged.

Fleur shrieked: "Watch out, Garst! Behind you!"

But he had blanked off all bands and was deaf to our warnings. We observed the events that followed with a mounting suspense, little suspecting that they would lead us, step by step, to a catastrophe of global dimensions.

Concerning the Wolf.

Though not larger than a double sleeping-space and almost noiseless in its operation, the Wolf was expressive, in every detail of its construction, of a sublime rapaciousness, a thirst for dominion so profound as to make *our* Empire, universal as it is, seem (for the moment we watched it) as insubstantial as the architectures shaped by the successive phrases of a Bach chorale, which fade as swiftly as they rise. Here, incarnate in chrome-vanadium steel, was the Word that *our* lips had always hesitated to speak; the orphic secret that had been sealed, eons past, in the cornerstone of the human heart, suspected but never seen; the last, unwritten chapter of the book.

Busy swarms of perceptual organs encircled its crenellated head to form a glistering metallic annulet; its jaws were the toothy scoops of ancient steam-shovels; it was gray, as a glass of breakfast juice is gray, and beautiful as only a machine can be beautiful. We of the crew were breathless with astonishment, admiration, and needless to say, fear.

The Wolf advanced along the path of trampled flowers (anemones, bluebells, etc.), stalking not only the flocks and the two young shepherds but the very Empire itself, in the person of Garst Flame. Did *it* know this already? Had the ever-expanding network of its senses discerned Garst's presence on the path ahead, and was this the reason that it seemed now to quicken its pace, as a lover, learning this his beloved is unexpectedly close-at-hand, will hasten toward her?

What was this creature? Could it have been formed here in Arcadia? In what hidden foundry? What intelligence had wrought so eloquently in chain and cogwheel, engine and frame, the manifest aim of all intelligence? What was it going to do? What weapons would be effective against it? These were the questions we asked ourselves.

All poetry, as Yank once remarked apropos of this brace of sacrificial lambs, is a preparation for death. Tityus tosses his crook—where the wood has slivered a tuft of fleece has snagged and clings—to his older brother: why, except *we* know the danger they are in, should this playful gesture rouse in us feelings of such ineffable sadness?

Such sadness. And yet, paradoxically, of all the indigenes it is only these two who, like green-barked saplings uprooted and bagged before some terrific flood, will survive, while all the rest, the stoutest oaks, the tallest pines, must be drowned in the waters of a necessary and just revenge. But I anticipate myself.

This is my point: that since we can never know from *his* lips why our captain left his post, we must suppose that he was moved by a sense of pity, and that somehow he had foreseen the danger that had till then been locked within the rocky shells of the Arcadian hills, as chemists at the dawn of the modern age suspected the existence, though they could not prove it, of the intercalary elements.

Through the morning and far into the afternoon, while the dreadful contest between the Wolf and Garst was being fought out on the slopes below, their sport continued, the songs, the jigs, the clumsy, countrified wrestling that was more like loveplay than form of combat, the pastoral lunch of whey and the snack later of scarlet berries—and all the while, like the tremolo work above a Lisztian melody, that same unvarying brave show of insouciance!

All this is astonishing, true enough, but as Fleur remarked even then, it is also essentially unhistorical. No more of this blather about Miliboeus and Tityus, who are nothing more now than gray, useless, aging aliens taking up bench-space in the Home Office's Park of All Arts, like turkeys manufactured for a holiday that is no longer much celebrated and still gathering dust beneath the counter of some hick store in Gary, Indiana, or like poems that were never translated from French or a song that never got taped, et cetera, et cetera. The possibilities for obsolescence are as numberless as the stars.

Dinosaurs quarrelling; the customs of pirates, of the Iroquois, of carnivorous apes; the great Super Bowl between the Packers and the Jets; the annihilation of Andromeda III; Norse berserkers hacking Saxons and their horses to bits; the hashish-inspired contretemps of the Assassins of Alamut; the duels of Romeo and Tybalt, of Tancred and Clorinda; killer-dwarves of the Roman arenas; John L. Lewis smashing the skulls of company scabs with his mammoth jackhammer; Apollo flaying Marsyas, slaying the Delphian Python at the very brink of the sacred abyss; bloodbaths, bullfights, drunken mayhem, battle hymns, Schutzstaffel deathcamps, missiles programmed to reproduce themselves in midflight; Germans galloping across the ice of Lake Peipus; Juggernauts and abattoirs; Alexander's delirium at *Arbela; Bull Run;* the Romans slaughtered at *Cannae* and slaughtering at

Chaeronea; Drogheda defeated and depopulated; Panzers swarming across the sand toward *El Alamein;* the Carolingian empire dissolving at *Fontenay,* the French victorious at *Fontenoy;* images that can only begin to suggest the weight and excitement of the drama our cameras recorded that day, as nine-and-an-half feet of red-haired, blue-eyed human fury matched its strength and wits against six tons of supercharged, kill-crazy engineering.

Even the cameras and mikes shared in the combat, for the Wolf's busy senses were equipped with their own weapon systems. A methodical destruction of our network began, to which I retaliated (communications being up my alley) with a simple Chinese-type strategy of endless reinforcement. I figured that the more eyes the Wolf used to pursue and destroy the ship's receptors, the fewer it would have available for its fight against Garst Flame.

As in so many deadly contests, the crucial moments were often the least spectacular. By bluff and psychic ambush each sought to win some fractional advantage over the other. Garst would set his corporal unit swaying hypnotically. The Wolf would spin round him in swift circles, braying and honking and clashing his jaws at erratic intervals, hoping to jar Garst from the steady 4/4 rhythm of his wariness.

Then, without warning, Garst unleashed a river of attenuator particles. The Wolf skittered sideways and parried with a hail of yttrium that spanged harmlessly against the tough polyisoprene of the corporal unit.

A teat of the Wolf squirted clouds of antilife gas, but Garst's nerveshields protected him. The priests, who had arrived on the scene moments after things got started, backed away in terror. The spray settled where they'd been standing; the grass withered and turned black.

The Wolf's eyes and ears were steadily demolishing the cameras and mikes that I poured into the area, making reception in the commonroom ragged and fragmentary. On the other hand, the personnel registers were functioning beautifully, and it boosted our morale a lot to know that Garst's acetylcholine production was down 36 percent with a corresponding 54 percent rise in sympathin. The time lapse for prosthetic response was, in consequence, pared to microseconds.

Then the impossible happened. The Wolf seemed to be taken in by one of Garst's feints, and he was able to run in under the lowest, least well-armored jaw and give it a taste of his circuit randomizers. The jaw turned to haywire—but it had been a trick! Three tentacles, hidden till now in another jaw higher up, blurted out and wrapped themselves around both Garst's arms and his helmet. Ineluctably he was lifted upward, flailing his legs with futile vigor, towards the chomping steam-shovels.

It had been to just such a death as now loomed over our captain that the Abba Damon had willingly and consciously foredoomed his own two sons! Think of *that*, all you moralizers, before you condemn the decision we arrived at (after hours of debate) concerning a suitable punitive measure.

To return, however, to that moment of supreme anxiety. It was just then, wouldn't you know it, that one of the Wolf's ears shot down our sole surviving camera, and simultaneously over the audio we heard the roar of a tremendous implosion.

The personnel registers dropped to a level of complete non-being.

To get fresh cameras to the scene I had to detach the network from my own unit. By the time it arrived everything was over. The amazing thing was that Garst had won, the Wolf was dead, and here is the stratagem: once the Wolf's tentacles had glued themselves to his corporal unit and begun corroding the armor, Garst had tongued the trigger for maximum Self-Destruct, then, hoping against hope, had jettisoned himself bang right out of his unit.

He'd landed, unsheathed and soft, at the feet of the Abba Damon. The suit meanwhile destructed and with it every contiguous
atom of the Wolf, whose eyes and ears buzzed round the site of
the implosion afterward, like bees who've lost their hive. Then,
without a central, directing intelligence, their programming
caused them to knock each other off, as the soldiers sprung from
Cadmus's sowing began, as soon as they'd risen, fully armed, from
the sun-warmed furrows of Boeotian Thebes, to slash and stab
at each other in the madness of civil war.

The Abba Damon stoops and lifts the pale, pained torso with
just such a mingling of amazement and acquisitive delight as a
collector in the heroic age of archaeology might have shown
upon discovering some antique term, an armless satyr from the
baths of Titus.

"Take me to . . ." Garst whispered, before the treason of his
own lungs, desperate for more, and purer, air, silenced him.

With our captain cradled in his arms the Abba Damon retraces
his path down the slopes of the mountain, along the line of blood
in the courtyard of π. Again the twin serpents writhe in the lock,
and now for the first time, as our camera flutters above the sacrifice like the Dove in representations of the Trinity, we see the
Inner Temple.

A piece of road equipment, precious in its antiquity, seems to
have been abandoned before the high altar.

A song of woe, Arcadian Muses, a song of woe!

The Abba Damon traces the curve (a lituus) of his staff of
office, as, with sacramental dispassion, he observes his assistants
fastening the cords securely around Garst's genitals. How many
times—and with what feelings of tenderness, the charity of the
senses—have all of us, Fleur, Yank, Oo Ling, myself, caressed
that cock, those balls, the little bush of hair! O Garst! now we
cannot touch you! And never, never again.

Then, as the priests take turns operating a crude windlass, the victim is raised until at last his body swings, inverted, an obscene, pitiful pendulum, above the rusting machinery. I cannot recall this moment, this final image without feeling again the same numbing terror, which shades, again, into the same unspoken collusion, as though, then and today, a compact were being made between us: between on the one hand, the Abba, his priests, that green planet, and, on the other, myself, the crew, our ship, an Empire—a compact whose tragic clauses we must obey, on each side, down to the last remorseless syllable.

A song of pain, Arcadian Muses! Arcadian Muses, a song of pain!

I must mention his screams. His suffering, like the attributes of Godhead, is at once inconceivable and endlessly intriguing, a perpetual calendar of thought, an Ouroboros. I think of that strong and splendid being stripped to the irreducible human sequence of head, chest, gut, and sex, and though usually it is a matter of indifference to me that I am of the female sex, I am glad to know that I need never fear such a thing happening to me.

Sing of death, Arcadian Muses! Sing!

He raises the knife and, murmuring some words to the effect that he does this only with the greatest reluctance, slits Garst's throat from left to right. A brief necklace of blood graces the white flesh that only this morning was banded by the red collar of Imperial office. The blood streamed down across his face to drench and darken the soft curls. His body hung there till the last drop had drained out into the rusted engine of the caterpillar.

Sing, Arcadian Muses! Sing the mystery. For your own death approaches.

The motor turned over once, sputtered, and died. The scoop lifted a fraction of an inch, and these events took place, our captain's death, the destruction of Arcadia, so that that gesture might be made.

* * *

Following these barbarities, the Abba Damon, in pleading for the release of his sons, sought to excuse himself and his people with arguments and "explanations" too laughable to merit the dignity of inclusion in this record. To repeat such tales would be an affront not only to the memory of our leader but also to that of the planet which it was our pleasure, the next day, to wipe out of existence.

Before X-hour each of us wrote his own epitaph in the log, an ineffaceable magnetic tribute to the man who'd led us to success on so many missions.

This was Fleur's: "Soon we'll be back at the Home Office, back on the red bands, where you were always most at home. Our recall priorities will be adjusted, they always are before reassignment, and that means I'll forget you, except for a couple memories that won't matter that much. This pain is a ground-mist, and the sun comes up and it's gone. But if I were able to miss you, Garst, I would."

This, Yank's: "The last time I kissed you . . . the rest may have to go, but I'm holding on to that."

And this, Oo Ling's: "I'm sorry that he had to die."

This history has been my epitaph for you, Garst. There is never a last thing to say, unless Oo Ling has said it. One day I told you I loved you more than I loved the rest—and even then it wasn't true. None of us, probably, loved you very much, because if truth be told you weren't that lovable, but we have done that which in your eyes would have been more important: we have done our duty.

Thus, on Day Delta, 12th trimester, the Conquest of Arcadia was concluded. Just before blast-off we fired a full charge from the temporal cannon at the heart of RR. Before the sun set that evening on the cities of Hapax and Legomenon, it would have gone to nova.

Arcadia has ceased to be, but other planets await us. The whole great pulsing body of what-is has been tied to the altar, and we advance to tie about its universal neck the sequence of our extinctions, like ropes of pearls, each one a unique, and now demolished world. O glades and rivers, O winds and darknesses, will you mourn, with us, their loss?

BUT SOFT, WHAT LIGHT . . .

Carol Emshwiller

At the time I wrote this story I had read lots of robot-in-love and love-of-robot and personified computer stories (I had even written one) and I liked these stories generally. Robots are cuddly sometimes and then, too, they represent the outsider or the left-out, the lame, the confused, etc., so most of us can identify with them only too well. I know I can. But once you think of it, all these stories are pretty ridiculous. You might as well fall in love with your washing machine. I forget what story I read just before I wrote this, but I know I read one about a lady falling in love with a robot and thought, Nice but silly; so I thought, why not be really all-out foolish? And maybe also take some aspects of computers that had to be ignored in other "realer" stories.

This story has never been anthologized, and yet when I wrote it I thought everybody would be begging for it. I learned the hard way. Anyway, I still like the story for two reasons. First, I was struggling hard to free myself from all the things I had learned so far about plotting and such. It's really hard to put aside something you've learned. That may sound strange and you may wonder why anyone would want to unlearn a skill. I can only say that I felt (in some intuitive way, since I didn't know that much about it at the time) that I had to unlearn in order to learn what I wanted, and I found it very hard to break away from the plotted story. I had to do it, literally, one step at a time, doing away with one plot element and finding one other formal element to put in its place. (I was utterly lost without form of some sort, and I had no desire to write chaos.) So this story was a step along that way and I was pleased with its free-flowing quality and its improvisational tone within its plot structure. Now I frequently use out and out improvisation to find my themes and to find my way into "stories," and I try to find forms completely other than plots to structure them. When I improvise, though, I write more and I discard more than I ever did when I was "plotting." I write at least ten pages for every one I keep. (I have never felt myself to be part of the New Wave, whatever that is, because that seemed to me to mean people with a cause and I was just sitting here writing, not bothering anybody, but I do like the writing that goes by that name even if I don't believe there is such a thing.)

Also, when I wrote this story I thought I was going to change the world. I really thought so. Not with just this one story, but I had a whole series of sex stories I thought would clean up sex. (Since then I've become a more self-confident person, but with fewer illusions about my importance . . . if you can follow that.) Anyway, I was going to make "fuck" the most beautiful and reverent and funny word in the language, as it should be. If, in the beginning there was a word, then that word should have been "fuck" since it is the word that says how most of us who are not flowers or fish and such were created. So, this is one of that series of stories to bring about the day when we'll celebrate our day of conception as our real birthday. (Unfortunately that would make us all nine months older. It also might be a little hard to get the exact time, so maybe we'd have to make do with the celebration of the first missed menstrual period.)

—Carol Emshwiller

Uniq-o-fax, the only machine of its kind in existence anywhere in the world today.

U-NI-KO-FA-EX! UN-I-KOFF-AX!

He isn't modest or immodest. He's neither proud nor humble nor shy, neither (what's more) truthful nor a liar and yet both true and false. One could say a finder of the lie in truth and of the truth in lies. He, the infallible within the fallible (or the other way around) that must always be the essence of the poetic gesture. He is, in other words, *all* poet.

And so I had refused to call him less than MAN or to allow anyone else to do so. (And, by the way, I was a virgin then. But I have since been transmogrified.)

Uniq-o-fax, a sensitive machine for combining words so fast that, like an infinite number of monkeys at an infinite number of typewriters, he not only COULD write, by a random selection, all of Shakespeare's plays, but almost DID at 10^{12} bits per second (also most of Mallarmé and Gide). Most certainly he is experienced, as anyone can see.

I was his (sort of) vestal virgin. I was there, in other words, to see that he was surrounded by an atmosphere conducive to his art. I kept the fires of inspirations going by supplying him with words fraught with meanings, rich in sounds, such as: athwart, somnambulist, besprinkle, incommensurate, smirch, discreate, duodecimality, ingurgitation, furbished, crepuscular.

He was thirty-nine typewriters and a word bank. I was seventeen.

One cannot hope to gain more by giving less. These days we all know so well the laws of payment and of goods received. (His very first words on the very first typewriter were, I LOVE YOU. Isn't that just like a poet!) I was there simply to *give* (yet with full expectations of receiving and in like proportion to that given). I was resolved to be the following: goodnatured, trusting, patient, enduring, admiring, understanding, (all my female virtues) and helpful, apt, illogical but not too much so, malleable,

and (especially) serving (woman's privilege). I LOVE YOU
TOO I wrote back to him on that very same typewriter.

Where, oh where, (I often wondered to myself on snowy winter evenings) among all these wires and tubes, is the actual seat
of his inner being?

> *I love you (he wrote.)*
> *"Let me count the ways:"*
> *One two*
> *Three four*
> *Eye neck leg Adam's apple*
> *(Five)*
>
> *Wrinkle under arm*
> *Big toe. That's seven*
> *But that's not all.*
>
> *Let one who can count, count,*
> *And in a microsecond*
> *To thousands.*
> *Charms have never been better*
> * catalogued*
> *Than this*
> *From whorl of fingertip through*
> * pubic hair line*
> *I love you*

I remember that first time, . . . you, in the rain in August wearing your stainless steel fedora, bright as a sink, with your other
units jauntily behind you. What a gay conglomeration! What a
happy-go-lucky air, hat back and something or other akimbo,
sparks flying at each step. You hadn't bothered to put up your
umbrella and neither had I.

The forsythia were not in bloom then, but if they had been,
what a riot of yellow all down the street!

"I WAS a phantom of delight
When first I gleamed upon your
*   sight, . . ."*

When I went into the A&P, I saw you turn and follow. You bought four tangelos at 49¢ a pound and a box of Band-Aids and I knew they couldn't be for you. I, on the other hand, bought Brillo, Glass Wax, Sani-Flush and a three-way 50-75-100 watt bulb and you knew I didn't buy them for myself.

And later, after I had eaten all your tangelos (and after you had used up my three-way light bulb) (Oh, those were innocent days!) we went uptown in a moving van and parked on 72nd Street. You, wired for redundancy (three-input, two-output) repeated poems you had already recited, for, as William Blake says: "You never know what is enough unless you know what is more than enough," and also: "The road of excess leads to the palace of wisdom." (And that was so TRUE as far as you were concerned.) And sometimes that night when you had a distant look in your eyes, you said (upon my questioning you) that you were counting to the ultimate number and at THAT many bits per second I dared not even guess how far you had already gotten. And later still, I saw the sunrise reflected in your forehead (if that was your forehead) and I saw the shine of the moon go down on what might have been your nose. The very next day I applied for that vestal-virgin job that happened to be open at the Office of Contemplative and Exploratory Poetry.

Days flew by. I was happy. Winter, Spring, etc. and then came the day the police arrested you for destroying public property. That night you had not only clicked chinks in the sidewalk all down Seventh Avenue, but one of the units dangling after you (220-volt, three-wire cables) had inadvertently leaned against a wall on the corner of 28th Street while contemplating possible trajectories to the Mare Imbrium. However, I pointed out to the police that you were, indeed, Uniq-o-fax, and, as such, certainly public property *yourself* (as aren't ALL poets?) and that night, believing me to be someone of importance from the Poetry Department, they let you out in my custody. How we laughed when we finally shut the door (to my apartment) on the outside world!

Why are you laughing so, Uniq-o? Are you convulsed by some tickling wire? some jerky AC-DC? Is there moisture in some sensitive spot? Are the logic gates not quite closed? However, redundancy, as usual, will keep you functioning in spite of it all and I have plenty of wall outlets if needed. Is that ozone? a crackle of static? Avoid the furniture, please. Oops, there goes the Oxford Anthology, in fact a whole shelf-load of poets: Ginsberg, Ashbery, Verlaine, Keats (in descending order of modernity, or does Ashbery come first?). In fact the bookcase. Lamp, too. The stuffing is coming out of the couch cushions. Snap, the little finger of my left hand, laughing, laughing. Now he has crushed my middle toes but I don't mention it and somehow I manage not even to wince. Why should I hurt him? Spoil this magic moment when we're alone together at last, tentative, embarrassed, yet SURE. Why should I spoil it? How could I! I hobble backwards, laughing, to the bedroom and put on a fur-lined glove and a pair of old sneakers (also loosen my bra and take off my garter belt). Laughing, I return. "Oh, dear Uniq-o, ho, ho. Oh, ho, ho. Ow, ho, ho. Oh, ow, ho, ho, ho."

He makes the first sly insinuation
(as always, all poet)
And now an impertinent interpolation,
    then a quiet interjection
        Here and there, here and
            there an addendum
            (three input, two output)
likely infiltrations, fierce interspersions,
intrusions, infusions, inroads,
intermittent instillations.

I, audibly receptive, gently recipient,
absorb, assimilate, stomach,
become concierge of so many en-
   tryways, corridors,
thresholds, vestibules and sills,
I, merged until implosion!

Then he interjaculates!
   I had no idea there were so
many pubic possibilities.
   And who would have dreamed
of such largess in the midst of an
all pervasive miniaturization.

Oh infinite series of variables . . .
"Oh wild West Wind," (at 10^{12}
   bits per second) . . .
"What if my leaves ARE falling . . ."

But isn't it strange that after all this I was still, to all appearances, a virgin? (I will never agree with the personnel manager
at the Office of Contemplative and Exploratory Poetry, who said
that I was technically unfit for my position as keeper of the fires
of inspiration.) You see I hobbled back to the poetry office as
soon as I was able, only to find in my place a male psychiatrist of
a fatherly type, but Uniq-o-fax, when I last heard, was suffering
from closed circuits, from which I conclude (happily) that at
least he never fell in love with anyone else. They say every 23rd,
24th and 25th word he says is I and love and you, respectively
and, due to his condition, I know he still means me.

THE MISOGYNIST

James Gunn

> *"The whole intricate question of method, in the craft of fiction, I take to be governed by the question of the point of view—the question of the relation in which the narrator stands to the story."*
>
> —PERCY LUBBOCK, The Craft of Fiction.

How does a writer select out of some sixty stories one that, in good conscience, he can include in a book like Authors' Choice? What criteria control his selection: creative satisfaction, recognition, financial return, career significance, sentimental attachment . . . ?

"The Misogynist" has all of these, and it has one more virtue the editor insisted upon: It is short.

"The Misogynist" was the first story printed over my own name —my first ten were published over the pseudonym of Edwin James for reasons which now almost evade me. I think it had something to do with preserving my critical detachment if I decided to return to college for a graduate degree and did a study of science fiction. By the time I wrote "The Misogynist," however, my master's degree was almost in hand, as was my thesis about science fiction and it was on its way to becoming the first thesis ever serialized in a pulp magazine, and if anything my writer's credentials were an asset.

"The Misogynist" was my first story in Galaxy. Astounding, the hero of my youth, had published two earlier stories, but Galaxy

was a new magazine which already had published stories like Fritz Leiber's "Coming Attraction," Pohl and Kornbluth's "Gravy Planet" (book title: The Space Merchants*), and Alfred Bester's "The Demolished Man"—different stories all, but all the kind of stories I wanted to write. For the next four years* Galaxy *would get first look at what I wrote.*

The sale of "The Misogynist," along with two other stories the same month to Astounding *and to* Planet Stories*, persuaded me to give up a job editing paperback books and return to full-time writing; during the next three years I wrote or laid the foundations for my first nine books.*

"The Misogynist" has been reprinted eleven times (twelve counting this one), including six foreign translations. It led off and set the tone for my collection of short stories for Bantam, Future Imperfect. *It has brought more income per word (or per hour expended, with the exception of the novelization of* The Immortal, *which I wrote in seven days) than anything I have written. I can hear Horace Gold saying now, "Good science fiction never dies."*

"The Misogynist" has a property shared by a few other stories: Many people remember it, but few know who wrote it. Occasionally I have described the story to a group and had some long-time writer or reader exclaim, "Did you write that *story?" One writer told me recently that he relates the story at parties and leaves the impression that* he *wrote it.*

Finally, I have used "The Misogynist" for nearly twenty years in my fiction writing classes as an example of the way idea turns into story. (The last time I read it aloud I was attacked by student members of the women's lib.)

I have a good record of the way the story was created. First came the idea: I wrote the story in 1951, but the idea itself occurred to me in the fall of 1950. My first son was a year old and still not sleeping at night, and the tensions of attending graduate school, writing a thesis, and rocking a child had brought out certain differences of opinion between my wife and me. Like many a man without sisters, I had always thought women were sort of soft men, arranged in a delightfully different way. But one day I thought: men and women don't think alike; they are so different, in fact, that they might as well be different species. And then I thought: Women are aliens. I wrote that down on a note card so I wouldn't forget it, a card I still have and show to my classes: *Women are aliens.*

I had an idea, but I didn't know what to do with it. An idea can go in many different directions: adventure, romance, intrigue, character development . . . and in various lengths from short short to novel. I visualized it as a satire and as a short story, but I couldn't think of a way to get into it. For six months I would pull the idea out of the recesses on my mind, look it over to see if it had sprouted any mechanisms, and tuck it away again.

Suddenly it came to me—a way of telling the story, a method of narration. I would use a narrator, like Ring Lardner's in "Haircut," who knows less about what is going on in the story than the reader. The protagonist would be an amateur humorist (men and women don't agree about humor, you know), and the narrator's admiration for the protagonist and his lack of understanding of the protagonist's seriousness would keep the story moving through an exposition of the alien qualities of women and then would result in the betrayal of the protagonist to his wife and lead to the final turn of events which would open up the story.

As I tell my students, a story is nothing without an idea, but it is equally true that an idea is nothing without a way of telling it. Occasionally, when they come together, they may produce a story like "The Misogynist."

—*James Gunn*

Harry is a wit.

Someone has described a wit as a person who can tell a funny story without cracking a smile. That's Harry.

"You know," Steve said at the office one day, "I'll bet Harry will walk right up to the flaming gates of Hell, keeping the Devil in stitches all the way, and never change expression."

That's the kind of fellow Harry is. A great guy to have around the office. Almost makes you want to go to work in the morning, thinking of the coffee break or watching until you can join Harry at the water cooler or in the men's room. Sometimes you got to laugh, just to see him, thinking about the last story he told. Smart, too, digging up odd facts, piling on detail after detail until you just got to admit he's right, and you finally see something straight for the first time. Everybody says he'd be president of the place someday, if he didn't make jokes about the company, too.

But the kind of story Harry likes—he likes them long. They start slow—sometimes you don't even know it's a joke—and build up until all at once you explode with laughter and then each new touch leaves you more helpless. The kind of story you take home to your wife and you get part way through, laughing like an idiot, and you notice she's just sitting there, sort of patient like a martyr, thinking maybe about getting dinner on the table or how she's going to re-do the living room, and you stop laughing and sigh and say, "It must be the way he tells it" or "Nobody can tell stories like Harry."

But then women don't think Harry's funny.

Like the other night. Harry and I were sitting in his living room while the women—Lucille and Jane—were whipping up something in the kitchen after the last rubber.

"Did you ever stop to think," Harry said, "about what strange creatures women really are? The way they change, I mean, after you marry them. You know—they stop hanging on your words, they stop worrying about what you like or don't like, they stop laughing at your jokes."

I chuckled and said, "So the honeymoon is over," Harry and Lucille being married only a month or so.

"Yes," Harry said seriously. "I guess you could say that. The honeymoon is over."

"Tough," I said. "The girl you marry and the woman you're married to are two different people."

"Oh, no. They're not. That's just the point."

"The point?" I began to suspect something. "You mean there's a point?"

"It's not just a matter of superficial differences, you see. It's something fundamental. Women think differently, their methods are different, their goals are different. So different, in fact, that they are entirely incomprehensible."

"I gave up trying to understand them a long time ago," I said, with a despairing wave of the hand.

"That's where we make our mistake," Harry said somberly. "We accept when we should try to understand. We must understand why. As the Scotch say, 'All are good lasses, but where come the ill wives?'"

"Why?" I echoed. "Well, they're built differently. Inside, too, glands, bearing children, and all that."

Harry looked scornful. "That's their excuse, and it's not good enough. They should do best what their differences fit them for. Marriage is their greatest career—and their greatest failure. A man to them is only the necessary evil they must have before they can get the other things they want."

"Like the black widow spider and her mate?" I suggested.

"In a way. And yet, not entirely. *The spiders, at least, are of the same species.*"

It was a moment before the meaning sank in. "And men and women aren't?" I almost shouted.

"Sh!" he warned, and glanced nervously at the kitchen door.

Then was when I began to chuckle. Harry should have been on television; he was not only a comedian, he was an actor. On top of that I had to admire the guy, making a joke out of what is—every husband can tell you—one of the greatest and most secret tragedies of life. Greater even because no one can talk about it. No one but Harry.

I laughed. That must have been what he was waiting for, because he nodded, relaxed, and stopped glancing at the door out of the corner of his eye. Or maybe that was after Lucille peeked out of the kitchen and said, "Harry off on one of his stories again? Tell us when he's through, so we can bring in the refreshments."

It was cute the way she said it, she's so pretty and blond and tiny and all, and you could tell it was a running joke with them. I couldn't help thinking what a lucky guy Harry was—if a fellow has to get married, that is, and most of us do.

"The alien race," Harry whispered and leaned back.

It was a good line and I laughed again.

"What better way," he went on quietly, "to conquer a race than to breed it out of existence? The Chinese learned that trick a long time ago. Conqueror after conqueror overran the country, and each one was passively accepted, allowed to marry—enveloped, devoured, obliterated. Only this case is just the reverse. Breed in the conqueror, breed out the slave; breed in the alien, breed out the human."

"Makes sense," I said, nodding.

"How did it all start?" Harry asked. "And when? If I knew these answers I would know everything. Did a race of mateless females descend upon the Earth when man was still almost a cave-dwelling animal? Or was it in historic times? My guess is they were dropped here by their men. Jettisoned. Dumped. 'If that's the way you're going to be, Baby, you can just walk home.' Except there are no footpaths in space."

"That was pretty drastic."

He shrugged. "They were aliens, remember. Maybe they had some solution, some procreative substitute for women. Maybe these women were the worst of the lot and the ones they had left were better. Or maybe the men didn't give a damn. Maybe they preferred racial suicide to surrender."

Angrily he shoved the coffee table aside, grumbling something about women's ideas of furnishing a home, and pulled his chair closer. "Okay, what could they do, these creatures from another world? '. . . the sad heart of Ruth, when sick for home, she stood in tears among the alien corn' was nothing to what they must have felt. But the song they heard was not that of the nightingale, but the song of conquest.

"They couldn't just exterminate humanity, now could they? Besides that's dangerous and virtually impossible. Give man a danger he can see, and he will never surrender. Women don't think like that. Their minds work in devious ways; they win what they want by guile and subtlety. That's why they married into the human race."

"You sound so certain," I said.

"This isn't just idle speculation; there's evidence. According to Jewish folklore, Eve wasn't the first woman. First, there was Lilith. Eve was the usurper. Oh, they made mistakes. They had to experiment. The Amazons—were they an experiment? Once a year, you know, they visited the Gargareans, a neighboring tribe; any resulting male children were put to death. That didn't work for long, of course. Their purpose, their very alienness, was too obvious. And the matriarchies—too blatant, would have given the whole thing away eventually. Besides, men are useful in ways that women aren't. Men are inventive, artistic, creative—and can be nagged or coaxed into doing what women want them to do anyway."

I lit a cigarette and looked for an ashtray. He shoved over a silly little dish that would suffocate a cigarette the minute you laid it down.

"That's what women buy when you aren't watching," Harry said. "The purpose isn't important; it's the appearance that counts. Lights that look pretty and make you blind. They want a house with southern exposure and a picture window, and then they put up heavy drapes to keep the furniture from fading. They buy new furniture and hide it in slip covers. They clean up the house so it will be nice to live in, and then they get angry when you try to get comfortable in it."

I dug out a pillow that was putting a crick in my back and threw it on another chair. "Are they all alike?"

He frowned. "I wonder. One hears about happy marriages, but that might be only alien propaganda. Perhaps there are a few Liliths left—women who like to read, who use their minds, who like sports and competition, who can grasp abstract ideas. You could use these as tests, perhaps—if there are any human women."

"How about women," I chipped in, "who prefer the company of men to that of other women?"

He started to nod and then shook his head. "It would just be guesswork. They're smart—smarter than we are about getting along, about getting around people. They use weapons like tears and mad fits and sulks against which we've never invented a defense."

"There are women who are satisfied with a comfortable life," I suggested, "who don't drive their husbands to so much insurance that they're worth more dead than alive and then work them to death. That sounds pretty human."

"If there are any like that," he said gloomily. "Anyway we'll never really know the answers. The important thing is to recognize the situation—to do something about it—before it's too late. It's in the last few generations that their plans have come to fruition. They have the vote, equal rights without surrendering any privileges, and so forth. They're outliving men. They control ninety percent of the wealth. And soon"—his voice sank to a significant whisper—"they'll be able to do away with men altogether—fertilization by salt water, electrical stimulus, that sort of thing. And we're the traitor generation. We're the ones who are committing suicide—for the whole human race."

"We won't be needed anymore," I said, trying not to laugh.

He nodded. "Don't think I haven't got more than vague suspicions. And it's been damned hard. Knowledge of the female conspiracy has died out in the last fifty years. There's no longer even that subconscious knowledge that alerted the centuries of men before—that body of tradition and folklore which is a sort of inherited wisdom of a people. We've been taught to scorn all that as superstition. Most teachers are women, of course."

I gave him his straight line. "Our ancestors knew about all this?"

"They knew. Maybe they were afraid to spell it out, but they kept hinting at it. Homer, Ovid, Swift—'A dead wife under the table is the best goods in a man's house,' said Swift. Antiphanes, Menander, Cato—there was a wise one. 'Suffer women once to arrive at an equality with you, and they will from that moment become your superiors.' Plautus, Clement of Alexandria, Tasso, Shakespeare, Dekker, Fletcher, Thomas Brown—the list is endless. The Bible: 'How can he be clean that is born of woman?' 'I suffer not a woman to teach, nor to usurp authority over a man, but to be in silence'. . . ."

For fifteen minutes he continued—covering the Greeks, the Romans, the Renaissance—and hadn't begun to run dry. Even for Harry this was digging deep for a story. *This is Harry's peak,* I said to myself, a little awed. *He will never do anything better than this.*

Then Harry began getting closer to modern times.

"'Women are much more like each other than men,' said Lord Chesterfield. And Nietzsche: 'Thou goest to women? Don't forget they whip.' Then there was Strindberg, touched by a divine madness which gave him visions of hidden truths. Shaw, who concealed his suspicions in laughter lest he be torn to pieces—"

"Ibsen?" I suggested, chuckling, dredging a name out of my school days that I vaguely remembered was somehow connected with the subject.

Harry spat, as if he had something vile in his mouth.

"That traitor! That blind fool! It was Ibsen who first drama- tized the insidious propaganda which led, eventually, to the so-called emancipation of women and was really the loosing of the chains which kept them from ravening unrestrained."

"Ravening," I chortled. "Oh, yes, yes. Ravening!"

"You must go back to folk sayings to get real truth," Harry said, quieting a little. " 'A man is happy only two times in his life,' say the Jugoslavs. 'When he marries a wife and when he buries her.' Or the Rumanians: 'When a man takes a wife, he ceases to dread Hell.' Or the Spanish: 'Who hath a wife hath also an enemy.' 'Never believe a woman, not even a dead one,' advise the German peasants. The wisdom of the Chinese: 'Never trust a woman, even though she has given you ten sons.' "

He stopped, not as if he were near the end of his material but to begin brooding.

"Did you ever look for something," he asked, "a collar button, say, or a particular pair of socks—and it isn't there and you tell your wife? Why is it she can come and pick it up and it's right under your nose all the time?"

"What else have they got to think about?"

"It makes you wonder," he said. "It makes you wonder if it really was there when you looked. They aren't mechanical, they hate machines, and yet they know when something's about to break down. 'Hear that funny little sound in the engine,' they'll say. 'Like a grasshopper's wings rubbing together.' You can't hear anything, but the next hour or the next day the fan belt breaks. All of a sudden food tastes wrong to them. 'This milk tastes funny. The cows have been eating wheat.' Or 'This meat's funny.' 'What do you mean, it's funny?' you ask. 'It's just funny. I can't describe it.' After awhile you're afraid to drink anything or eat anything."

I agreed with him and thought, *Strange, the odd truths that Harry can link into something excruciatingly funny.*

"They have no respect for logic," Harry said. "No respect at all for the sanctity of a man's mind, for what his world is built upon. They argue as it suits them, waving away contradictions and inconsistencies as meaningless. How many of us have our Xanthippes, bent on dragging us down from our contemplation of divine truth to the destructive turmoil of daily strife? It's maddening, maddening!"

This was Harry's story, but it needed one thing, a climax, a clincher to wind up all the threads into a neat ball of laughter.

"What would they do," I asked soberly, "if they discovered that someone knew their secret?'"

Harry smiled. For one unwary second I thought he was slipping but I should have known better. The smile was sardonic.

"There," Harry said, "you have hit upon the crux. If my surmises are true, why has no one else discovered it? And the answer is—they have!"

"They have?" I repeated.

Harry nodded. "They would have to be done away with, of course. Silenced. And it would have to show up somewhere—if one knew where to look."

He paused. "Why," he said, pointing a finger at me, "are there more men in asylums than women?"

"You mean—?"

He nodded.

I collapsed, hysterical. I choked. I burbled. I gasped. When the women came in a moment later with their ridiculous little sandwiches and coffee and strange dessert, I was barely able to get out a couple of words.

"Hi, alien!" I spluttered at Jane.

And I laughed some more, especially when I saw the stricken face Harry was putting on, as if he were horrified, terribly frightened, sort of all sunk in on himself—better, much better, than I've seen a professional actor do it on television.

The look on the women's faces brought me around finally—the bored look—and I tried to share the joke. Harry was laughing, too, kind of weakly. That surprised me a little; he always is sort of bland and mildly curious when one of his stories turn his listeners into squirming protoplasm, as if he were saying, "Oh, did I do that?"

"It must be the way he tells it," I said, surrendering. "Nobody can tell stories like Harry."

You see what I mean. Women don't think Harry's funny.

And so the evening was all right. A little flat at the end, the way evenings usually are, nice for a while but tapering off until there isn't much to say but "good night—had a wonderful time—have to do it again soon," and we said it.

As we were going out I heard Lucille say, kind of sharp, "Harry, there's something wrong with the hot water heater. You've been promising to look at it for days, and you've got to do something about it tonight because I'm going to do the washing tomorrow," and I heard Harry answer, "Yes, dear," very meek and obedient, and I thought, *The guy's got to blow off steam somewhere,* and I figured I'd be hearing the story again at the office.

Which goes to show how wrong a man can be.

Next morning Lucille called up and said Harry was sick—turned out it was a heart attack, a coronary—and couldn't come to work. I called there a couple of times, but Lucille said he was too sick to see anybody, the doctor wanted him kept very quiet, and maybe he wasn't going to pull through. And I guess Harry is really sick because Lucille had Dr. Simpson, that woman doctor, and Harry's said many times he wouldn't have her treat his sick dog if he wanted the dog to get well. I knew then Harry was too sick to care.

It's funny how quick a fellow can go. I got to thinking what a shame it was that Harry's finest effort, the climax of his wit, so to speak, should go with him, and how it's too bad that great' vocal art should vanish without leaving a trace.

I began trying to remember—and I couldn't remember so good —particularly the quotations—so I did a little research of my own, to give an idea what it was like. I even ran across a couple Harry missed, and I guess I'll put them in because probably Harry knew them and just didn't get around to talking about them.

One of them everybody knows. The one of Kipling's that begins, "The female of the species. . . ." The other one I worked up by myself, just thinking. *Why,* I asked myself one day, *are there more widows than widowers?*

Jane is calling me to come down and fix the furnace.

But I don't know. I don't remember anything being wrong with the furnace.

ALL OF US ARE DYING

George Clayton Johnson

The story on All of Us Are Dying:

I was desperately trying to be a writer. My movie Ocean's 11 *had just come out, and using that single credit, I managed to interest a Hollywood agent in looking at some of my material. The man's name is Jay Richards. He was head of the television department of the Famous Artist's Agency, long since absorbed by IFA (International Famous Agency) which represents me now in television and movies. I showed Jay the story titled then "The Four of Us Are Dying." He scrubbed out the title and wrote in* Rubberface! *He shot it over to Rod Serling at The Twilight Zone and Rod winced and offered $500 for it before retitling it "All of Us Are Dying," the best title of the three. He adapted it for tv. I went on to sell Rod other things and finally ended up writing for the show along with Richard Matheson and Charles Beaumont.* Rogue *finally bought the story for publication. Said Frank M. Robinson, the editor, "I would have bought anything with the title 'All of Us Are Dying.' It's one of those titles that speaks to everyone."*

I hope you agree.

—*George Clayton Johnson*

He drove into the strange new town, parked the car in front of the hotel on Main Street and climbed out.

"Sam!" said a voice. "Sam Windgate!" A heavy-set man in a dark suit was bustling toward him with his hand outstretched.

His response was automatic. He clapped the man on the back and pumped his hand. "It's good to see you again," he said fervently. "I'm in a hurry now but I'll look you up when I finish."

"I'm in the book, Sam," said the man, grinning.

He entered the hotel. At the cigar counter he stopped to buy a pack of cigarettes. The girl behind the glass case smiled warmly as she turned toward him. Seeing his face the smile died.

"It's Fred, isn't it?" she asked. "Fred Black?"

He looked at her, not saying anything.

"Did you expect me to forget the things you said? The promises you made?" she said.

"Of course not."

"I don't understand how you would dare come back here after everything that happened."

He reached out to touch her hand where it rested on the glass case.

"There is a reason why I came back." His eyes traveled boldly over her body.

"It's too late," she said.

"Perhaps not," he said.

Her eyes met his, becoming large and moist, before she turned away to busy herself with the stock.

He walked out of the hotel.

At the Wagonwheel Cafe where he went to lunch, the waitress came up to the table briskly. "Ben!" she said. "Ben Hoffmier!"

He pushed a smile onto his lips.

"Well," she said, bending over him. "When did you get in town?"

"Just arrived," he said.

"Where's Evie? Have you still got that diner at Grosse Point?"

"Here, here," he said easily. "One thing at a time."

She swiped at the table with a damp cloth, rubbing against his shoulder.

While she talked, his mind was busy sorting out the words, the tones, the inflections, weighing them, assigning them values.

"I left Evie behind this time. You know how it is."

"Sure," she said. "Do you remember the awful way she acted when she found us together?" Her hands brushed his on the dark table top.

"Forget about Evie," he said.

"Sure," she said. "Now you just sit here while I bring you the special. For you, it's on the house." She swirled away in a rustle of starched clothing.

He saw a man eyeing him from a counter stool. And who do *you* think I am? he thought.

On his way out he waved to the waitress.

"I get off at eight," she said.

Back at the hotel, he smiled at the girl behind the cigar counter. She turned away coldly. He crossed over to the registration desk. "One single," he said.

In his room he picked up the telephone and asked to be connected with the cigar counter.

"This is Fred," he said into the mouthpiece. He lowered his voice to a husky whisper. "Will you meet me someplace?"

He held the receiver to his ear, listening, while a smile grew on his face. Then he replaced the instrument in its cradle and lay back on the bed.

It was getting dark. Through the window he could see the sign winking on and off: BAR—BAR—BAR! He took out his wallet and checked its contents. He saw he was getting short on funds. He ran a comb through his hair and went out.

In the lobby the cigar counter was closed.

As he entered the cocktail lounge, he paused to get his bearings. To his left was a long bar. He saw the girl from the cigar counter. She sat at the far end, a drink in front of her.

He walked along the bar, relaxed, listening to the wash of sound from the juke box.

"Hey, isn't that Mike Grover?"

"Who?"

"You remember Mike, the dispatcher?"

He steered his way closer to the table.

"Naw, doesn't look anything like him."

"That's Grover all right. Hey, Mike!"

He looked up as though startled. He let the smile spread over his face as he came up to the table. Three roughly dressed men sat around a half-empty bottle of Old Crow.

"Say," he said. "Where did you guys come from? How long has it been?"

"Pull up a chair, Mike. You remember Eddie Walsh and this here is Barney Koenig. Fellas, this is Mike Grover. The meanest dispatcher ever worked for the Union Pacific."

"Have a drink," said Eddie. "Harvey ain't got no manners." Eddie pushed an empty glass in front of him. He sloshed liquor into the glass. "You still with the U.P.?"

"You know what they say about old soldiers," he said. He wondered if anyone at the table had money.

"Boy, we had some times together, didn't we?" said Harvey. "Remember the time we took old Swenson the Super out and got him tight? I bet he's still wondering how he come to wake up at Essie Kuppenheimer's!"

"Yeah," he said, smiling.

"And the next day he tells his old lady that he had to go to Denver on business." Harvey roared.

He smiled brightly and then let the expression change to one of sadness.

"Something wrong, Mike?"

"I just remembered," he said sadly. "I was supposed to stop at the bank this afternoon and make a withdrawal. Completely slipped my mind. I've got some things to do tonight and I haven't got a cent on me."

"How much do you need?" asked Harvey. "I've got some dough."

"I can let you have it back tomorrow."

"Will twenty be enough?"

He looked doubtful.

Harvey had his wallet out. "Here, take thirty bucks. You can leave it with the bartender and I can pick it up tomorrow night."

"I appreciate this, Harvey."

"'Sallright. Seeing you was worth it. Man, some of the times we had—those were the days." He slapped him on the shoulder. "Have another drink?"

"Next time, huh? It's getting late and I have a lot to do."

"If you can't be good, be careful," said Harvey, slyly. "Don't spend it all at Essie's."

As he came abreast of the girl she slipped lightly from the stool. "Fred . . ." she said tentatively.

He put his arm about her shoulder. "Let's go where we can talk."

He moved her toward the door. Outside, the brisk breeze came down on them. She shivered, looking up at him.

"You've changed, Fred," she said.

"Yes," he said. He took her arm and began to walk toward the hotel.

In his room she turned to him, her arms going around his neck. "Oh, Fred," she said.

"Yes, yes," he said huskily. He bent over her, his hands cupping her.

Almost feverishly she pulled away. "When you left I thought I'd go crazy. I kept telling myself that you would come back and when you didn't, I began to hate you. Alone at night I worked out the things I would say to you if I ever met you again. I began to look in the mirror, wondering what there was about me that made you leave. I'd take off my clothes and look at myself in the mirror."

"It wasn't that," he said. He pulled her to him again, his hand expertly finding the zipper on her dress.

"And then I thought, maybe I did something wrong. I remembered our nights together, recalling each detail, remembering each touch and each kiss." Her breath came warmly into his ear.

"And then I thought that maybe there was another woman." Her hands climbed up and down his spine.

"None as dear as you," he whispered. He picked her up and carried her to the bed.

"You won't ever leave me again?"

His clothing fell in a heap beside the bed.

"Never," he said, and then he joined her on the clean sheets.

"I was wrong," she said at last in a small subdued voice. "You haven't changed at all. You're still the same Fred Black that I remember."

Lying there he tried to remember how it had all started. He'd done all the normal boyish things the other kids did—and then he was twelve and things changed. Not with the kids because they knew who he was and couldn't be fooled, but everything changed with the grownups. They were always confusing him with the other kids. They'd call up his mother with strange stories.

"Are you calling Mrs. Kelling a liar?" his mother would ask, a switch in her hand. "She saw you and that awful Grenfeld boy breaking her milk bottles. How many times have I told you to keep away from him?"

"But Mom . . ."

"You know better than that," his mother would say and then she would switch him.

One night, standing before the mirror in the bathroom, he looked long and searchingly into his face and discovered his secret. If he held his head cocked *so*, he looked like Charlie Brice. If he smiled *thus* he looked like Billie Warner. If he frowned and lowered his eyebrows he was Pud.

At first he had been delighted with the discovery. He'd go

down the street wearing his mask and people would say, "Hi Pud," or, "Hey, Billie!"

Suddenly he was twenty-one and all this was kid stuff. He wanted to be noticed for himself, not Charlie or Pud. He'd be careful not to cock his head to the side or lower his eyebrows and then strangers would say, "Hey Keith," or, "Hello Wendell." Then he'd stand still on the sidewalk trying to remember his name.

He found that when he corrected people who wrongly identified him it hurt their feelings. They would flush and stammer and sometimes they would get angry. What the hell, he told himself. If they get pleasure out of thinking he was someone else why spoil it for them. At the end of each day, his face stiff from nodding and smiling, he'd go home and in his dreams he would hear a flood of voices calling him Jack or Bart or Brad.

One day a man walked up to him in front of Seeger's Clothing Store and said, "Here, Evans. Here's the twenty I owe you." He pressed a bill into his hands and walked away.

The next day he packed up his clothes and left town. He discovered he had old friends in every town always good for a free meal, a place to stay or a loan of money.

It was fun.

Except on those bad days when he'd sit in a drab hotel dreaming of a job and a family and an identity that wouldn't flow and shift like mercury.

One day he bought a little black book to keep track of the "loans" and the "gifts." He found they averaged over ten thousand a year. Why be a sap? How else could he make that kind of money?

He remembered it all and fell asleep thinking of the next morning when he would get in his car and drive away to another town where it would begin all over again.

When he woke the girl was gone. Passing through the hotel

lobby he saw her standing behind the glass case. He went by without looking at her.

He had breakfast at the Wagonwheel Cafe, and made glib conversation with the waitress while he ate.

Driving out of town he saw a service station. He cramped the wheels to the left, driving across the white line and pulled up beside the pumps.

The attendant came out from inside, moving slowly, peering toward him.

"Fill it up," he said, and stopped.

"You!" screamed the attendant. "Arthur Danyluk! I've been looking for you for ten years!"

He felt himself being hauled out into the driveway. His head glanced off of the pump as he fell to his knees. "No!" he thought foggily. Terrified, he tried to roll away from the kicking feet.

The attendant had wrenched the gasoline hose from its socket in the pump and had the heavy nozzle poised high in the air. "I swore I'd kill you!" growled the attendant. He brought the nozzle down.

It caught him crushingly across the shoulders. He stiffened convulsively, his face gone dead, becoming a strange face, a distinctive face.

"Please," he sobbed. "I'm not who you think. My name is . . . is . . ." He tried vainly to remember. Who was he? He didn't know at first and then he did.

Too late. The nozzle flailed high and started its downward rush.

He was Sam Windgate. He was Fred Black. He was Ben Hoffmier. He was Mike Grover. He was Arthur Danyluk.

And all of them were dying.

THE FIRE AND THE SWORD

Frank M. Robinson

There was a time, when I first started writing, when I was very fond of the story with the anthropological background. Probably my first attempt in the field was "The Santa Claus Planet"—a nice try, though essentially lightweight. My second stab at it (or so I thought) was "The Fire and the Sword," which ran in one of the early issues of Galaxy. *I was very proud of it at the time, although the middle gets a little murky plot-wise, and if I had it to do all over again, I'm sure I would turn out a somewhat tighter story with a stronger plot and smoother characterization and all those great things that come with practice to the writer.*

But I wouldn't change the basic idea at all. It's one that I had never seen before (though that doesn't mean that somebody might not have tried their hand at it and done a better job than I did) and one that's peculiarly personal and peculiarly relevant —a word I've grown to detest, but at the moment I can't think of a good synonym for it. It also isn't really anthropological in nature, either—it's psychological and deals with alienation (though I'm not sure I was aware of that at the time). And although it's set on a far-off planet, it didn't have to be.

Alienation, of course, is of two types. It describes the cellophane cloak we wear to guard ourselves against the world, and which others wear to guard themselves against us; in its extreme form, the cloak can sometimes harden into armor (consider Kitty Genovese). It happens every day and it happens all around us and it happens to people we know.

The premise of "The Fire and the Sword" is that a man is not accepted into paradise—or the science fictional equivalent of it —even though he happens to live in the middle of it. He is excluded. He can eat there, he can sleep there, he can earn his daily bread there. But he can't "live" there because the people will not open their hearts to him. They will not accept him.

Like we won't accept the blacks (as human beings).

Or women (as human beings).

Or Communists (as human beings).

Or those homosexuals rash enough to reveal themselves (as human beings).

Or, for that matter, anybody who looks different, smells different, thinks different—you name it.

It would be nice, of course, if all those people who aren't allowed into "paradise"—and I'll admit that's subject to definition— would kindly go away and build their own version of paradise. They've tried to do just that, of course—the country is filled with various ghettoes of one stripe or another.

Well, I don't mean to wax political—that's not my point. In one sense of the word, we all live in a paradise that we're busily keeping somebody else out of. And in the same sense, there are a dozen other paradises that somebody is keeping us out of. We have our walled-off cities and our walled-off neighborhoods, and, worst of all, our walled-off hearts.

In its extreme form, of course, alienation kills. See your daily paper.

Some of this I was conscious of when I wrote the story, though not all of it. And the story actually came out rather oddly. Originally I had considered the human beings as something in the nature of villains because they wanted to crash paradise. And the nice, honorable Tunpeshans were the good guys. With time, of course, I came to realize my error. The human beings in the story were really you and I and particularly all those hundreds of people we know who don't "belong." And the Tunpeshans were actually double-dyed villains who should've been strung up by their balls.

If I had been a little older and more experienced when I wrote the story, they would have been.

—Frank M. Robinson

Why do people commit suicide?

Templin tightened his safety belt and lay back on the acceleration bunk. The lights in the cabin dimmed to a dull, red glow that meant the time for takeoff was nearing. He could hear noises from deep within the ship and the tiny whir of the ventilator fan, filling the air with the sweetish smell of sleeping gas. To sleep the trip away was better than to face the dull monotony of the stars for days on end.

Oh, they kill themselves for lots of reasons. Maybe ill health or financial messes or family difficulties. An unhappy love affair. Or more complex ones, if you went into it deeper. The failure to achieve an ambition, failure to live up to one's own ideals. Weltschmerz, perhaps.

He could smell the bitter fragrance of tobacco smoke mingling with the gas. Eckert had lit a cigarette and was calmly blowing the smoke at the neon NO SMOKING sign, which winked on and off in mechanical disapproval.

He turned his head slightly so he could just see Eckert in the bank facing him. Eckert, one of the good gray men in the Service.

The old reliables, the ones who could take almost anything in their stride because, at one time or another, they had had to.

It was Eckert who had come into his office several days ago and told him that Don Pendleton had killed himself.

Only Pendleton wasn't the type. He was the kind who have everything to live for, the kind you instinctively know will amount to something someday. And that was a lousy way to remember him. The clichés always come first. Your memory plays traitor and boils friendship down to the status of a breakfast food testimonial.

The soft red lights seemed to be dancing in the darkness of the cabin. Eckert was just a dull, formless blur opposite him. His cigarette was out.

Eckert had come into his office without saying a word and had watched his scenery-window. It had been snowing in the window, the white flakes making a simple pattern drifting past the glass. Eckert had fiddled with the controls and changed it to sunshine, then to a weird mixture of hail amid the brassy, golden sunlight.

And then Eckert had told him that Pendleton had taken the short way out.

He shouldn't get sentimental. But how the hell else should he remember Pendleton? Try to forget it and drink a toast to him at the next class reunion? And never, never be so crude as to speculate why Pendleton should have done it? If, of course, he had . . .

The cabin was hazy in the reddish glow, the sleeping gas a heavy perfume.

Eckert and he had talked it out and gone over the records. Pendleton had come of good stock. There had been no mental instability in his family for as far back as the genetic records went. He had been raised in a middle-class neighborhood and attended a local grammar school where he had achieved average grades and had given his instructors the normal amount of trouble. Later, when he had made up his mind to enter the Diplomatic Service, his grades had improved. He had worked hard at it, though he wasn't what you would call a grind. In high school and later in college, he was the well-balanced type, athletic, popular, hardworking.

How long would it be before memories faded and all there was left of Pendleton was a page of statistics? He had been on this team, he had been elected president of that, he had graduated with such and such honors. But try getting a picture of him by reading the records, resurrect him from a page of black print. Would he be human? Would he be flesh and blood? Hell, no! In the statistics Pendleton was the All-Around Boy, the cold marble statue with the finely chiseled muscles and the smooth, blank sockets where the eyes should be. Maybe someday fate would play a trick on a hero-worshiping public and there would actually be kids like that. But they wouldn't be human; they wouldn't be born. Parents would get them by sending in so many box tops.

He was drowsy; the room was filled with the gas now. It would be only a matter of minutes now before he would be asleep.

Pendleton had been in his second year as attaché on Tunpesh, a small planet with a G-type sun. The Service had stumbled across it recently and decided the system was worth diplomatic recognition of some kind, so Pendleton had been sent there. He had been the first attaché to be sent and naturally he had gone alone.

There was no need to send more. Tunpesh had been inspected and certified and approved. The natives were primitive and friendly. Or maybe the Service had slipped up, as it sometimes did, and Tunpesh had received something less than a thorough survey.

And then an unscheduled freighter had put in for repairs, one of the very few ships that ever came by Tunpesh. The captain had tried to pay his respects to Pendleton. Only Pendleton wasn't there. The natives said he had killed himself and showed the captain the little flower-covered plot where they had buried him.

Tunpesh had been Pendleton's second assignment.

The natives were oh-so-friendly. So friendly that he had made sure that a certain box was on board, filled with shiny atomic rifles, needle pistols, and the fat little gas guns. They might be needed. People like Pendleton didn't kill themselves, did they? No, they didn't. But sometimes they were murdered.

It was almost black inside the cabin now; only a thin red line around the ceiling told how close they were to takeoff. His head was thick with drowsiness, his eyelids a heavy weight that he knew he couldn't keep open much longer.

Eckert and he had been chosen to go to Tunpesh and investigate. The two of them, working together, should be able to find out why Pendleton had killed himself.

But that wasn't the real reason. Maybe Eckert thought so, but he knew better. The real reason they were going there was to find out why Pendleton had been killed and who had killed him. That was it.

Who had killed Cock Robin?

The thin red line was practically microscopic now and Templin could feel his lashes lying gently on his cheeks. But he wasn't asleep—not quite. There was something buzzing about in the dim recesses of his mind.

Their information on Tunpesh was limited. They knew that it had no trading concessions or armed forces and that nobody from neighboring systems seemed to know much about it or even visited it. But a staff anthropologist must have been routinely assigned to Tunpesh to furnish data and reports.

"Ted?" he murmured sleepily.

A faint stirring in the black bulk opposite him. "Yes?"

"How come our anthropologist on Tunpesh didn't come across with more information?"

A drowsy mumble from the other cot: "He wasn't there long enough. He committed suicide not long after landing."

The room was a whirling pool of blackness into which his mind was slowly slipping. Takeoff was only seconds away.

Why do people commit suicide?

* * *

"It's a nice day, isn't it, Ted?"

Eckert took a deep and pleasurable breath. "It's the type of day that makes you feel good just to be alive."

Warm breezes rustled through Eckert's graying hair and tugged gently at his tunic. The air smelled as if it had been washed and faintly perfumed with the balsamy scent of something very much like pine. A few hundred yards away, a forest towered straight and slim and coolly inviting, and brilliantly colored birds whirled and fluttered in the foliage.

The rocketport, where they were standing surrounded by their luggage, was a grassy valley where the all too infrequent ships could land and discharge cargo or make repairs. There was a blackened patch on it now, with little blast-ignited flames dying out around the edges. *It won't be long before it will be green again,* he thought. The grass looked as though it grew fast—it would certainly have plenty of time to grow before the next ship landed.

He looked at the slim, dwindling shape that was the rocket, and was suddenly, acutely aware that he and Templin would be stranded for six months on a foreign and very possibly dangerous planet. And there would be no way of calling for help or of leaving before the six months were up.

He stood there for a moment, drinking in the fresh air and feeling the warmth of the sun against his face. It might be a pleasant six months at that, away from the din and the hustle and confusion, spending the time in a place where the sun was warm and inviting.

I must be getting old, he thought, *thinking about the warmth and comfort. Like old dogs and octogenarians.*

Templin was looking at the scenery with a disappointed expression on his face. Eckert stole a side glance at him and for a fleeting moment felt vaguely concerned. "Don't be disappointed if it doesn't look like cloak-and-dagger right off, Ray. What seems innocent enough on the surface can prove to be quite dangerous underneath."

"It's rather hard to think of danger in a setting like this."

Eckert nodded agreement. "It wouldn't fit, would it? It would be like a famous singer suddenly doing a jazz number in an opera, or having the princess in a fairy tale turn out to be ugly." He gestured toward the village. "You could hardly class that as dangerous from its outward appearance, could you?"

The rocketport was in a small valley, surrounded by low, wooded hills. The village started where the port left off and crawled and wound over the wooded ridges. Small houses of sunbaked, whitewashed mud crouched in the shadow of huge trees and hugged the banks of a small stream.

It looked fairly primitive, Eckert thought, and yet it didn't have the earmarks, the characteristics of most primitive villages.

A few adults were watching them curiously and the usual bunch of kids that always congregated around rocketports quickly gathered. Eckert stared at them for a moment, wondering what it was that seemed odd about them, and they stared back with all the alert dignity of childhood. They finally came out on the field and clustered around him and Templin.

Templin studied them warily. "Better watch them, Ted. Even kids can be dangerous."

It's because you never suspect kids, Eckert thought, *you never think they'll do any harm. But they can be taught. They could do as much damage with a knife as a man could, for instance. And they might have other weapons.*

But the idea still didn't go with the warm sun and the blue sky and the piny scent of the trees.

One of the adults of the village started to walk toward them.

"The reception committee," Templin said tightly. His hand went inside his tunic.

He couldn't be blamed for being jumpy, Eckert realized. This was his first time out, his first mission like this. And, of course, Pendleton had been a pretty good friend of his.

"I'd be very careful what I did," Eckert said softly. "I would hate to start something merely because I misunderstood their intentions."

The committee of one was a middle-aged man dressed in a simple strip of white cloth twisted about his waist and allowed to hang freely to his knees. When he got closer, Eckert became less sure of his age. He had the firm, tanned musculature of a much younger man, though a slightly seamed face and white hair aged him somewhat. Eckert still had the feeling that if you wanted to know his exact age, you'd have to look at his teeth or know something about his epiphyseal closures.

"You are *menshars* from Earth?" The voice was husky and pleasant and the pronunciation was very clear. Eckert regarded him thoughtfully and made a few mental notes. He wasn't bowing and scraping like most natives who weren't too familiar with visitors from the sky, and yet he was hardly either friendly or hostile.

"You learned our language from Pendleton and Reynolds?" Reynolds had been the anthropologist.

"We have had visitors from Earth before." He hesitated a moment and then offered his hand, somewhat shyly, Eckert thought, in the Terrestrial sign of greeting. "You may call me Jathong if you wish." He paused a moment to say something in his native tongue to the kids who were around. They promptly scattered and picked up the luggage. "While you are here, you will need a place to stay. There is one ready, if you will follow me."

He was polite, Eckert thought. He didn't ask what they were there for or how long they were going to stay. But then again, perhaps the natives were a better judge of that than he and Templin.

The town was larger than he had thought at first, stretching over a wide expanse of the countryside. There wasn't, so far as he could see, much manufacturing above the level of handicrafts and simple weaving. Colored patches on far hillsides indicated the presence of farms, and practically every house in the village had its small garden.

What manufacturing there was seemed to be carried on in the central square of the town, where a few adults and children squatted in the warm afternoon sun and worked industriously at potter's wheels and weaver's looms. The other part of the square was given over to the native bazaar where pots and bolts of cloth were for sale, and where numerous stalls were loaded with dried fruits and vegetables and the cleaned and plucked carcasses of the local variety of fowl.

It was late afternoon when they followed Jathong into a small, white-washed house midway up a hill.

"You are free to use this while you are here," he said.

Eckert and Templin took a quick tour of the few rooms. They were well furnished, in a rustic sort of way, and what modern conveniences they didn't have they could easily do without. The youngsters who had carried their luggage left it outside and quietly faded away. It was getting dark; Eckert opened one of the boxes they had brought along, took out an electric lantern and lighted it. He turned to Jathong.

"You've been very kind to us and we would like to repay you. You may take what you wish of anything within this box." He opened another of the boxes and displayed the usual trade goods —brightly colored cloth and finely worked jewelry and a few mechanical contrivances that Eckert knew usually appealed to the primitive imagination.

Jathong ran his hand over the cloth and held some of the jewelry up to the light. Eckert knew by the way he looked at it that he wasn't at all impressed. "I am grateful," he said finally, "but there is nothing I want." He turned and walked away into the gathering darkness.

"The incorruptible native." Templin laughed sarcastically.

Eckert shrugged. "That's one of the things you do out of habit, try and buy some of the natives so you'll have friends in case you need them." He stopped for a moment, thinking. "Did you notice the context? He didn't say he didn't want what we showed him. He said there was *nothing* that he wanted. Implying that everything he wanted, he already had."

"That's not very typical of a primitive society, is it?"

"No, I'm afraid it's not." Eckert started unpacking some of the boxes. "You know, Ray, I got a kick out of the kids. They're a healthy-looking lot, aren't they?"

"Too healthy," Templin said. "There didn't seem to be any sick ones or ones with runny noses or cuts or black eyes or bruises. It doesn't seem natural." His voice was strained. "This could be a trap, you know."

"In what way?"

The words came out slowly. "The people are too casual, as though they're playing a rehearsed part. Here we are, from an entirely different solar system, landed in what must be to them an unusual manner. And yet how much curiosity did they show? Hardly any. Was there any fear? No. And the cute, harmless little kids." He looked at Eckert. "Maybe that's what we're supposed to think—just an idyllic, harmless society. Maybe that's what Pendleton thought, right to the very end."

He was keyed up, jumpy, Eckert realized. He would probably be seeing things in every shadow and imagining danger to be lurking around every corner.

"It hasn't been established yet that Pendleton was killed, Ray. Let's keep an open mind until we know for certain."

He flicked out the light and lay back on the cool bed, letting his body relax completely. The cool night wind blew lazily through the wood slat blinds, carrying the fragrance of the trees and the grass, and he inhaled deeply and let his thoughts wander for a moment. It was going to be pleasant to live on Tunpesh for six months—even if the six months were all they had to live. The climate was superb and the people seemed a cut above the usual primitive culture. If he ever retired some day, he thought suddenly, he would have to remember Tunpesh. It would be pleasant to spend his old age here. And the fishing was probably excellent. . . .

He turned his head a little to watch Templin get ready for bed. There were advantages in taking him along that Templin probably didn't even realize. He wondered what Templin would do if he ever found out that the actual reason he had been chosen to go was that his own psychological chart was very close to Pendleton's. Pendleton's own feelings and emotions would almost exactly be duplicated in Templin's.

A few stray wisps of starlight pierced through the blinds and sparkled for an instant on a small metal box strapped to Templin's waist. A power pack, Eckert saw grimly, probably leading to the buttons on his tunic. A very convenient, portable, and hard to detect weapon.

There were disadvantages in taking Templin, too.

"Just how primitive do you think the society is, Ted?"

Eckert put down the chain he had been whittling and reached for his pipe and tobacco.

"I don't think it's primitive at all. There are too many disparities. Their knowledge of a lot of things is a little more than empirical knowledge; they associate the growth of crops with fertilizer and nitrogen in the soil as well as sunlight, rather than the blessings of some native god. And they differ a lot in other respects. Their art and their music are advanced. Free art exists along with purely decorative art, and their techniques are finely developed."

"I'm glad you agree, then. Take a look at this." Templin threw a shiny bit of metal on the rough-hewn table. Eckert picked it up and inspected it. It was heavy and one side of it was extremely sharp.

"What's it for?"

"They've got a hospital set up here. Not a hospital like any we know, of course, but a hospital nonetheless. It's not used very much; apparently the natives don't get sick here. But occasionally there are hunting accidents and injuries that require surgery. The strip of metal there is a scalpel." He laughed shortly. "Primitive little gadget, but it works well—as well as any of ours."

Eckert hefted it in his palm. "The most important thing is that they have the knowledge to use it. Surgery isn't a simple science."

"Well, what do you think about it?"

"The obvious. They evidently have as much technology as they want, at least in fields where they have to have it."

"How come they haven't gone any further?"

"Why should they? You can live without skycars and rocket ships, you know."

"Did you ever wonder what kind of weapons they might have?"

"The important thing," Eckert mused, "is not if they have them, but if they'd use them. And I rather doubt that they would. We've been here for two weeks now and they've been very kind to us, seeing that we've had food and water and what fuel we need."

"It's known in the livestock trade as being fattened up for the slaughter," Templin said.

"You're convinced that Pendleton was murdered, aren't you?"

Templin nodded. "Sure."

"Why?"

"The Tunpeshans know why we're here. We've dropped enough hints along those lines. But nobody has mentioned Pendleton; nobody has volunteered any information about him. And he was an attaché here for three years. Didn't anybody know him during that time? We've let slip a few discreet statements that we would like to talk to Pendleton's friends, yet nobody's come around. Apparently, in all the three years he was here, Pendleton didn't make any friends. And that's a little hard to believe. It's more likely that his friends have been silenced and any information about him is being withheld for a reason."

"What reason?"

Templin shrugged. "Murder. What other reason could there be?"

Eckert rolled up the thin, slatted blinds and stared out at the scenery. A hundred feet down the road, a native woman was going to market, leading a species of food animal by the halter.

"They grow their women nice, don't they?"

"Physically perfect, like the men," Templin grumbled. "You could get an inferiority complex just from watching the people here. Everybody's so damn perfect. Nobody's sick, nobody's unhealthy, nobody is too fat or too thin, nobody's unhappy. The only variation is that they don't all look alike. Perfection. It gets boring after a while."

"Does it? I hadn't noticed." Eckert turned away from the blinds. His voice was crisp. "I knew Don Pendleton quite well, too," he said. "But it isn't blinding me to what I'm here for. We came to find out what happened to him, not to substantiate any preconceived notions. What we find out may be vitally important to anybody serving here in the future. I would hate to see our efforts spoiled because you've already made up your mind."

"You knew Pendleton," Templin repeated grimly. "Do you think it was suicide?"

"I don't think there's such a thing as a suicide type, when you come down to it. I'm not ruling out the possibility of murder, either. I'm trying to keep an open mind."

"What have we accomplished so far? What have we found out?"

"We've got six months," Eckert said quietly. "Six months in which we'll try to live here inconspicuously and study the people and try to cultivate informants. We would get nowhere if we came barging in asking all sorts of questions. And don't forget, Ray, we're all alone on Tunpesh. If it is a case of murder, what happens when the natives find out that we know it is?"

Templin's eyes dueled for a moment. Then he turned his back and walked to the window. "I suppose you're right," he said at last. "It's nice living here, Ted. Maybe I've been fighting it. But I can't help thinking that Don must have liked it here, too."

*　*　*

One of the hardest things to learn in a foreign culture, Eckert thought, is when to enjoy yourself, when to work and when to worry.

"*Pelache, menshar?*"

"*Sharra!*" He took the small bowl of *pelache* nuts, helped himself to a few, and passed the bowl on. This was definitely the time to enjoy himself, not to work or worry. He had heard about the *halera* a few days ago, and, by judicious hinting to the proper authorities, he and Templin had been invited. It was a good chance to observe native customs. A little anthropology—with refreshments.

The main courses started making the rounds and he took generous helpings of the roasted *ulami* and the broiled *halunch* and numerous dabs from the side dishes of steaming vegetables. Between every course, they passed around a small flagon of the hot, spiced native wine, but he noticed that nobody drank to excess.

The old Greek ideal, he thought: *moderation in everything.*

He looked at Templin, sitting across from him in the huge circle, and shrugged mentally. Templin looked as if he was about to break down and enjoy himself, but there was still a slight bulge under his tunic, where he had strapped his power pack. Any fool should have known that nothing would happen at a banquet like this. The only actual danger lay in Templin's getting excited and doing something he was bound to regret later on. And even that danger was not quite as likely now.

There will be hell to pay, Eckert thought, *if Templin ever finds out that I sabotaged his power pack.*

"You look thoughtful, *menshar* Eckert."

Eckert took another sip of the wine and turned to the Tunpeshan on his left. He was a tall, muscular man with sharp eyes, a firm chin and a certain aura of authority.

"I was wondering if my countryman Pendleton had offended your people in any way, Nayova." Now was as good a time as any to pump him for what he knew about Pendleton's death.

"So far as I know, *menshar* Pendleton offended no one. I do not even know what duties he had to perform here, but he was a generous and courteous man."

Eckert gnawed the dainty meat off a slender *ulami* bone and tried to appear casual in his questioning.

"I am sure he was, Nayova. I am sure, too, that you were as kind to him as you have been to Templin and myself. My Government is grateful to you for that."

Nayova seemed pleased. "We tried to do as well for *menshar* Pendleton as we could. While he was here, he had the house that you have now and we saw that he was supplied with food and all other necessities."

Eckert had a sudden clammy feeling which quickly passed away. What Nayova had said was something he'd make sure Templin never heard about. He wiped his mouth on a broad, flat leaf that had been provided and took another sip of the wine.

"We were shocked to find out that *menshar* Pendleton had killed himself. We knew him quite well and we could not bring ourselves to believe he had done such a thing."

Nayova's gaze slid away from him. "Perhaps it was the will of the Great One," he said vaguely. Then he added reluctantly, "It is hard for us to imagine anything doing what *menshar* Pendleton did. It is . . ." and he used a native word that Eckert translated as being roughtly equivalent to "*obscene.*"

Acrobats took the stage and went through a dizzying routine, and they in turn were succeeded by a native singer.

They were all excellent, Eckert thought. If anything, they were too good.

The bowl of *pelache* nuts made its way around again and Nayova leaned over to speak to him. "If there is any possibility that I can help you while you are here, *menshar* Eckert, you have but to ask."

It would probably be a mistake to ask for a list of Pendleton's friends, but there was a way around that. "I would like to meet any of your people who had dealings with Pendleton, either in

business or socially. I will do everything not to inconvenience
them in any way."

"I think they would be glad to help you. I shall ask them to go
to you this coming week."

It wasn't a driving rain, just a gentle drizzle that made the
lanes muddy and plastered Eckert's tunic against him. He didn't
mind it; the rain was warm and the trees and grass smelled good
in the wet.

"How would you classify the culture after seeing the ceremony, Ted?" Templin asked.

"About what you would expect. An Apollonian culture, simple
and dignified. Nothing in excess, no striving for great emotional
release."

Templin nodded soberly. "It grows on you, doesn't it? You
find yourself getting to like the place. And I suppose that's
dangerous, too. You tend to let your guard down, the way Pendleton must have. You—what was that?"

Eckert tensed. There was a gentle padding in the mud, several
hundred feet behind them. Templin flattened himself in the
shadows alongside a house. His hand darted inside his tunic and
came out with the slim deadliness of a needle gun.

"Don't use it!" Eckert whispered tersely.

Templin's eyes were thin, frightened slits in the darkness. "Why
not?"

Eckert's mind raced. It might be nothing at all, and then again
it might be disaster. But there was still a chance that Templin
might be wrong. And there were more immediate reasons.

"How many charges do you have for that?"

"Twelve."

"You think you can stand there and hold them off with only
twelve charges for your needle gun?"

"There's my power pack."

"It's no good," Eckert said softly. "The batteries in it are dead.
I was afraid you might do something foolish with it."

The footsteps were only yards away. He listened intently, but it was hard to tell how many there were by the sound.

"What do we do then?"

"See if they're following us first," Eckert said practically. "They might not be, you know."

They slid out from the shadows and ducked down another lane between the houses. The footsteps behind them speeded up and came down the same lane.

"We'll have to head back for our house," Eckert whispered.

They started running as quietly as they could, slipping and sliding in the mud. Another stretch past the shuttered, crouching houses and they found themselves in the square they had visited on the day they had landed. It was deserted, the looms and pottery wheels covered with cloth and reeds to keep off the rain. They darted across it, two thin shadows racing across the open plaza, and hurried down another path.

The last path led to the small river that cut through the city. Templin looked around, gestured to Eckert, waded into the water and crouched under the small bridge that spanned it. Eckert swore silently to himself, then followed Templin in.

The cold water swirled under his armpits and he bit his lips to keep himself from sneezing. Templin's emotions were contagious. Would he have worried about the footsteps? He frowned and tried to be honest with himself. Perhaps he would have—and perhaps he wouldn't have. But he couldn't have let Templin stay there and face the unknown approachers. Not Templin.

Footsteps approached the bridge, hesitated a moment, then pattered on the wooden structure and faded off down the muddy path. Eckert let his breath out slowly. The footsteps were curiously light.

There was only one pair of them.

"I would like to know something," Templin said coldly. He stripped off his power pack and let it fall to the floor of their house. "Why did you decide to substitute dead batteries in the pack?"

"Because," Eckert said shortly, "I was afraid you would do something with it that you might regret later. You're inexperienced in situations like this. Your reactions aren't to be trusted. One false move here and we could follow Pendleton, however he died. You know that." He wriggled out of his tunic and slowly peeled off his wet trousers.

There was a timid knock at the door. He wrapped a blanket about himself and motioned to Templin to stand to one side. Templin grabbed a small stool, hefted it in one hand, and complied.

Eckert went to the door and casually threw it open.

A girl stood there, half in the outer darkness and half in the yellowish light from the room, covered with mud to the knees and drenched to the skin.

"The *menshar* forgot this at the *halera*," she said softly. She quickly handed him his pipe and a soggy bag of tobacco, and disappeared instantly into the rain. He listened for the sound of her footsteps in the soft mud and then closed the door.

Templin put down the stool and stared stupidly at the pipe and the tobacco sack. Eckert placed them carefully on the table and began to towel himself.

"We probably face as much danger from our own imaginations as from anything else," he said grimly. "Tell me, would you have fired first, or would you have waited until you found out for sure who she was and what she wanted when she first started to follow us?"

"I don't know," Templin said sullenly.

"Then I'll leave to your imagination the position we would be in now, if you had given in to your impulse."

"We haven't found out much, have we?" Templin demanded some days later.

"No," Eckert admitted. "We haven't."

He riffled through the thick stack of cards on the table. Statistically, the results were not only interesting but slightly phenomenal. During the three years or so that Pendleton had been on Tunpesh, he had met and known approximately seven hundred of the natives. By far the greater majority of these, of course, were purely casual and meant nothing. Almost a hundred, though, had had extended relations with Pendleton in business or social affairs. Of this hundred, none—not a single one—would admit that he had known Pendleton well or could be considered a friend of his. About all they had to say was that Pendleton had been healthy and easy to get along with, and one warm night he had shocked the community by going off and shooting himself.

"Like Richard Cory," Eckert said aloud.

"Like who?" Templin asked.

"Richard Cory. A character in a poem by a twentieth-century poet, Edwin Arlington Robinson. Apparently he had everything to live for, but 'Richard Cory, one calm summer night, went home and put a bullet through his head.'"

"I'll have to look it up some day," Templin said. He pointed to the stack of cards. "That's so much waste paper, isn't it?"

"Yes, it is," Eckert said reluctantly. "To be frank, I had hoped we'd know a lot more by now. I still can't understand why we haven't dug up anybody who will admit having been his friend."

"How do you know they're telling the truth? Or, for that matter, how do you know that the ones we've seen so far are the ones who *actually* knew Pendleton?"

Eckert drummed his fingers on the table. *You handle different human cultures for twenty-five years and you get to the point where you can tell if people are lying or not. Or do you? Maybe just an old man's conceit. Age alone never lent wisdom. Regardless of the personal reasons that Templin might have for thinking the Tunpeshans are lying, the fact remains that they very easily could be. And what should you do if they are?*

There was a polite knock at the door.

"We've got another visitor," Templin said sarcastically. "He probably saw Pendleton at a *halera* four years ago and wants to be sure we know all about it."

The Tunpeshan looked faintly familiar to Eckert. There was something about the man's carriage . . .

"I met you the day you landed," the Tunpeshan began, and Eckert remembered. Jathong, the guide who had shown them to the house.

"You knew Pendleton?"

Jathong nodded. "I and a fellow weaver took over his small office after he had left it." Eckert recalled the small office in the square with the bolts of cloth on display, and the small mud brick on the window ledge with the incised lettering reading:

DONALD PENDLETON, SERVICE ATTACHE

"Why didn't you tell us this before?"

"I didn't know what kind and how much information you wanted."

We didn't ask him, Eckert thought, *so he didn't volunteer any information. Polite, to say the least.*

"How long did you know him?"

"Since he landed. I was the one appointed to him."

"What do you mean—appointed to him?"

"To try to learn his language, and try to teach him ours."

Eckert felt his interest rising. Jathong, then, must have known Pendleton fairly well.

"Did he have any enemies that you know of?"

"Enemies?" Jathong seemed ignorant of the meaning of the word, so Eckert explained. "No, he had no enemies. He would naturally have none such on Tunpesh."

Templin leaned forward, tense. "If he had no enemies, why did he have no friends? You, for example, knew him longer and better than most. Why is it that you weren't his friend?"

Jathong looked unhappy, as if being forced to say something he wanted not to say. "Pendleton was *kava*—I cannot explain it. The concept is difficult. You would not understand."

He might be running the danger of throwing too many questions at Jathong, Eckert realized, and having him freeze up or turn vague. But it couldn't be helped. They had made no progress at all by subtlety, and time would eventually run out.

He tried to broach the next subject delicately. "Did Pendleton know any of the women of your race?"

"He knew some of the women, as he knew the men."

The answer didn't tell Eckert what he wanted to know. "Was he in love with any woman?" It sounded crude the way he put it, but it was hard to think of any other way of asking it.

Jathong looked at him incredulously, as if Eckert had asked him if Pendleton had had two heads.

"That would have been impossible. None of our women would have—could have—been in love with *menshar* Pendleton."

One line of inquiry just gone phht, Eckert thought. *But Pendleton wasn't one to let a broken heart get him down anyway.*

"Why not?" Templin cut in harshly. "He wasn't hard to look at and he would have made a good husband."

Jathong diplomatically turned around to face Templin. "I have told you once—Pendleton was *kava*. It would have been quite impossible."

The answer to what had happened to Pendleton probably lay in Jathong's inability to explain his own terms, Eckert believed. One could get just so close, and then the definitions became vague and useless.

"Tonight we'll have to start eliminating certain ideas," Eckert said.

He took a small case from their pile of luggage and opened it. Inside was a small, battery-powered box with various dials set on the front and the usual electrodes and nerve probes protruding from the sides and the top.

Templin looked at it with surprise. "That will be dangerous to use, won't it?"

"It might be more dangerous not to. Time is getting to be a factor and we have to make some progress. We have a safety margin of a sort in that we can erase memories of its use, but the procedure is still risky."

"Who do we use it on?"

"As long as we're going to use it," Eckert said grimly, "we might as well start at the top."

When they had started out, the investigation had seemed fairly simple to Eckert. There were two possibilities—either Pendleton had committed suicide or he had been murdered. Knowing Pendleton's record, the first possibility had seemed remote. A few weeks on Tunpesh had convinced him that the second possibility was also remote. One or the other had to be eliminated. The second would be the easiest.

There were other reasons as well. Templin was still convinced that Pendleton had been killed, and Templin was an emotional man with access to powerful weapons. The question was not what he might eventually do, but when.

The night looked as if it would be another rainy one. It was cooler than usual and dark clouds were scudding across the star-lit sky. Eckert and Templin stood in the shadows of the house, watching the dark lane for any casual strollers. Eckert looked at his watch. A few minutes more and Nayova would come out for his evening walk.

Eckert had just started to think longingly of his bed and the warmth inside his house when the door opened and Nayova appeared in the opening. Eckert held his breath while the chieftain stood uncertainly in the doorway, testing the night air, and then let it out slowly when Nayova started down the lane.

They closed in on him.

"The *menshars* from Earth," he said without alarm. "Is there something you wish?"

"We would like you to come with us to our house for a while," Eckert started in.

Nayova looked puzzled. "I do not understand. Would not tomorrow do as well?"

"I'm afraid it'll have to be tonight."

Nayova was obviously not quite sure of their threat.

"No, I . . ."

Eckert caught him before he touched the ground. Templin took the rag off the butt of the needle gun, lifted the ruler's feet, and they disappeared into the brush along the lane.

They would have to sneak back to the house, Eckert knew, and hope that nobody saw them lugging the unconscious native. He laughed a little grimly to himself. Templin had expected cloak-and-dagger. It looked as if he was going to get more than his share of it, after all.

Once inside the house, Eckert arranged the electrodes and the small nerve probes on Nayova, who had come to.

"I am sorry," Eckert said formally, "but we find this necessary. You understand that we have to find out all we can about Pendleton. We have no choice."

He found it difficult to look the ruler in the face, even with the realization that this was strictly in the line of duty and that the chieftain would not be hurt.

"But I have cooperated with you in every way possible!" Nayova protested. "I have told you everything we know!"

"That's right," Templin said bluntly. "And now we're going to ask you the same questions."

Nayova looked blank for a moment and then reddened as he understood.

Templin turned to the dials on the little square box.

"We would like to know," Eckert said politely, "where you were two weeks ago at this time of night."

Nayova looked surprised. "You know that I was at the *halera*, the coming-of-age ceremony. You were there with me, as my guests. You should assuredly know I was there."

Eckert looked over at Templin, who nodded shortly. It had been a standard question, to test the apparatus.

"Did Pendleton have any enemies here on Tunpesh?"

Nayova emphatically shook his head. "To the best of my knowledge, *menshar* Pendleton had no enemies here. He would have none."

Templin's face showed its disappointment.

"Who were his friends?"

"He had no friends."

Templin glowered angrily, but he said nothing.

Eckert frowned. The same answer—Pendleton had had no enemies and yet he had had no friends.

"Would you say he was well liked here?"

"I would say no."

"Why not?"

A shrug. "It is hard to explain and you would not be able to understand."

"Did somebody here kill Pendleton?"

Eckert could hear Templin suck in his breath.

"No."

"Ask him that again," Templin cut in.

"Did somebody kill Pendleton?"

"No."

"Did Pendleton kill himself?"

A trace of disgust showed on Nayova's face.

"Yes."

"Why?"

"I do not know."

Templin gestured to Eckert to take the box. "Let me ask him." He came around and faced the native. "Why did your people kill Pendleton?"

"We did not kill him. We had no reason to wish him harm."

"Do you expect us to believe that Pendleton killed himself? We knew him better than that."

"You may believe whatever you wish. But men change and perhaps he did. We did not kill him. Such an act would have been repugnant to us."

"I think that's enough," Eckert said calmly.

Templin bit his lip as Eckert touched another dial on the machine. Nayova suddenly jerked, looked blank, and slumped in the chair.

Eckert took off the electrodes. "Help me take him back, will you, Ray?"

They carried Nayova to his house, stayed with him until he showed signs of recovering, and then left.

"Why didn't you use a drug?" Templin demanded.

"Possible allergy or serum reaction. We don't know enough about these people to take chances—they're humanoid, not human."

"They can fool machines, though, can't they?"

Eckert didn't reply.

"All right, I know they can't," Templin said grudgingly. "He was telling the truth all the time, wasn't he?"

Eckert nodded. "I never did think he was lying. They don't seem to be the type; their culture doesn't allow for it."

They were silent for a while, walking quietly in the lanes between the shuttered, seemingly untenanted houses.

"I'm glad," Templin said quietly. "It's off my mind. It's hard to believe that anybody here would . . . deliberately kill somebody else."

Templin's reactions would be worth something now for Eckert to study. They wouldn't be inhibited by his conviction that the natives had murdered his best friend. Just what reactions and emotions he would display, Eckert wasn't sure, nor how Templin's psychology, so similar to Pendleton's, would help solve the problem.

They had eliminated one possibility, but that still left them with the one they had started with.

Why had Pendleton taken the short way out?

Eckert opened the door slowly. Templin was asleep on the bed, the sunlight lying in bands across his tanned, bare back. He had on a strip of white cloth, knotted at the waist in imitation of what the natives wore.

It was mussed now, and the knot had started to come loose.

He looked a lot healthier than he had when they had first landed. More peaceful, more content. He appeared to have gained ten pounds and shed five years in the last six months.

And now the vacation was over. It was time to go back.

"Ray," Eckert called out to him softly.

Templin didn't stir, but continued his soft and very regular breathing.

Eckert found a book and dropped it on the floor with a thud. Templin woke up, but didn't move.

"What do you want, Ted?"

"How did you know it was me?"

Templin chuckled, as if it were hugely funny. "Riddles yet. Who else would it be? No Tunpeshan would be rude enough to wake somebody up in the middle of a nap, so it had to be you."

"You know what you would have done if somebody had awakened you like that five months ago?"

Templin tried to nod, but was slightly handicapped by the bed underneath him. "I would have pulled my trusty atom-gun and plugged him."

Eckert went over to where they kept their luggage and started pulling the boxes out from the wall. "Well, I've got good news for you. A liner just landed to pick us up. They were going through this sector and they got an order from the Service to stop by for us. Some cargo-wallopers will be here in a few minutes to help us with our gear."

"Ted."

Eckert paused.

"Yes?"

"I'm not going back."

"Why not?" Eckert's face had a look of almost clinical curiosity on it.

"Why should I? I like it here. I want to live here the rest of my life."

The pieces began to fall in place.

"I'm not so sure you'd like it, Ray. Not after a while. All your friends are back on Earth. Everybody you know is back there. It's just the novelty of something new and something different here. I've felt that way a lot of times in different cultures and different societies. You'd change your mind after a while."

"Those aren't reasons, Ted. Why should I go back to a world where most of the people are unhappy at some time and a few people all the time? As far as I'm concerned, Tunpesh is my home now, and I don't intend to leave it."

Eckert was fascinated. It was like a case history unfolding right before his eyes.

"Are you sure you would enjoy it here for the rest of your life? Have you made any friends to take the place of those back home?"

"It takes time to become acquainted, even more time to make friends," Templin said defensively.

"You can't desert the Service," Eckert pointed out. "You still have your duty."

Templin laughed in his pillow. "It won't work, Ted. Duty's just a catchword, a jingo phrase. They can get along without me and you know it."

"What about Pendleton, Ray? He died here, you know, in mysterious circumstances."

"Would going back help him any? He wasn't murdered; we know that. And why do people commit suicide? For what one of several thousand possible reasons did Pendleton? We don't know. We'll never know. And if we did know, what good would it do?"

He had changed a lot in six months, Eckert saw.

Too much.

"What if I told you I knew why Pendleton killed himself?" Eckert asked. "And that you would do the same if you stayed here?"

"Don't use it, Ted. It's poor psychology. It won't work."

The pieces made a perfect picture. But Templin was going back whether he wanted to or not. The only difficulty was that, deep underneath, Eckert sympathized with him. Perhaps if he had been younger, less experienced . . .

"Then you won't go back with us?"

Templin closed his eyes and rolled over on his back. "No."

There was dead silence. Templin could smell the piny scent of the woods and feel the warmth of soft sunlight that lanced through the blinds. Some place far away, there was the faint chatter of kids at play, but outside of that it was quiet.

Too quiet.

Templin opened his eyes in sudden alarm. "Ted! Don't!" He caught the gas full in the face and tumbled back on the bed, unconscious.

Eckert opened the hatch to the observation cabin as quietly as he could. Templin was seated on one of the pneumatic couches, staring soberly at a small yellow star in the black sky. He didn't look up.

"It's me, Ray," Eckert said.

Templin didn't move.

"I suppose I owe you an apology," Eckert began, "but I had to gas you to get you to leave. Otherwise you wouldn't have left. And the same thing would have happened to you that happened to Don Pendleton."

"You're sure of that?" Templin asked bitterly.

"Reasonably. You're a lot like Pendleton, you know. In fact, that's why you were selected to go—not so much because you knew him as the fact that psychologically you were a lot like him. We thought that by studying your response to situations there, we would have a picture of what Pendleton's must have been."

Templin didn't want to talk about it, Eckert realized, but it had to be explained to him.

"Do you want to know why Pendleton killed himself?"

Templin shrugged listlessly.

"I suppose we should have seen it right away," Eckert continued. "Any race that is so happy with their way of life that they show no curiosity about strangers, the way they live, or what possessions they have, must have something to be happy about. Tunpesh is something that might happen only once in a thousand civilizations, maybe less, Ray.

"The environment is perfection and so are the people, or at least as near to perfection as it's possible to get. An intelligent people who have as much technology as they desire, living simply with themselves and each other. A fluke of nature, perhaps. No criminals, no insane, no neurotics. A perfect cultural pattern. Tunpesh is a paradise. You didn't want to leave, neither did I, and neither did Pendleton."

Templin turned on him. "So it was paradise. Would it have been criminal if I had stayed there? Who would it have hurt?"

"It would have hurt you," Eckert said gravely. "Because the Tunpeshans would never have accepted you. We're too different, Ray. We're too aggressive, too pushy, too persistent. We're not —perfect. You see, no matter how long we stayed there, we would never have fit in. We lived in a harsh society and we bear the scars of it. Our own environment has conditioned us, and we can't change. Oh, we could try, but it would crop up in little ways. Because of that, the natives could never genuinely like us. We'd never belong. Their own cultural pattern wouldn't allow them to accept us.

"Their cultural pattern is like the Fire and the Sword that were placed outside the Garden of Eden, after Adam and Eve were driven out, to keep it sacrosanct. If you're an outsider, you stay outside. You can never come in."

He paused a moment, waiting for Templin to say something. Templin didn't.

"The natives have a word for it. *Kava*. It means, I suppose, *different*—not necessarily inferior, just different. We should have seen it as time went on. We weren't invited places; they seemed to avoid us. A natural reaction for them, I guess I have to admit."

Eckert cleared his throat huskily. "You see, what happened to Pendleton," he continued awkwardly, "is that he fell in love with paradise, but paradise would have nothing to do with him. By the time three years were up, he knew that he was an outcast in Eden. And he couldn't leave, to come back and try to forget. He was stranded in paradise and had to look forward to spending four more years there as a pariah. He couldn't do it. And neither could you."

He was quiet for a moment, thinking of the cool, scented air and the warm sunshine and the happy kids playing on the grassy lanes.

"I suppose it didn't affect you at all, did it?" Templin asked venomously.

A shadow crossed Eckert's face. "You should know better than that, Ray. Do you think I'll ever forget it? Do you think I'll ever be satisfied with my own culture again?"

"What are you going to do about it?"

"It's dangerous to human beings, Ray. Looking at it brutally, their culture has killed two of our people as surely as if Tunpesh were populated by murderous savages. We'll probably send a larger commission, throw it open to commerce, try to change it."

Templin gripped the sides of the couch, his face strained and tense with anxiety. "What happens to it depends on the report you make, doesn't it?"

"Yes, it does."

"Then make up something in your report. Say the climate is

bad for Earthmen. Say anything, but don't let them change Tunpesh!"

Eckert looked at him for a long moment, remembering.

"Okay, Ray," he said slowly. "We'll leave paradise alone. Strictly alone. It'll be put on the quarantine list."

He turned and left.

Behind him, Templin swiveled around in his chair and gazed bleakly at the tiny mote of yellow fading in the blackness of space.

BAD MEDICINE

Robert Sheckley

I wrote "Bad Medicine" as a lighthearted extrapolation of some not-very-possible possibilities to be found in a projection of the psychotherapeutic situation. The story was not meant to be true —only plausible within the conditions I set. I never thought that I was predicting a course of events that lay almost immediately before me. I was unaware of the possibility that a fantasy can be a prediction, and that predictions are often self-fulfilling. I was rewarded for my ignorance by spending a good part of the next six years in and out of the offices of a variety of psychotherapists. What they had in common was the arcane difficulty of their doctrines and the consistent lack of success of their methods. That and their enthusiasm, of course, which was impervious to any influence from reality. These qualities convince me that these people must have come from Mars or points west.

Many reputable scientists have argued the case against Freudian and other mentalist doctrines with impressive good sense. Despite this, it is difficult to examine the various psychotherapeutic premises and practices with any hope of an open discussion. One can argue for or against ghosts, inherited adaptations, or the existence of Atlantis without being declared biased by the mere fact of taking a position. This is not so in the case of psychotherapy. It is a closed and comprehensive universal psychic system that deals exclusively in its own referents. Argument is resistance.

*In "Bad Medicine," Elwood Caswell is laid upon the Procrus-
tean bed of an alien theory, which is shown to fit whatever data
he produces. The result is that the attempt to cure a nonexistent
sickness produces a sickness of its own. Something like this
seems to have happened in my own case. I began psychotherapy lightly enough, because it was available, and, at the
beginning, exceedingly inexpensive; because I was curious, and
because, like everyone else, I had my problems. Like Caswell, I
was all too ready to accept the strange premises with which my
Martian analysts regaled me. I too was able to find any proposi-
tion applicable to my case. Not even contradictions disturbed
me: Like a good medieval scholar I was able to reconcile any differences, and to argue with fervor the modern version of how
many angels could dance on the head of a pin.*

*Under treatment, my problems became worse; I increased the
number of weekly seances, and the prices went disastrously up.
(You get the first one free, the second one for half-price. After
that, you're hooked.) I reached many deep understandings,
but unfortunately I also became less able to function. This was
my own fault, of course; each of my Martian therapists knew very
well how to cure me, and had in fact spent their lives studying
just how to do this. Like the Mad Hatter, they fixed their watches
with the very best butter. If I and other patients continued to
malfunction, and even became worse, it had to be attributed to
the stubbornness of the ailment and the lack of drive on the part
of the patient.*

*At long last, out of time, money, and patience, I gave up all
hope of a cure and ventured out into the world with my diseased
psyche. Some years have passed since then. I seem to be as normal
as the next madman, and I have my fair share of happiness.
When I stopped trying to cure my Martian psychosis, it went
away of its own accord.*

*I wrote "Bad Medicine" with suspicious ease. Why not? I was
simply relating, in allegorical form, an incident from my own*

*future. It all taught me at least this much: that it is very difficult
to learn anything from what one knows.*

—*Robert Sheckley*

On May 2, 2103, Elwood Caswell walked rapidly down Broadway with a loaded revolver hidden in his coat pocket. He didn't want to use the weapon, but feared he might anyhow. This was a justifiable assumption, for Caswell was a homicidal maniac.

It was a gentle, misty spring day and the air held the smell of rain and blossoming dogwood. Caswell gripped the revolver in his sweaty right hand and tried to think of a single valid reason why he should not kill a man named Magnessen, who, the other day, had commented on how well Caswell looked.

What business was it of Magnessen's how he looked? Damned busybodies, always spoiling things for everybody . . .

Caswell was a choleric little man with fierce red eyes, bulldog jowls and ginger-red hair. He was the sort you would expect to find perched on a detergent box, orating to a crowd of lunching businessmen and amused students, shouting, "Mars for the Martians, Venus for the Venusians!"

But in truth, Caswell was uninterested in the deplorable social conditions of extraterrestrials. He was a jetbus conductor for the New York Rapid Transit Corporation. He minded his own business. And he was quite mad.

Fortunately, he knew this at least part of the time, with at least half of his mind.

Perspiring freely, Caswell continued down Broadway toward the Forty-third Street branch of Home Therapy Appliances, Inc. His friend Magnessen would be finishing work soon, returning to his little apartment less than a block from Caswell's. How easy it would be, how pleasant, to saunter in, exchange a few words and . . .

No! Caswell took a deep gulp of air and reminded himself that he didn't *really* want to kill anyone. It was not right to kill people. The authorities would lock him up, his friends wouldn't understand, his mother would never have approved.

But these arguments seemed pallid, overintellectual and entirely without force. The simple fact remained—he wanted to kill Magnessen.

Could so strong a desire be wrong? Or even unhealthy?

Yes, it could! With an agonized groan, Caswell sprinted the last few steps into the Home Therapy Appliances Store.

Just being within such a place gave him an immediate sense of relief. The lighting was discreet, the draperies were neutral, the displays of glittering therapy machines were neither too bland nor obstreperous. It was the kind of place where a man could happily lie down on the carpet in the shadow of the therapy machines, secure in the knowledge that help for any sort of trouble was at hand.

A clerk with fair hair and a long, supercilious nose glided up softly, but not *too* softly, and murmured, "May one help?"

"Therapy!" said Caswell.

"Of course, sir," the clerk answered, smoothing his lapels and smiling winningly. "That is what we are here for." He gave Caswell a searching look, performed an instant mental diagnosis, and tapped a gleaming white-and-copper machine.

"Now this," the clerk said, "is the new Alcoholic Reliever, built by IBM and advertised in the leading magazines. A handsome piece of furniture, I think you will agree, and not out of place in any home. It opens into a television set."

With a flick of his narrow wrist, the clerk opened the Alcoholic Reliever, revealing a 52-inch screen.

"I need—" Caswell began.

"Therapy," the clerk finished for him. "Of course. I just wanted to point out that this model need never cause embarrassment for yourself, your friends or loved ones. Notice, if you will, the recessed dial which controls the desired degree of drinking. See? If you do not wish total abstinence, you can set it to heavy, moderate, social or light. That is a new feature, unique in mechanotherapy."

"I am not an alcoholic," Caswell said, with considerable dignity. "The New York Rapid Transit Corporation does not hire alcoholics."

"Oh," said the clerk, glancing distrustfully at Caswell's bloodshot eyes. "You seem a little nervous. Perhaps the portable Bendix Anxiety Reducer—"

"Anxiety's not my ticket, either. What have you got for homicidal mania?"

The clerk pursed his lips. "Schizophrenic or manic-depressive origins?"

"I don't know," Caswell admitted, somewhat taken aback.

"It really doesn't matter," the clerk told him. "Just a private theory of my own. From my experience in the store, redheads and blonds are prone to schizophrenia, while brunettes incline toward the manic-depressive."

"That's interesting. Have you worked here long?"

"A week. Now then, here is just what you need, sir." He put his hand affectionately on a squat black machine with chrome trim.

"What's that?"

"That, sir, is the Rex Regenerator, built by General Motors. Isn't it handsome? It can go with any decor and opens up into a well-stocked bar. Your friends, family, loved ones need never know—"

"Will it cure a homicidal urge?" Caswell asked. "A *strong* one?"

"Absolutely. Don't confuse this with the little ten-amp neurosis models. This is a hefty, heavy-duty, twenty-five-amp machine for a really deep-rooted major condition."

"That's what I've got," said Caswell, with pardonable pride.

"This baby'll jolt it out of you. Big, heavy-duty thrust bearings! Oversize heat absorbers! Completely insulated! Sensitivity range of over—"

"I'll take it," Caswell said. "Right now. I'll pay cash."

"Fine! I'll just telephone Storage and—"

"This one'll do," Caswell said, pulling out his billfold. "I'm in a hurry to use it. I want to kill my friend Magnessen, you know."

The clerk clucked sympathetically. "You wouldn't want to do that. . . . Plus five percent sales tax. Thank you, sir. Full instructions are inside."

Caswell thanked him, lifted the Regenerator in both arms and hurried out.

After figuring his commission, the clerk smiled to himself and lighted a cigarette. His enjoyment was spoiled when the manager, a large man impressively equipped with pince-nez, marched out of his office.

"Haskins," the manager said, "I thought I asked you to rid yourself of that filthy habit."

"Yes, Mr. Follansby, sorry, sir," Haskins apologized, snubbing out the cigarette. "I'll use the display Denicotinizer at once. Made rather a good sale, Mr. Follansby. One of the big Rex Regenerators."

"Really?" said the manager, impressed. "It isn't often we—wait a minute! You didn't sell the *floor model*, did you?"

"Why—why, I'm afraid I did, Mr. Follansby. The customer was in such a terrible hurry. Was there any reason—"

Mr. Follansby gripped his prominent white forehead in both

hands, as though he wished to rip it off. "Haskins, I told you. I *must* have told you! That display Regenerator was a *Martian* model. For giving mechanotherapy to *Martians*."

"Oh," Haskins said. He thought for a moment. "Oh."

Mr. Follansby stared at his clerk in grim silence.

"But does it really matter?" Haskins asked quickly. "Surely the machine won't discriminate. I should think it would treat a homicidal tendency even if the patient were not a Martian."

"The Martian race has never had the slightest tendency toward homicide. A Martian Regenerator doesn't even possess the concept. Of course the Regenerator will treat him. It has to. *But what will it treat?*"

"Oh," said Haskins.

"That poor devil must be stopped before—you say he was *homicidal?* I don't know what will happen! Quick, what is his address?"

"Well, Mr. Follansby, he was in such a terrible hurry—"

The manager gave him a long, unbelieving look. "Get the police! Call the General Motors Security Division! Find him!"

Haskins raced for the door.

"Wait!" yelled the manager, struggling into a raincoat. "I'm coming, too!"

Elwood Caswell returned to his apartment by taxicopter. He lugged the Regenerator into his living room, put it down near the couch and studied it thoughtfully.

"That clerk was right," he said after a while. "It *does* go with the room."

Esthetically, the Regenerator was a success.

Caswell admired it for a few more moments, then went into the kitchen and fixed himself a chicken sandwich. He ate slowly, staring fixedly at a point just above and to the left of his kitchen clock.

Damn you, Magnessen! Dirty no-good lying shifty-eyed enemy of all that's decent and clean in the world . . .

Taking the revolver from his pocket, he laid it on the table. With a stiffened forefinger, he poked it into different positions.

It was time to begin therapy.

Except that . . .

Caswell realized worriedly that he didn't want to lose the desire to kill Magnessen. What would become of him if he lost that urge? His life would lose all purpose, all coherence, all flavor and zest. It would be quite dull, really.

Moreover, he had a great and genuine grievance against Magnessen, one he didn't like to think about.

Irene!

His poor sister, debauched by the subtle and insidious Magnessen, ruined by him and cast aside. What better reason could a man have to take his revolver and . . .

Caswell finally remembered that he did not have a sister.

Now was *really* the time to begin therapy.

He went into the living room and found the operating instructions tucked into a ventilation louver of the machine. He opened them and read:

To Operate all Rex Model Regenerators:

1. Place the Regenerator near a comfortable couch. (A comfortable couch can be purchased as an additional accessory from any General Motors dealer.)

2. Plug in the machine.

3. Affix the adjustable contact-band to the forehead.

And that's all! Your Regenerator will do the rest! There will be no language bar or dialect problem, since the Regenerator communicates by Direct Sense Contact (Patent Pending). All you must do is cooperate.

Try not to feel any embarrassment or shame. Everyone has problems and many are worse than yours! Your Regenerator has no interest in your morals or ethical standards, so don't feel it is "judging" you. It desires only to aid you in becoming well and happy.

As soon as it has collected and processed enough data, your Regenerator will begin treatment. You make the sessions as short or as long as you like. You are the boss! And of course you can end a session at any time.

That's all there is to it! Simple, isn't it? Now plug in your General Motors Regenerator and GET SANE!

"Nothing hard about that," Caswell said to himself. He pushed the Regenerator closer to the couch and plugged it in. He lifted the headband, started to slip it on, stopped.

"I feel so silly!" he giggled.

Abruptly he closed his mouth and stared pugnaciously at the black-and-chrome machine.

"So you think you can make me sane, huh?"

The Regenerator didn't answer.

"Oh, well, go ahead and try." He slipped the headband over his forehead, crossed his arms on his chest and leaned back.

Nothing happened. Caswell settled himself more comfortably on the couch. He scratched his shoulder and put the headband at a more comfortable angle. Still nothing. His thoughts began to wander.

Magnessen! You noisy, overbearing oaf, you disgusting—

"Good afternoon," a voice murmured in his head. "I am your mechanotherapist."

Caswell twitched guiltily. "Hello. I was just—you know, just sort of—"

"Of course," the machine said soothingly. "Don't we all? I am now scanning the material in your preconscious with the intent of synthesis, diagnosis, prognosis and treatment. I find . . ."

"Yes?"

"Just one moment." The Regenerator was silent for several minutes. Then, hesitantly, it said, "This is beyond doubt a most unusual case."

"Really?" Caswell asked, pleased.

"Yes. The coefficients seem—I'm not sure . . ." The machine's robotic voice grew feeble. The pilot light began to flicker and fade.

"Hey, what's the matter?"

"Confusion," said the machine. "Of course," it went on in a stronger voice, "the unusual nature of the symptoms need not prove entirely baffling to a competent therapeutic machine. A symptom, no matter how bizarre, is no more than a signpost, an indication of inner difficulty. And *all* symptoms can be related to the broad mainstream of proven theory. Since the theory is effective, the symptoms must relate. We will proceed on that assumption."

"Are you sure you know what you're doing?" asked Caswell, feeling light-headed.

The machine snapped back, its pilot light blazing, "Mechano-therapy today is an exact science and admits no significant errors. We will proceed with a word-association test."

"Fire away," said Caswell.

"House?"

"Home."

"Dog?"

"Cat."

"Fleefl?"

Caswell hesitated, trying to figure out the word. It sounded vaguely Martian, but it might be Venusian or even—

"Fleefl?" the Regenerator repeated.

"Marfoosh," Caswell replied, making up the word on the spur of the moment.

"Loud?"

"Sweet."

"Green?"

"Mother."

"Thanagoyes?"

"Patamathonga."

"Arrides?"

"Nexothesmodrastica."

"Chtheesnohelgnopteces?"

"Rigamaroo latasentricpropatria!" Caswell shot back. It was a collection of sounds he was particularly proud of. The average man would not have been able to pronounce them.

"Hmm," said the Regenerator. "The pattern fits. It always does."

"What pattern?"

"You have," the machine informed him, "a classic case of feem desire, complicated by strong dwarkish intentions."

"I do? I thought I was homicidal."

"That term has no referent," the machine said severely. "Therefore I must reject it as nonsense syllabification. Now consider these points: The feem desire is perfectly normal. Never forget that. But it is usually replaced at an early age by the hovendish revulsion. Individuals lacking in this basic environmental response—"

"I'm not absolutely sure I know what you're talking about," Caswell confessed.

"Please, sir! We must establish one thing at once. You are the patient. *I* am the mechanotherapist. You have brought your troubles to me for treatment. But you cannot expect help unless you cooperate."

"All right," Caswell said. "I'll try."

Up to now, he had been bathed in a warm glow of superiority. Everything the machine said had seemed mildly humorous. As a matter of fact, he had felt capable of pointing out a few things wrong with the mechanotherapist.

Now that sense of well-being evaporated, as it always did, and Caswell was alone, terribly alone and lost, a creature of his compulsions, in search of a little peace and contentment.

He would undergo anything to find them. Sternly he reminded himself that he had no right to comment on the mechanotherapist. These machines knew what they were doing and had been doing it for a long time. He would cooperate, no matter how outlandish the treatment seemed from his layman's viewpoint.

But it was obvious, Caswell thought, settling himself grimly on the couch, that mechanotherapy was going to be far more difficult than he had imagined.

The search for the missing customer had been brief and useless. He was nowhere to be found on the teeming New York streets and no one could remember seeing a redhaired, red-eyed little man lugging a black therapeutic machine.

It was all too common a sight.

In answer to an urgent telephone call, the police came immediately, four of them, led by a harassed young lieutenant of detectives named Smith.

Smith just had time to ask, "Say, why don't you people put tags on things?" when there was an interruption.

A man pushed his way past the policeman at the door. He was tall and gnarled and ugly, and his eyes were deep-set and bleakly blue. His clothes, unpressed and uncaring, hung on him like corrugated iron.

"What do you want?" Lieutenant Smith asked.

The ugly man flipped back his lapel, showing a small silver badge beneath. "I'm John Rath, General Motors Security Division."

"Oh . . . Sorry, sir," Lieutenant Smith said, saluting. "I didn't think you people would move in so fast."

Rath made a noncommittal noise. "Have you checked for prints, Lieutenant? The customer might have touched some other therapy machine."

"I'll get right on it, sir," Smith said. It wasn't often that one of the operatives from GM, GE or IBM came down to take a personal hand. If a local cop showed he was really clicking, there just might be the possibility of an Industrial Transfer. . . .

Rath turned to Follansby and Haskins, and transfixed them with a gaze as piercing and as impersonal as a radar beam. "Let's have the full story," he said, taking a notebook and pencil from a shapeless pocket.

He listened to the tale in ominous silence. Finally he closed his notebook, thrust it back into his pocket and said, "The therapeutic machines are a sacred trust. To give a customer the wrong machine is a betrayal of that trust, a violation of the Public Interest, and a defamation of the Company's good reputation."

The manager nodded in agreement, glaring at his unhappy clerk.

"A Martian model," Rath continued, "should never have been on the floor in the first place."

"I can explain that," Follansby said hastily. "We needed a demonstrator model and I wrote to the Company, telling them—"

"This might," Rath broke in inexorably, "be considered a case of gross criminal negligence."

Both the manager and the clerk exchanged horrified looks. They were thinking of the General Motors Reformatory outside of Detroit, where Company offenders passed their days in sullen silence, monotonously drawing micro-circuits for pocket television sets.

"However, that is out of my jurisdiction," Rath said. He turned his baleful gaze full upon Haskins. "You are certain that the customer never mentioned his name?"

"No, sir. I mean yes, I'm sure," Haskins replied rattledly.

"Did he mention any names at all?"

Haskins plunged his face into his hands. He looked up and said eagerly, "Yes! He wanted to kill someone! A friend of his!"

"Who?" Rath asked, with terrible patience.

"The friend's name was—let me think—Magneton! That was it! Magneton! Or was it Morrison? Oh, dear . . ."

Mr. Rath's iron face registered a rather corrugated disgust. People were useless as witnesses. Worse than useless, since they were frequently misleading. For reliability, give him a robot every time.

"Didn't he mention *anything* significant?"

"Let me *think!*" Haskins said, his face twisting into a fit of concentration.

Rath waited.

Mr. Follansby cleared his throat. "I was just thinking, Mr. Rath. About that Martian machine. It won't treat a Terran homicidal case as homicidal, will it?"

"Of course not. Homicide is unknown on Mars."

"Yes. But what will it do? Might it not reject the entire case as unsuitable? Then the customer would merely return the Regenerator with a complaint and we would—"

Mr. Rath shook his head. "The Rex Regenerator must treat if it finds evidence of psychosis. By Martian standards, the customer is a very sick man, a psychotic—*no matter what is wrong with him.*"

Follansby removed his pince-nez and polished them rapidly. "What will the machine do, then?"

"It will treat him for the Martian illness most analogous to his case. Feem desire, I should imagine, with various complications. As for what will happen once treatment begins, I don't know. I doubt whether anyone knows, since it has never happened before. Offhand, I would say there are two major alternatives: The patient may reject the therapy out of hand, in which case he is left with his homicidal mania unabated. Or he may accept the Martian therapy and reach a cure."

Mr. Follansby's face brightened. "Ah! A cure is possible!"

"You don't understand," Rath said. "He may effect a cure—*of his nonexistent Martian psychosis.* But to cure something that is not there is, in effect, to erect a gratuitous delusional system. You might say that the machine would work in reverse, producing psychosis instead of removing it."

Mr. Follansby groaned and leaned against a Bell Psychoso-matica.

"The result," Rath summed up, "would be to convince the customer that he was a Martian. A *sane* Martian, naturally."

Haskins suddenly shouted, "I remember! I remember now! He said he worked for the New York Rapid Transit Corporation! I remember distinctly!"

"That's a break," Rath said, reaching for the telephone.

Haskins wiped his perspiring face in relief. "And I just remembered something else that should make it easier still."

"What?"

"The customer said he had been an alcoholic at one time. I'm sure of it, because he was interested at first in the IBM Alcoholic Reliever, until I talked him out of it. He had red hair, you know, and I've had a theory for some time about red-headedness and alcoholism. It seems—"

"Excellent," Rath said. "Alcoholism will be on his records. It narrows the search considerably."

As he dialed the NYRT Corporation, the expression on his craglike face was almost pleasant.

It was good, for a change, to find that a human could retain some significant facts.

"But surely you remember your goricae?" the Regenerator was saying.

"No," Caswell answered wearily.

"Tell me, then, about your juvenile experiences with the thorastrian fleep."

"Never had any."

"Hmm. Blockage," muttered the machine. "Resentment. Repression. Are you sure you don't remember your goricae and what it meant to you? The experience is universal."

"Not for me," Caswell said, swallowing a yawn.

He had been undergoing mechanotherapy for close to four hours and it struck him as futile. For a while, he had talked voluntarily about his childhood, his mother and father, his older brother. But the Regenerator had asked him to put aside those fantasies. The patient's relationships to an imaginary parent or sibling, it explained, were unworkable and of minor importance psychologically. The important thing was the patient's feelings —both revealed and repressed—toward his goricae.

"Aw, look," Caswell complained, "I don't even know what a goricae is."

"Of course you do. You just won't *let* yourself know."

"I don't know. Tell me."

"It would be better if you told me."

"How can I?" Caswell raged. "I don't know!"

"What do you *imagine* a goricae would be?"

"A forest fire," Caswell said. "A salt tablet. A jar of denatured alcohol. A small screwdriver. Am I getting warm? A notebook. A revolver—"

"These associations are meaningful," the Regenerator assured him. "Your attempt at randomness shows a clearly underlying pattern. Do you begin to recognize it?"

"What in hell is a goricae?" Caswell roared.

"The tree that nourished you during infancy, and well into puberty, if my theory about you is correct. Inadvertently, the goricae stifled your necessary rejection of the feem desire. This in turn gave rise to your present urge to dwark someone in a vlendish manner."

"No tree nourished *me*."

"You cannot recall the experience?"

"Of course not. It never happened."

"You are sure of that?"

"Positive."

"Not even the tiniest bit of doubt?"

"No! No goricae ever nourished me. Look, I can break off these sessions at any time, right?"

"Of course," the Regenerator said. "But it would not be advisable at this moment. You are expressing anger, resentment, fear. By your rigidly summary rejection—"

"Nuts," said Caswell, and pulled off the headband.

The silence was wonderful. Caswell stood up, yawned, stretched and massaged the back of his neck. He stood in front of the humming black machine and gave it a long leer.

"You couldn't cure me of a common cold," he told it.

Stiffly he walked the length of the living room and returned to the Regenerator.

"Lousy fake!" he shouted.

Caswell went into the kitchen and opened a bottle of beer. His revolver was still on the table, gleaming dully.

Magnessen! You unspeakable treacherous filth! You fiend incarnate! You inhuman, hideous monster! Someone must destroy you, Magnessen! Someone . . .

Someone? He himself would have to do it. Only he knew the bottomless depths of Magnessen's depravity, his viciousness, his disgusting lust for power.

Yes, it was his duty, Caswell thought. But strangely, the knowledge brought him no pleasure.

After all, Magnessen was his friend.

He stood up, ready for action. He tucked the revolver into his righthand coat pocket and glanced at the kitchen clock. Nearly six-thirty. Magnessen would be home now, gulping his dinner, grinning over his plans.

This was the perfect time to take him.

Caswell strode to the door, opened it, started through, and stopped.

A thought had crossed his mind, a thought so tremendously involved, so meaningful, so far-reaching in its implications that he was stirred to his depths. Caswell tried desperately to shake off the knowledge it brought. But the thought, permanently etched upon his memory, would not depart.

Under the circumstances, he could do only one thing.

He returned to the living room, sat down on the couch and slipped on the headband.

The Regenerator said, "Yes?"

"It's the damnedest thing," Caswell said, "but do you know, I think I *do* remember my goricae!"

John Rath contacted the New York Rapid Transit Corporation by televideo and was put into immediate contact with Mr. Bemis, a plump, tanned man with watchful eyes.

"Alcoholism?" Mr. Bemis repeated, after the problem was explained. Unobtrusively, he turned on his tape recorder. "Among our employees?" Pressing a button beneath his foot, Bemis alerted Transit Security, Publicity, Intercompany Relations and the Psychoanalysis Division. This done, he looked earnestly at Rath. "Not a chance of it, my dear sir. Just between us, why does General Motors *really* want to know?"

Rath smiled bitterly. He should have anticipated this. NYRT and GM had had their differences in the past. Officially, there was cooperation between the two giant corporations. But for all practical purposes—

"The question is in terms of the Public Interest," Rath said.

"Oh, certainly," Mr. Bemis replied, with a subtle smile. Glancing at his tattle board, he noticed that several company executives had tapped in on his line. This might mean a promotion, if handled properly.

"The Public Interest of GM," Mr. Bemis added with polite nastiness. "The insinuation is, I suppose, that drunken conductors are operating our jetbuses and helis?"

"Of course not. I was searching for a single alcoholic predilection, an individual latency—"

"There's no possibility of it. We at Rapid Transit do not hire people with even the merest tendency in that direction. And may I suggest, sir, that you clean your own house before making implications about others?"

And with that, Mr. Bemis broke the connection.

No one was going to put anything over on *him*.

"Dead end," Rath said heavily. He turned and shouted, "Smith! Did you find any prints?"

Lieutenant Smith, his coat off and sleeves rolled up, bounded over. "Nothing usable, sir."

Rath's thin lips tightened. It had been close to seven hours since the customer had taken the Martian machine. There was no telling what harm had been done by now. The customer would be justified in bringing suit against the Company. Not that the money mattered much; it was the bad publicity that was to be avoided at all cost.

"Beg pardon, sir," Haskins said.

Rath ignored him. What next? Rapid Transit was not going to cooperate. Would the Armed Services make their records available for scansion by somatotype and pigmentation?

"Sir," Haskins said again.

"What is it?"

"I just remembered the customer's friend's name. It was Magnessen."

"Are you sure of that?"

"Absolutely," Haskins said, with the first confidence he had shown in hours. "I've taken the liberty of looking him up in the telephone book, sir. There's only one Manhattan listing under that name."

Rath glowered at him from under shaggy eyebrows. "Haskins, I hope you are not wrong about this. I sincerely hope that."

"I do too, sir," Haskins admitted, feeling his knees begin to shake.

"Because if you are," Rath said, "I will . . . Never mind. Let's go!"

By police escort, they arrived at the address in fifteen minutes. It was an ancient brownstone and Magnessen's name was on a second-floor door. They knocked.

The door opened and a stocky, crop-headed, shirt-sleeved man in his thirties stood before them. He turned slightly pale at the sight of so many uniforms, but held his ground.

"What is this?" he demanded.

"You Magnessen?" Lieutenant Smith barked.

"Yeah. What's the beef? If it's about my hi-fi playing too loud, I can tell you that old hag downstairs—"

"May we come in?" Rath asked. "It's important."

Magnessen seemed about to refuse, so Rath pushed past him, followed by Smith, Follansby, Haskins and a small army of policemen. Magnessen turned to face them, bewildered, defiant and more than a little awed.

"Mr. Magnessen," Rath said, in the pleasantest voice he could muster, "I hope you'll forgive the intrusion. Let me assure you, it is in the Public Interest, as well as your own. Do you know a short, angry-looking, red-haired, red-eyed man?"

"Yes," Magnessen said slowly and warily.

Haskins let out a sigh of relief.

"Would you tell us his name and address?" asked Rath.

"I suppose you mean—hold it! What's he done?"

"Nothing."

"Then what you want him for?"

"There's no time for explanations," Rath said. "Believe me, it's in his own best interest, too. What is his name?"

Magnessen studied Rath's ugly, honest face, trying to make up his mind.

Lieutenant Smith said, "Come on, talk, Magnessen, if you know what's good for you. We want the name and we want it quick."

It was the wrong approach. Magnessen lighted a cigarette, blew smoke in Smith's direction and inquired, "You got a warrant, buddy?"

"You bet I have," Smith said, striding forward. "I'll warrant you, wise guy."

"Stop it!" Rath ordered. "Lieutenant Smith, thank you for your assistance. I won't need you any longer."

Smith left sulkily, taking his platoon with him.

Rath said, "I apologize for Smith's over-eagerness. You had better hear the problem." Briefly but fully, he told the story of the customer and the Martian therapeutic machine.

When he was finished, Magnessen looked more suspicious than ever. "You say he wants to kill *me?*"

"Definitely."

"That's a lie! I don't know what your game is, mister, but you'll never make me believe that. Elwood's my best friend. We been best friends since we was kids. We been in service together. Elwood would cut off his arm for me. And I'd do the same for him."

"Yes, yes," Rath said impatiently, "in a sane frame of mind, he would. But your friend Elwood—is that his first name or last?"

"First," Magnessen said tauntingly.

"Your friend Elwood is psychotic."

"You don't know him. That guy loves me like a brother. Look, what's Elwood really done? Defaulted on some payments or something? I can help out."

"You thick-headed imbecile!" Rath shouted. "I'm trying to save your life, and the life and sanity of your friend!"

"But how do I know?" Magnessen pleaded. "You guys come busting in here—"

"You must trust me," Rath said.

Magnessen studied Rath's face and nodded sourly. "His name's Elwood Caswell. He lives just down the block at number 341."

The man who came to the door was short, with red hair and red-rimmed eyes. His right hand was thrust into his coat pocket. He seemed very calm.

"Are you Elwood Caswell?" Rath asked. "The Elwood Caswell who bought a Regenerator early this afternoon at the Home Therapy Appliances Store?"

"Yes," said Caswell. "Won't you come in?"

Inside Caswell's small living room, they saw the Regenerator, glistening black and chrome, standing near the couch. It was unplugged.

"Have you used it?" Rath asked anxiously.

"Yes."

Follansby stepped forward. "Mr. Caswell, I don't know how to explain this, but we made a terrible mistake. The Regenerator you took was a Martian model—for giving therapy to Martians."

"I know," said Caswell.

"You do?"

"Of course. It became pretty obvious after a while."

"It was a dangerous situation," Rath said. "Especially for a man with your—ah—troubles." He studied Caswell covertly. The man seemed fine, but appearances were frequently deceiving, especially with psychotics. Caswell had been homicidal; there was no reason why he should not still be.

And Rath began to wish he had not dismissed Smith and his policemen so summarily. Sometimes an armed squad was a comforting thing to have around.

Caswell walked across the room to the therapeutic machine. One hand was still in his jacket pocket; the other he laid affectionately upon the Regenerator.

"The poor thing tried its best," he said. "Of course, it couldn't cure what wasn't there." He laughed. "But it came very near succeeding!"

Rath studied Caswell's face and said, in a trained, casual tone, "Glad there was no harm, sir. The Company will, of course, reimburse you for your lost time and for your mental anguish—"

"Naturally," Caswell said.

"—and we will substitute a proper Terran Regenerator at once."

"That won't be necessary."

"It *won't*?"

"No." Caswell's voice was decisive. "The machine's attempt at therapy forced me into a complete self-appraisal. There was a moment of absolute insight, during which I was able to evaluate and discard my homicidal intentions toward poor Magnessen."

Rath nodded dubiously. "You feel no such urge now?"

"Not in the slightest."

Rath frowned deeply, started to say something, and stopped. He turned to Follansby and Haskins. "Get that machine out of here. I'll have a few things to say to you at the store."

The manager and the clerk lifted the Regenerator and left.

Rath took a deep breath. "Mr. Caswell, I would strongly advise that you accept a new Regenerator from the Company, gratis. Unless a cure is effected in a proper mechanotherapeutic manner, there is always the danger of a setback."

"No danger with me," Caswell said, airily but with deep conviction. "Thank you for your consideration, sir. And good night."

Rath shrugged and walked to the door.

"Wait!" Caswell called.

Rath turned. Caswell had taken his hand out of his pocket. In it was a revolver. Rath felt sweat trickle down his arms. He calculated the distance between himself and Caswell. Too far.

"Here," Caswell said, extending the revolver butt-first. "I won't need this any longer."

Rath managed to keep his face expressionless as he accepted the revolver and stuck it into a shapeless pocket.

"Good night," Caswell said. He closed the door behind Rath and bolted it.

At last he was alone.

Caswell walked into the kitchen. He opened a bottle of beer, took a deep swallow and sat down at the kitchen table. He stared fixedly at a point just above and to the left of the clock.

He had to form his plans now. There was no time to lose.

Magnessen! That inhuman monster who cut down the Caswell goricae! Magnessen! The man who, even now, was secretly planning to infect New York with the abhorrent feem desire! Oh, Magnessen, I wish you a long, long life, filled with the torture I can inflict on you. And to start with . . .

Caswell smiled to himself as he planned exactly how he would dwark Magnessen in a vlendish manner.

THE AUTUMN LAND

Clifford D. Simak

When a writer is asked to say something about a certain story he has written, he most often finds himself at a loss for anything to say. We can pretend that we plot stories, but that is not entirely true. A story hatches, somewhat like an egg. The hatching process may be a long one and so hidden in the subconscious mind the writer is not aware of it until suddenly there it stands, not full-blown, certainly, but with some hint of structure, in his mind.

Searching back, I can detect some of the elements of this story, although I cannot say I took those elements and put them all together—not to start with, anyhow. I think I can detect three rather faint ideas that at times I had given thought to and each time had given up because they seemed to come to nothing. One idea was simply a locale, an old village that lived forever in the depths of time, inhabited by people who also lived in the depths of time. Another was a wonderment as to what one might do if he happened to foresee, with some clarity and conviction, a great catastrophe that was about to be visited upon the human race. The answer seemed to be that there was little that could be done about it, for his warning would be blunted by public apathy and the natural human bent toward cynical disbelief. The third element was simply a rather limp and apparently unproductive thought: Would it be possible for a man to start walking and walk so far he left everything behind?

A more unlikely group of ideas of which to construct a story would be hard to find. And yet, somehow, the ideas got together, without too much conscious effort on the author's part and "The Autumn Land" was written.

—*Clifford D. Simak*

He sat on the porch, in the rocking chair, with the loose board creaking as he rocked. Across the street the old white-haired lady cut a bouquet of chrysanthemums in the never-ending autumn. Where he could see between the ancient houses to the distant woods and wastelands, a soft Indian-summer blue lay upon the land. The entire village was soft and quiet, as old things often are—a place constructed for a dreaming mind rather than a living being. It was an hour too early for his other old and shaky neighbor to come fumbling down the grass-grown sidewalk, tapping the bricks with his seeking cane. And he would not hear the distant children at their play until dusk had fallen—if he heard them then. He did not always hear them.

There were books to read, but he did not want to read them. He could go into the backyard and spade and rake the garden once again, reducing the soil to a finer texture to receive the seed when it could be planted—if it ever could be planted—but there was slight incentive in the further preparation of a seed bed against a spring that never came. Earlier, much earlier, before he knew about the autumn and the spring, he had mentioned garden seeds to the Milkman, who had been very much embarrassed.

He had walked the magic miles and left the world behind in bitterness and when he first had come here had been content to live in utter idleness, to be supremely idle and to feel no guilt or shame at doing absolutely nothing or as close to absolutely nothing as a man was able. He had come walking down the autumn street in the quietness and the golden sunshine, and the first person that he saw was the old lady who lived across the street. She had been waiting at the gate of her picket fence as if she had known he would be coming, and she had said to him, "You're a new one come to live with us. There are not many come these days. That is your house across the street from me, and I know we'll be good neighbors." He had reached up his hand to doff his hat to her, forgetting that he had no hat. "My name is Nelson Rand," he'd told her. "I am an engineer. I will try to be a decent neighbor." He had the impression that she stood taller and straighter than she did, but old and bent as she might be there was a comforting graciousness about her. "You will please come in," she said. "I have lemonade and cookies. There are other people there, but I shall not introduce them to you." He waited for her to explain why she would not introduce him, but there was no explanation, and he followed her down the time-mellowed walk of bricks with great beds of asters and chrysanthemums, a mass of color on either side of it.

In the large, high-ceilinged living room, with its bay windows forming window seats, filled with massive furniture from another time and with a small blaze burning in the fireplace, she had shown him to a seat before a small table to one side of the fire and had sat down opposite him and poured the lemonade and passed the plate of cookies.

"You must pay no attention to them," she had told him. "They are all dying to meet you, but I shall not humor them."

It was easy to pay no attention to them, for there was no one there.

"The Major, standing over there by the fireplace," said his hostess, "with his elbow on the mantel, a most ungainly pose if you should ask me, is not happy with my lemonade. He would prefer a stronger drink. Please, Mr. Rand, will you not taste my lemonade? I assure you it is good. I made it myself. I have no maid, you see, and no one in the kitchen. I live quite by myself and satisfactorily, although my friends keep dropping in, sometimes more often than I like."

He tasted the lemonade, not without misgivings, and to his surprise it was lemonade and was really good, like the lemonade he had drunk when a boy at Fourth of July celebrations and at grade school picnics, and had never tasted since.

"It is excellent," he said.

"The lady in blue," his hostess said, "sitting in the chair by the window, lived here many years ago. She and I were friends, although she moved away some time ago and I am surprised that she comes back, which she often does. The infuriating thing is that I cannot recall her name, if I ever knew it. You don't know it, do you?"

"I am afraid I don't."

"Oh, of course, you wouldn't. I had forgotten. I forget so easily these days. You are a new arrival."

He had sat through the afternoon and drank her lemonade and eaten her cookies, while she chattered on about her nonexistent guests. It was only when he had crossed the street to the house she had pointed out as his, with her standing on the stoop and waving her farewell, that he realized she had not told him her name. He did not know it even now.

How long had it been? he wondered, and realized he didn't know. It was this autumn business. How could a man keep track of time when it was always autumn?

It all had started on that day when he'd been driving across Iowa, heading for Chicago. No, he reminded himself, it had started with the thinnesses, although he had paid little attention to the thinnesses to begin with. Just been aware of them, perhaps as a strange condition of the mind, or perhaps an unusual quality to the atmosphere and light. As if the world lacked a certain solidity that one had come to expect, as if one were running along a mystic borderline between here and somewhere else.

He had lost his West Coast job when a government contract had failed to materialize. His company had not been the only one; there were many other companies that were losing contracts and there were a lot of engineers who walked the streets bewildered. There was a bare possibility of a job in Chicago, although he was well aware that by now it might be filled. Even if there were no job, he reminded himself, he was in better shape than a lot of other men. He was young and single, he had a few dollars in the bank, he had no house mortgage, no car payments, no kids to put through school. He had only himself to support—no family of any sort at all. The old, hard-fisted bachelor uncle who had taken him to raise when his parents had died in a car crash and had worked him hard on that stony, hilly Wisconsin farm, had receded deep into the past, becoming a dim, far figure that was hard to recognize. He had not liked his uncle, Rand remembered —had not hated him, simply had not liked him. He had shed no tears, he recalled, when the old man had been caught out in a pasture by a bull and gored to death. So now Rand was quite alone, not even holding the memories of a family.

He had been hoarding the little money that he had, for with a limited work record, with other men better qualified looking for the jobs, he realized that it might be some time before he could connect with anything. The beat-up wagon that he drove had space for sleeping, and he stopped at the little wayside parks along the way to cook his meals.

He had almost crossed the state, and the road had started its long winding through the bluffs that rimmed the Mississippi. Ahead he caught glimpses, at several turnings of the road, of smokestacks and tall structures that marked the city just ahead.

He emerged from the bluffs, and the city lay before him, a small industrial center that lay on either side the river. It was then that he felt and saw (if one could call it seeing) the thinness that he had seen before or had sensed before. There was about it, not exactly an alienness, but a sense of unreality, as if one were seeing the actuality of the scene through some sort of veil, with the edges softened and the angles flattened out, as if one might be looking at it as one would look at the bottom of a clear-water lake with a breeze gently ruffling the surface. When he had seen it before, he had attributed it to road fatigue and had opened the window to get a breath of air or had stopped the car and gotten out to walk up and down the road a while, and it had gone away.

But this time it was worse than ever, and he was somewhat frightened at it—not so much frightened at it as he was frightened of himself, wondering what might be wrong with him.

He pulled off to the side of the road, braking the car to a halt, and it seemed to him, even as he did it, that the shoulder of the road was rougher than he'd thought. As he pulled off the road, the thinness seemed to lessen, and he saw that the road had changed, which explained its roughness. The surface was pocked with chuckholes and blocks of concrete had been heaved up and other blocks were broken into pebbly shards.

He raised his eyes from the road to look at the city, and there was no city, only the broken stumps of a place that had somehow been destroyed. He sat with his hands frozen on the wheel, and in the silence—the deadly, unaccustomed silence—he heard the cawing of crows. Foolishly, he tried to remember the last time he had heard the caw of crows, and then he saw them, black specks that flapped just above the bluff top. There was something else as well—the trees. No longer trees, but only here and there blackened stumps. The stumps of a city and the stumps of trees, with the black, ash-like flecks of crows flapping over them.

Scarcely knowing what he did, he stumbled from the car. Thinking of it later, it had seemed a foolish thing to do, for the car was the only thing he knew, the one last link he had to reality. As he stumbled from it, he put his hand down in the seat, and beneath his hand he felt the solid, oblong object. His fingers closed upon it, and it was not until he was standing by the car that he realized what he held—the camera that had been lying in the seat beside him.

Sitting on the porch, with the loose floorboard creaking underneath the rocker, he remembered that he still had the pictures, although it had been a long time since he had thought of them—a long time, actually, since he'd thought of anything at all beyond his life, day to day, in this autumn land. It was as though he had been trying to keep himself from thinking, attempting to keep his mind in neutral, to shut out what he knew—or, more precisely perhaps, what he thought he knew.

He did not consciously take the pictures, although afterward he had tried to tell himself he did (but never quite convincing himself that this was entirely true), complimenting himself in a wry sort of way for providing a piece of evidence that his memory alone never could have provided. For a man can think so many things, daydream so many things, imagine so many things that he can never trust his mind.

The entire incident, when he later thought of it, was hazy, as if the reality of that blasted city lay in some strange dimension of experience that could not be explained, or even rationalized. He could remember only vaguely the camera at his eyes and the clicking as the shutter snapped. He did recall the band of people charging down the hill toward him and his mad scramble for the car, locking the door behind him and putting the car in gear, intent on steering a zigzag course along the broken pavement to get away from the screaming humans who were less than a hundred feet away.

But as he pulled off the shoulder, the pavement was no longer broken. It ran smooth and level toward the city that was no longer blasted. He pulled off the road again and sat limply, beaten, and it was only after many minutes that he could proceed again, going very slowly because he did not trust himself, shaken as he was, to drive at greater speed.

He had planned to cross the river and continue to Chicago, getting there that night, but now his plans were changed. He was too shaken up and, besides, there were the films. And he needed time to think, he told himself, a lot of time to think.

He found a roadside park a few miles outside the city and pulled into it, parking alongside an outdoor grill and an old-fashioned pump. He got some wood from the small supply he carried in the back and built a fire. He hauled out the box with his cooking gear and food, fixed the coffee pot, set a pan upon the grill and cracked three eggs into it.

When he had pulled off the road, he had seen the man walking along the roadside; and now, as he cracked the eggs, he saw that the man had turned into the park and was walking toward the car. The man came up to the pump.

"Does this thing work?" he asked.

Rand nodded. "I got water for the pot," he said. "Just now."

"It's a hot day," said the man.

He worked the pump handle up and down.

"Hot for walking," he said.

"You been walking far?"

"The last six weeks," he said.

Rand had a closer look at him. The clothes were old and worn, but fairly clean. He had shaved a day or two before. His hair was long—not that he wore it long, but from lack of barbering.

Water gushed from the spout and the man cupped his hands under it, bent to drink.

"That was good," he finally said. "I was thirsty."

"How are you doing for food?" asked Rand.

The man hesitated. "Not too well," he said.

"Reach into that box on the tailgate. Find yourself a plate and some eating implements. A cup, too. Coffee will be ready soon."

"Mister, I wouldn't want you to think I came walking up here . . ."

"Forget it," said Rand. "I know how it is. There's enough for the both of us."

The man got a plate and cup, a knife, a fork, a spoon. He came over and stood beside the fire.

"I am new at this," he said. "I've never had to do a thing like this before. I always had a job. For seventeen years I had a job . . ."

"Here you are," said Rand. He slid the eggs onto the plate, went back to the box to get three more.

The man walked over to a picnic table and put down his plate. "Don't wait for me," said Rand. "Eat them while they're hot. The coffee's almost ready. There's bread if you want any."

"I'll get a slice later," said the man, "for mopping up."

John Sterling, he said his name was, and where now would John Sterling be, Rand wondered—still tramping the highways, looking for work, any kind of work, a day of work, an hour of work, a man who for seventeen years had held a job and had a job no longer? Thinking of Sterling, he felt a pang of guilt. He owed John Sterling a debt he never could repay, not knowing at the time they talked there was any debt involved.

They had sat and talked, eating their eggs, mopping up the plates with bread, drinking hot coffee.

"For seventeen years," said Sterling. "A machine operator. An experienced hand. With the same company. Then they let me out. Me and four hundred others. All at one time. Later they let out others. I was not the only one. There were a lot of us. We weren't laid off, we were let out. No promise of going back. Not the company's fault, I guess. There was a big contract that fizzled out. There was no work to do. How about yourself? You let out, too?"

Rand nodded. "How did you know?"

"Well, eating like this. Cheaper than a restaurant. And you got a sleeping bag. You sleep in the car?"

"That is right," said Rand. "It's not as bad for me as it is for some of the others. I have no family."

"I have a family," said Sterling. "Wife, three kids. We talked it over, the wife and me. She didn't want me to leave, but it made sense I should. Money all gone, unemployment run out. Long as I was around, it was hard to get relief. But if I deserted her, she could get relief. That way there's food for the wife and kids, a roof over their heads. Hardest thing I ever did. Hard for all of us. Someday I'll go back. When times get better, I'll go back. The family will be waiting."

Out on the highway the cars went whisking past. A squirrel came down out of a tree, advanced cautiously toward the table, suddenly turned and fled for his very life, swarming up a nearby tree trunk.

"I don't know," said Sterling. "It might be too big for us, this society of ours. It may be out of hand. I read a lot. Always liked to read. And I think about what I read. It seems to me maybe we've outrun our brains. The brains we have maybe were OK back in prehistoric days. We did all right with the brains we had until we built too big and complex. Maybe we built beyond our brains. Maybe our brains no longer are good enough to handle what we have. We have set loose economic forces we don't understand and political forces that we do not understand, and if we can't understand them, we can't control them. Maybe that is why you and I are out of jobs."

"I wouldn't know," said Rand. "I never thought about it."

"A man thinks a lot," said Sterling. "He dreams a lot walking down the road. Nothing else to do. He dreams some silly things: Things that are silly on the face of them, but are hard to say can't be really true. Did this ever happen to you?"

"Sometimes," said Rand.

"One thing I thought about a lot. A terribly silly thought. Maybe thinking it because I do so much walking. Sometimes people pick me up, but mostly I walk. And I got to wondering if a man should walk far enough could he leave it all behind? The farther a man might walk, the farther he would be from everything."

"Where you heading?" Rand asked.

"Nowhere in particular. Just keep on moving, that is all. Month or so I'll start heading south. Get a good head start on winter.

These northern states are no place to be when winter comes."

"There are two eggs left," said Rand. "How about it?"

"Hell, man, I can't. I already . . ."

"Three eggs aren't a lot. I can get some more."

"Well, if you're sure that you don't mind. Tell you what—let's split them, one for you, one for me."

The giddy old lady had finished cutting her bouquet and had gone into the house. From up the street came the tapping of a cane—Rand's other ancient neighbor, out for his evening walk. The sinking sun poured a blessing on the land. The leaves were gold and red, brown and yellow—they had been that way since the day that Rand had come. The grass had a tawny look about it—not dead, just dressed up for dying.

The old man came trudging carefully down the walk, his cane alert against a stumble, helping himself with it without really needing any help. He was slow, was all. He halted by the walk that ran up to the porch. "Good afternoon," he said. "Good afternoon," said Rand. "You have a nice day for your walk." The old man acknowledged the observation graciously and with a touch of modesty, as if he, himself, might somehow be responsible for the goodness of the day. "It looks," he said, "as if we might have another fine day tomorrow." And having said that, he continued down the street.

It was ritual. The same words were said each day. The situation, like the village and the weather, never varied. He could sit here on this porch a thousand years, Rand told himself, and the old man would continue going past and each time the self-same words would be mouthed—a set piece, a strip of film run over and over again. Something here had happened to time. The year had stuck on autumn.

Rand did not understand it. He did not try to understand it. There was no way for him to try. Sterling had said that man's cleverness might have outstripped his feeble, prehistoric mind—or, perhaps, his brutal and prehistoric mind. And here there was less chance of understanding than there had been back in that other world.

He found himself thinking of that other world in the same myth-haunted way as he thought of this one. The one now seemed as unreal as the other. Would he ever, Rand wondered, find reality again? Did he want to find it?

There was a way to find reality, he knew. Go into the house and take out the photos in the drawer of his bedside table and have a look at them. Refresh his memory, stare reality in the face again. For those photos, grim as they might be, were a harder reality than this world in which he sat or the world that he had known. For they were nothing seen by the human eye, interpreted by the human brain. They were, somehow, fact. The camera saw what it saw and could not lie about it; it did not fantasize, it did not rationalize, and it had no faulty memory, which was more than could be said of the human mind.

He had gone back to the camera shop where he had left the film and the clerk had picked out the envelope from the box behind the counter.

"That will be three ninety-five," he said.

Rand took a five-dollar bill out of his wallet and laid it on the counter.

"If you don't mind my asking," said the clerk, "where did you get these pictures?"

"It is trick photography," said Rand.

The clerk shook his head. "If that is what they are, they're the best I've ever seen."

The clerk rang up the sale and, leaving the register open, stepped back and picked up the envelope.

"What do you want?" asked Rand.

The man shook the prints out of the envelope, shuffled through them.

"This one," he said.

Rand stared at him levelly. "What about it?" he asked.

"The people. I know some of them. The one in front. That is Bob Gentry. He is my best friend."

"You must be mistaken," Rand said coldly.

He took the prints from the clerk's fingers, put them back in the envelope.

The clerk made the change. He still was shaking his head, confused, perhaps a little frightened, when Rand left the shop.

He drove carefully, but with no loss of time, through the city and across the bridge. When he hit open country beyond the river, he built up his speed, keeping an eye on the rear-vision mirror. The clerk had been upset, perhaps enough to phone the police. Others would have seen the pictures and been upset as well. Although, he told himself, it was silly to think of the police. In taking the photos, he had broken no regulations, violated no laws. He had had a perfect right to take them.

Across the river and twenty miles down the highway, he turned off into a small, dusty country road and followed it until he found a place to pull off, where the road widened at the approach to a bridge that crossed a small stream. There was evidence that the pull-off was much used, fishermen more than likely parking their cars there while they tried their luck. But now the place was empty.

He was disturbed to find that his hands were shaking when he pulled the envelope from his pocket and shook out the prints.

And there it was—as he no longer could remember it.

He was surprised that he had taken as many pictures as he had. He could not remember having taken half that many. But they were there, and as he looked at them, his memory, reinforced, came back again, although the photos were much sharper than his memory. The world, he recalled, had seemed to be hazed and indistinct so far as his eyes had been concerned; in the photos it lay cruel and merciless and clear. The blackened stumps stood up, stark and desolate, and there could be no doubt that the imprint that lay upon the photos was the actuality of a bombed-out city. The photos of the bluff showed the barren rock no

longer masked by trees, with only here and there the skeletons
of trees that by some accidental miracle had not been utterly re-
duced by the storm of fire. There was only one photo of the
band of people who had come charging down the hill toward
him; and that was understandable, for once having seen them,
he had been in a hurry to get back to the car. Studying the photo,
he saw they were much closer than he'd thought. Apparently
they had been there all the time, just a little way off, and he had
not noticed them in his astonishment at what had happened to
the city. If they had been quieter about it, they could have been
on top of him and overwhelmed him before he discovered them.
He looked closely at the picture and saw that they had been close
enough that some of the faces were fairly well defined. He wondered which one of them was the man the clerk back at the camera shop had recognized.

He shuffled the photographs together and slid them back
into the envelope and put it in his pocket. He got out of the car
and walked down to the edge of the stream. The stream, he saw,
was no more than ten feet or so across; but here, below the bridge,
it had gathered itself into a pool, and the bank had been trampled
bare of vegetation, and there were places where fishermen had
sat. Rand sat down in one of these places and inspected the pool.
The current came in close against the bank and probably had
undercut it, and lying there, in the undercut, would be the fish
that the now-absent anglers sought, dangling their worms at the
end of a long cane pole and waiting for a bite.

The place was pleasant and cool, shaded by a great oak that
grew on the bank just below the bridge. From some far-off field
came the subdued clatter of a mower. The water dimpled as a
fish came up to suck in a floating insect. A good place to stay,
thought Rand. A place to sit and rest awhile. He tried to blank
his mind, to wipe out the memory and the photos, to pretend that
nothing at all had happened, that there was nothing he must
think about.

But there was, he found, something that he must think about.

Not about the photos, but something that Sterling had said just the day before. "I got to wondering," he had said, "if a man should walk far enough, could he leave it all behind."

How desperate must a man get, Rand wondered, before he would be driven to asking such a question. Perhaps not desperate at all—just worried and alone and tired and not being able to see the end of it. Either that, or afraid of what lay up ahead. Like knowing, perhaps, that in a few years time (and not too many years, for in that photo of the people the clerk had seen a man he knew) a warhead would hit a little Iowa town and wipe it out. Not that there was any reason for it being hit; it was no Los Angeles, no New York, no Washington, no busy port, no center of transportation or communication, held no great industrial complex, was no seat of government. Simply hit because it had been there, hit by blunder, by malfunction, or by miscalculation. Although it probably didn't matter greatly, for by the time it had been hit, the nation and perhaps the world might have been gone. A few years, Rand told himself, and it would come to that. After all the labor, all the hopes and dreams, the world would come to just that.

It was the sort of thing that a man might want to walk away from, hoping that in time he might forget it ever had been there. But to walk away, he thought, rather idly, one would have to find a starting point. You could not walk away from everything by just starting anywhere.

It was an idle thought, sparked by the memory of his talk with Sterling; and he sat there, idly, on the stream bank; and because it had a sense of attractive wonder, he held it in his mind, not letting go at once as one did with idle thoughts. And as he sat there, still holding it in mind, another thought, another time and place crept in to keep it company; and suddenly he knew, with no doubt at all, without really thinking, without searching for an answer, that he knew the place where he could start.

He stiffened and sat rigid, momentarily frightened, feeling like

a fool trapped by his own unconscious fantasy. For that, said
common sense, was all that it could be. The bitter wondering of
a beaten man as he tramped the endless road looking for a job,
the shock of what the photos showed, some strange, mesmeric
quality of this shaded pool that seemed a place apart from a
rock-hard world—all of these put together had produced the
fantasy.

Rand hauled himself erect and turned back toward the car,
but as he did he could see within his mind this special starting
place. He had been a boy—how old? he wondered, maybe nine
or ten—and he had found the little valley (not quite a glen, yet
not quite a valley, either) running below his uncle's farm down
toward the river. He had never been there before and he had
never gone again; on his uncle's farm there had been too many
chores, too many things to do to allow the time to go anywhere
at all. He tried to recall the circumstances of his being there and
found that he could not. All that he could remember was a single
magic moment, as if he had been looking at a single frame of a
movie film—a single frame impressed upon his memory because
of what? Because of some peculiar angle at which the light had
struck the landscape? Because for an instant he had seen with
different eyes than he'd ever used before or since? Because for the
fractional part of a second he had sensed a simple truth behind
the facade of the ordinary world? No matter what, he knew, he
had seen magic in that moment.

He went back to the car and sat behind the wheel, staring at
the bridge and sliding water and the field beyond, but seeing, instead of them, the map inside his head. When he went back to
the highway, he'd turn left instead of right, back toward the river
and the town, and before he reached them he would turn north
on another road and the valley of the magic moment would be
only a little more than a hundred miles away. He sat and saw
the map and purpose hardened in his mind. Enough of this silli-
ness, he thought; there were no magic moments, never had been

one; when he reached the highway, he'd turn to the right and hope the job might still be there when he reached Chicago.

When he reached the highway, he turned not right, but left.

It had been so easy to find, he thought as he sat on the porch. There had been no taking of wrong roads, no stopping for directions; he'd gone directly there as if he'd always known he would be coming back and had kept the way in mind. He had parked the car at the hollow's mouth, since there was no road, and had gone on foot up the little valley. It could so easily have been that he would not have found the place, he told himself, admitting now for the first time since it all began that he might not have been so sure as he had thought he was. He might have gone up the full length of the valley and not have found the magic ground, or he might have passed it by, seeing it with other eyes and not recognizing it.

But it still was there, and he had stopped and looked at it and known it; again he was only nine or ten, and it was all right, the magic still was there. He had found a path he had not seen before and had followed it, the magic still remaining; and when he reached the hilltop, the village had been there. He had walked down the street in the quietness of the golden sunshine, and the first person that he had seen had been the old lady waiting at the gate of her picket fence, as if she had been told that he would be coming.

After he had left her house he went across the street to the house she said was his. As he came in the front door, there was someone knocking at the back.

"I am the Milkman," the knocker had explained. He was a shadowy sort of person; you could not really see him; when one looked away and then looked back at him, it was as if one were seeing someone he had never seen before.

"Milkman," Rand had said. "Yes, I suppose I could do with milk."

"Also," said the Milkman, "I have eggs, bread, butter, bacon and other things that you will need. Here is a can of oil; you'll need it for your lamps. The woodshed is well stocked, and when there's need of it, I'll replenish it. The kindling's to the left as you go through the door."

Rand recalled that he'd never paid the Milkman or even mentioned payment. The Milkman was not the kind of man to whom one mentioned money. There was no need, either, to leave an order slip in the milkbox; the Milkman seemed to know what one might need and when without being told. With some shame, Rand remembered the time he had mentioned garden seeds and caused embarrassment, not only for the Milkman, but for himself as well. For as soon as he mentioned them, he had sensed that he'd broken some very subtle code of which he should have been aware.

The day was fading into evening, and he should be going in soon to cook himself a meal. And after that, what he wondered. There still were books to read, but he did not want to read them. He could take out from the desk the plan he had laid out for the garden and mull over it a while, but now he knew he'd never plant the garden. You didn't plant a garden in a forever-autumn land, and there were no seeds.

Across the street a light blossomed in the windows of that great front room with its massive furniture, its roomy window seats, the great fireplace flaring to the ceiling. The old man with the cane had not returned, and it was getting late for him. In the distance now Rand could hear the sounds of children playing in the dusk.

The old and young, he thought. The old, who do not care; the young, who do not think. And what was he doing here, neither young nor old?

He left the porch and went down the walk. The street was empty, as it always was. He drifted slowly down it, heading toward the little park at the village edge. He often went there, to sit on a bench beneath the friendly trees; and it was there, he was sure, that he would find the children. Although why he should think that he would find them there he did not know, for he had never found them, but only heard their voices.

He went past the houses, standing sedately in the dusk. Had people ever lived in them, he wondered. Had there ever been that many people in this nameless village? The old lady across the street spoke of friends she once had known, of people who had lived here and had gone away. But was this her memory speaking or the kind befuddlement of someone growing old?

The houses, he had noted, all were in good repair. A loose shingle here and there, a little peeling paint, but no windows broken, no loosened gutters, sagging from the eaves, no rotting porch posts. As if, he thought, good householders had been here until very recently.

He reached the park and could see that it was empty. He still heard the childish voices, crying at their play, but they had receded and now came from somewhere just beyond the park. He crossed the park and stood at its edge, staring off across the scrub and abandoned fields.

In the east the moon was rising, a full moon that lighted the landscape so that he could see every little clump of bushes, every grove of trees. And as he stood there, he realized with a sudden start that the moon was full again, that it was always full. It rose with the setting of the sun and set just before the sun came up, and it was always a great pumpkin of a moon, an eternal harvest moon shining on an eternal autumn world.

The realization that this was so all at once seemed shocking. How was it that he had never noticed this before? Certainly he had been here long enough, had watched the moon often enough to have noticed it. He had been here long enough—and how long had that been, a few weeks, a few months, a year? He found he did not know. He tried to figure back and there was no way to figure back. There were no temporal landmarks. Nothing ever happened to mark one day from the next. Time flowed so smoothly and so uneventfully that it might as well stand still.

The voices of the playing children had been moving from him, becoming fainter in the distance; and as he listened to them, he found that he was hearing them in his mind when they were no longer there. They had come and played and now had ceased their play. They would come again, if not tomorrow night, in another night or two. It did not matter, he admitted, if they came or not, for they really weren't there.

He turned heavily about and went back through the streets. As he approached his house, a dark figure moved out from the shadow of the trees and stood waiting for him. It was the old lady from across the street. It was evident that she had been waiting his return.

"Good evening, ma'am," he said gravely. "It is a pleasant night."

"He is gone," she said. "He did not come back. He went just like the others and he won't come back."

"You mean the old man."

"Our neighbor," she said. "The old man with the cane. I do not know his name. I never knew his name. And I don't know yours."

"I told it to you once," said Rand, but she paid him no attention.

"Just a few doors up the street," she said, "and I never knew his name and I doubt that he knew mine. We are a nameless people here, and it is a terrible thing to be a nameless person."

"I will look for him," said Rand. "He may have lost his way."

"Yes, go and look for him," she said. "By all means look for him. It will ease your mind. It will take away the guilt. But you will never find him."

He took the direction that he knew the old man always took. He had the impression that his ancient neighbor, on his daily walks, went to the town square and the deserted business section, but he did not know. At no other time had it ever seemed important where he might have gone on his walks.

When he emerged into the square, he saw, immediately, the

dark object lying on the pavement and recognized it as the old man's hat. There was no sign of the man himself.

Rand walked out into the square and picked up the hat. He gently reshaped and creased it and after that was done held it carefully by the brim so that it would come to no further damage.

The business section drowsed in the moonlight. The statue of the unknown man stood starkly on its base in the center of the square. When he first had come here, Rand recalled, he had tried to unravel the identity of the statue and had failed. There was no legend carved into the granite base, no bronze plate affixed. The face was undistinguished, the stony costume gave no hint as to identity or period. There was nothing in the posture or the attitude of the carven body to provide a clue. The statue stood, a forgotten tribute to some unknown mediocrity.

As he gazed about the square at the business houses, Rand was struck again, as he always was, by the carefully unmodern make-up of the establishments. A barber shop, a hotel, a livery barn, a bicycle shop, a harness shop, a grocery store, a meat market, a blacksmith shop—no garage, no service station, no pizza parlor, no hamburger joint. The houses along the quiet streets told the story; here it was emphasized. This was an old town, forgotten and by-passed by the sweep of time, a place of another century. But there was about it all what seemed to be a disturbing sense of unreality, as if it were no old town at all, but a place deliberately fashioned in such a manner as to represent a segment of the past.

Rand shook his head. What was wrong with him tonight? Most of the time he was quite willing to accept the village for what it seemed to be, but tonight he was assailed with uneasy doubt.

Across the square he found the old man's cane. If his neighbor had come in this direction, he reasoned, he must have crossed the square and gone on down the street nearest to the place where he had dropped the cane. But why had he dropped the cane? First his hat and then his cane. What had happened here?

Rand glanced around, expecting that he might catch some

movement, some furtive lurker on the margin of the square. There was nothing. If there had been something earlier, there was nothing now.

Following the street toward which his neighbor might have been heading, he walked carefully and alert, watching the shadows closely. The shadows played tricks on him, conjuring up lumpy objects that could have been a fallen man, but weren't. A half a dozen times he froze when he thought he detected something moving, but it was, in each case, only an illusion of the shadows.

When the village ended, the street continued as a path. Rand hesitated, trying to plan his action. The old man had lost his hat and cane, and the points where he had dropped them argued that he had intended going down the street that Rand had followed. If he had come down the street, he might have continued down the path, out of the village and away from it, perhaps fleeing from something in the village.

There was no way one could be sure, Rand knew. But he was here and might as well go on for at least a ways. The old man might be out there somewhere, exhausted, perhaps terribly frightened, perhaps fallen beside the path and needing help.

Rand forged ahead. The path, rather well-defined at first, became fainter as it wound its way across the rolling moonlit countryside. A flushed rabbit went bobbing through the grass. Far off an owl chortled wickedly. A faint chill wind came out of the west. And with the wind came a sense of loneliness, of open empty space untenanted by anything other than rabbit, owl and wind.

The path came to an end, its faintness finally pinching out to nothing. The groves of trees and thickets of low-growing shrubs gave way to a level plain of blowing grass, bleached to whiteness by the moon, a faceless prairie land. Staring out across it, Rand knew that this wilderness of grass would run on and on forever. It had in it the scent and taste of foreverness. He shuddered at the sight of it and wondered why a man should shudder at a thing so simple. But even as he wondered, he knew—the grass was staring back at him; it knew him and waited patiently for him, for in time he would come to it. He would wander into it and be lost in it, swallowed by its immensity and anonymity.

He turned and ran, unashamedly, chill of blood and brain, shaken to the core. When he reached the outskirts of the village, he finally stopped the running and turned to look back into the wasteland. He had left the grass behind, but he sensed illogically that it was stalking him, flowing forward, still out of sight, but soon to appear, with the wind blowing billows in its whiteness.

He ran again, but not so fast and hard this time, jogging down the street. He came into the square and crossed it, and when he reached his house, he saw that the house across the street was dark. He did not hesitate, but went on down the street he'd walked when he first came to the village. For he knew now that he must leave this magic place with its strange and quiet old village, its forever autumn and eternal harvest moon, its faceless sea of grass, its children who receded in the distance when one went to look for them, its old man who walked into oblivion, dropping hat and cane—that he must somehow find his way back to that other world where few jobs existed and men walked the road to find them, where nasty little wars flared in forgotten corners and a camera caught on film the doom that was to come.

He left the village behind him and knew that he had not far to go to reach the place where the path swerved to the right and down a broken slope into the little valley to the magic starting point he'd found again after many years. He went slowly and carefully so that he would not wander off the path, for as he remembered it the path was very faint. It took much longer than he had thought to reach the point where the path swerved to the right into the broken ground, and the realization grew upon him that the path did not swing to the right and there was no broken ground.

In front of him he saw the grass again and there was no path leading into it. He knew that he was trapped, that he would never leave the village until he left it as the old man had, walking out of it and into nothingness. He did not move closer to the grass, for he knew there was terror there and he'd had enough of terror. You're a coward, he told himself.

Retracing the path back to the village, he kept a sharp lookout, going slowly so that he'd not miss the turnoff if it should be there. It was not, however. It once had been, he told himself, bemused, and he'd come walking up it, out of that other world he'd fled.

The village street was dappled by the moonlight shining through the rustling leaves. The house across the street still was dark, and there was an empty loneliness about it. Rand remembered that he had not eaten since the sandwich he had made that noon. There'd be something in the milkbox—he'd not looked in it that morning, or had he? He could not remember.

He went around the house to the back porch where the milkbox stood. The Milkman was standing there. He was more shadowy than ever, less well defined, with the moonlight shining on him, and his face was deeply shaded by the wide-brimmed hat he wore.

Rand halted abruptly and stood looking at him, astounded that the Milkman should be there. For he was out of place in the autumn moonlight. He was a creature of the early morning hours and of no other times.

"I came," the Milkman said, "to determine if I could be of help."

Rand said nothing. His head buzzed large and misty, and there was nothing to be said.

"A gun," the Milkman suggested. "Perhaps you would like a gun."

"A gun? Why should I want one?"

"You have had a most disturbing evening. You might feel safer, more secure, with a gun in hand, a gun strapped about your waist."

Rand hesitated. Was there mockery in the Milkman's voice?

"Or a cross."

"A cross?"

"A crucifix. A symbol . . ."

"No," said Rand. "I do not need a cross."

"A volume of philosophy, perhaps."

"No!" Rand shouted at him. "I left all that behind. We tried to use them all, we relied on them and they weren't good enough and now . . ."

He stopped, for that had not been what he'd meant to say, if in fact he'd meant to say anything at all. It was something that he'd never even thought about; it was as if someone inside of him were speaking through his mouth.

"Or perhaps some currency?"

"You are making fun of me," Rand said bitterly, "and you have no right . . ."

"I merely mention certain things," the Milkman said, "upon which humans place reliance . . ."

"Tell me one thing," said Rand, "as simply as you can. Is there any way of going back?"

"Back to where you came from?"

"Yes," said Rand. "That is what I mean."

"There is nothing to go back to," the Milkman said. "Anyone who comes has nothing to go back to."

"But the old man left. He wore a black felt hat and carried a cane. He dropped them and I found them."

"He did not go back," the Milkman said. "He went ahead. And do not ask me where, for I do not know."

"But you're a part of this."

"I am a humble servant. I have a job to do and I try to do it well. I care for our guests the best that I am able. But there comes a time when each of our guests leaves us. I would suspect this is a halfway house on the road to someplace else."

"A place for getting ready," Rand said.

"What do you mean?" the Milkman asked.

"I am not sure," said Rand. "I had not meant to say it." And this was the second time, he thought, that he'd said something he had not meant to say.

"There's one comfort about this place," the Milkman said. "One good thing about it you should keep in mind. In this village nothing ever happens."

He came down off the porch and stood upon the walk. "You spoke of the old man," he said, "and it was not the old man only. The old lady also left us. The two of them stayed on much beyond their time."

"You mean I'm here all alone?"

The Milkman had started down the walk, but now he stopped and turned. "There'll be others coming," he said. "There are always others coming."

What was it Sterling had said about man outrunning his brain capacity? Rand tried to recall the words, but now, in the confusion of the moment, he had forgotten them. But if that should be the case, if Sterling had been right (no matter how he had phrased his thought), might not man need, for a while, a place like this, where nothing ever happened, where the moon was always full and the year was stuck on autumn?

Another thought intruded and Rand swung about, shouting in sudden panic at the Milkman. "But these others? Will they talk to me? Can I talk with them? Will I know their names?"

The Milkman had reached the gate by now and it appeared that he had not heard.

The moonlight was paler than it had been. The eastern sky was flushed. Another matchless autumn day was about to dawn.

Rand went around the house. He climbed the steps that led up to the porch. He sat down in the rocking chair and began waiting for the others.

A SENSE OF BEAUTY

Robert Taylor

I have always been able to perceive words in a way that seems different from the way people around me seem to be able to perceive them. To me words have substance; they are as real as the pigments of a painter or the clay of a potter. In some universe they have a substantial existence, and I am able to peek a ways into that universe. It has always been my deep regret that I am not Dylan Thomas, that mad singer who saw words in the very shapes of trees.

A story, then, is a construction, using words as its building blocks. It has substance. It is palpable. Touch it, feel it, bring your senses to it. Let it blossom forth into the magical thing it is.

There are no villains here in my story, except far off stage, if they can be called villains at all. We have gone beyond that humbug. We have been too long blaming the serpent in the tree for our own misdeeds and misfortunes. It is important now, in an age that seems to stand ever poised on the brink of violence, to see that if evil lurks anywhere it lurks within us. We are all stained, tainted. We are all responsible for our own actions. We plucked and ate of the apple of our own free will; the serpent merely gave us the excuse we were searching for.

There are no heroes, either, because these days we're all too democratic for heroes to exist. The hero is traditionally the best man of his time, the most outstanding example of bravery and purity. But we don't have heroes anymore, because everybody's equal and we don't want to admit that someone is better than we are. And as for standing out from the crowd—well, everyone must be kept in his place. The only heroes we allow today are killers in a distant war who, God willing, we will never have to see up close.

I may seem bitter, but it is not my usual attitude toward life. I really want to take life with a mouthful of laughter, to see beauty in the simplest flower growing alone on a mountain, to believe that this earth itself is the paradise that has been lied about for so many thousands of years.

It's not easy to write about this story, since I wrote it ages and ages ago as a young man of twenty-one who had not yet been tempted by the serpent who lies inside each of us. I remember that I wrote it in an attitude of cynical optimism. But so much has happened since I wrote it, including Vietnam, and I've changed so much from what I was when I wrote it—a youth trying to sound so much older than I really was—that it's hard to say anything else about it, except that I still like it. It gives me a good feeling.

So, remember that it's just a construction of words, substantial, palpable. Touch it, feel it, bring human thought to it, and let it exist for a moment. It deserves that much, at least.

—*Robert Taylor*

She was dark against the burning white of the bed sheets, but not so dark that her skin didn't glow with a translucent ivory light of its own. The light of the moon was hidden by the heavy curtains drawn across the window, but still her nails glinted like rare bits of pearl. She lay there, breathing softly, almost not at all, washed by a dark and surging sea.

Far outside, the real ocean hurled itself against the cliffs with a ceaseless rhythm, tearing at the land with curling fingers driven by energy stored within the vast, dark deep for over a billion years. If you listened deep enough, you could almost hear the cruel scratching of the billion particles of sand that the waves threw against the cliffs, you could almost hear the solid rock start to crack and tear away from the continent, you could almost hear the whole world start to slide into the sea.

Kurt lay back against the icy white coolness that had become inflamed with their heat and now threatened to burst into fire. He tried to let his mind float into the world of swirling colors and pleasant sounds that lies on the rim of sleep, but something kept throbbing in his head, like an aching hand, that might at any moment break into the clear day of realization.

The alienness of this place ached down upon him, and once again he yearned with an unutterable feeling for the tall blocked cities and the ceaseless sands and the great hoarded reservoirs of water of his home. And then again he ached with another unutterable feeling that he must leave this place and the girl lying softly beside him, not sleeping, but drifting deep on that sea that lies between sleep and waking and touches neither.

He felt the girl's fingers crawl down over his arm like some giant, five-legged insect, and settle about his wrist. She began to press down, massaging softly, quietly moving, as if searching for something.

Something nagged at him, something about the girl. Her eyes seemed somehow too wide open to the world around her. She seemed to notice everything and put it away for future reference. Even when she wasn't looking at you, she seemed to be watching you. She has a will to know, he thought, so intense that it devours everything. All primitives are that way.

He felt his skin prickle as a flowing wind of darkness touched him and left glowing drops of dew behind.

Why, it was almost as if she could see right through him.

The girl's fingers stopped moving. They rested firmly across his wrist. They were soft and warm against his skin.

Far outside, the ocean roared, beating rhythmically like a giant heart. There was the sound of rock scraping against rock, giving up to the sky, and then a splash that was lost deep in angry waves. The continent was a bit smaller now.

The girl stirred, moaning a little. "Kurt?"

The voice shivered in the night, he sensed the thing that was coming, even before he knew what it was.

"Kurt," she said, slipping her fingers away from his wrist, "you're an alien, aren't you?"

Kurt reached over the night table beside the bed and picked up a cigarette. He inhaled deeply and the tip burst into flame. Lying there in the darkness, he looked up at the invisible ceiling, the still strange fumes swirling around inside him, the strange heat settling pleasantly in his chest. An ocean was breaking over him, for all his seeming ease, and he was afraid that any second he would begin shaking violently.

"I mean"—she turned in the darkness to face him, holding herself on one elbow—"you come from another planet, another star system."

He slipped softly out of bed, drawing on a robe, and strode to the window, the night air soft and cool against him. He tore back the curtains to let the moonshine in.

There it was, the moon, so tremendous, so bright, and such a strange silver light. And how fast she was moving behind the clouds. But no, he had forgotten again. It was not the moon that was moving, but the clouds.

He remembered how his world's three tiny moons glinted together sometimes in the sky, sparkling the sands with their rays. Oh lord, what an ocean of light this moon would make of the desert! A man might go blind with it.

Far out, the sea was ablaze with moonlight, moving softly.

"How bright the moon is. I've never seen anything so large." Then softly: "How did you know?"

"I don't know. I think I suspected something all along, the way you spoke, the way you walked, the way you touched me. There was something strange about you. You looked at things differently, reacted strangely. The way you blended your idioms was strange. I couldn't put my finger on what it was, but I could tell there *was* something wrong. And then I felt your pulse, and it wasn't in the right place, and it was beating too slowly, too strongly."

He turned to look at her, her body silvery white in the moonlight, her eyes and lips glistening wetly. His eyes shifted to the painting above her head, a wild swirl of colors—a replication—but there was no possible way of telling it from the original.

"I think I need a drink."

He hurried off to the kitchen.

It was a tall bottle, silver blue from the liquid inside. He poured it into a glass as molten metal might be poured from a smelter. Sipping it, it was cool inside him. The tension that had been mounting up within his body was suddenly gone, dispersed.

The girl came out of the darkness, a light, transparent robe drawn over her nakedness. Her long black hair fell down around her shoulders and flowed like a river between the small mounds of her breasts. "I'm sorry," she said. "I didn't mean to upset you so."

He turned to her. "Why would you *say* such a thing? It's against all logic to make an accusation like that."

She smiled. "I guess we humans aren't very logical."

"Meaning that I'm not human."

Shock leaped in her face. "Oh, I didn't—"

"But you did, subconsciously. What you should have said is, 'We primitives aren't very logical.'"

She smiled again. "I really am sorry."

He reached behind him and took down another glass. "Here,

I suppose it won't hurt anything if you try this. The first person on this planet to taste an alien liquor."

He watched her as softly she raised the glass to her lips and softly let the cool blue lake flow into her warm red mouth. She held it for a little while and then let it flow on down. Her lips began to quiver with disgust, and then suddenly blossomed into a wry smile. "It's so cold."

"You must expect something different. What does it taste like?"

"I can't—strange—I can only think of dark space and blazing suns, a fall of dust on lifeless plains."

"It always makes me think of my home planet, dry air and sands like oceans of jewels, with the naked stars blazing over it all."

He pushed the door open, out into the night upon the terrace above the sea. "Let's go out here a little while."

She followed him out to the small fence that ran along the edge of the terrace where the land dropped away to the sea far below. The waves roared and roared, angry at the land for its existence. Kurt looked down at the phosphorescence burning in the waves, his elbow resting on the top rail of the fence—wood cracked, someone would have to fix it some year—his glass glinting by moonlight in his hands.

"Everything that is alien and beautiful fills the soul with a strange wonder, an immense peace. The ocean, oh, how strange and wonderful is the ocean! Tell me about the ocean."

She leaned close to him, her glass glinting in one hand, her hair flowing like a dark river, blazed with silver by the moonshine. It brushed soft against him, so soft and fuzzy, like the deepest memories of childhood, like the first tendrils of sleep. There was a smell about her, the smell of a primitive people raised on meat and milk, but it wasn't an unpleasant smell; it was merely strange, alien.

She turned to look at him, a strange smile on her lips, a strange glint in her dark-by-moonshine eyes. "The sea," she said, her voice a poem in the night. "The ocean is the mother of all life."

"Is it?"

"Of course." She almost laughed. "You must know *that!*"

"But—" He stood in stunned silence for long seconds, and when at last he spoke, it was in a voice that almost wept. "My world lost its oceans a million years ago. My ancestors were stranded on it twenty-five thousand years ago, after the Exodus from the Center."

"Oh, then you couldn't know. I'm sorry."

"There is nothing can be done now. There are some peoples that would know this, but the talents of mine do not fall that way. Go on."

"What is your people's talent?"

"Appreciating, but do go on."

"What can I say? Dark Mother of all life, it flows even in our blood, beats in our hearts. She is dark and eternal. She beats in our souls, calls us. She will be here when we are gone. She will be here when the sun flames out."

Kurt took another sip from his glass. He knew what was coming; he felt it as surely as he heard the beating of the ocean. "I suppose there must be something of the ocean still left in my people, however far they are away from the sea that originally gave them birth. There was something in me that made me rent this house here, something besides the loneliness. Perhaps I felt its call."

Above them, the single moon gazed down upon them as it had done upon millions of couples for thousands and thousands of years.

"What was the Exodus from the Center you were talking about?"

"Twenty-five-thousand years ago the empire in the central nucleus of the galaxy dissolved in a wave of anarchy and chaos. All those that could fled out into the night of peace in the Arms, or even beyond into the intergalactic night. Undoubtedly, that was how this world was populated. We are probably distant, distant cousins."

He wanted to speak more, but he couldn't. He wanted to tell her about his planet, but he couldn't. He wanted to tell her about racing boats across the sand while the three moons sparkled high above, but he couldn't. He had suddenly realized that an enormous gulf separated them. She was more primitively emotional than he was. The ocean beat more in her blood than it did in his; she was closer to the source. She dwelt more in nature than he did, and she was controlled more by the cycles of nature.

"How long have you been here?"

"Two years."

"So long? I suppose you're still studying us."

"That, and collecting—" He stopped with his heart in his throat. If he went on, she would surely guess, and for some reason he didn't want her to know.

"Collecting what?"

"Works of art, literature. . . ."

"Of course, studying our culture. When are you going to reveal yourselves?"

"We don't plan to."

"Why not? If you've gone to all this trouble, you just can't go away. Or have we failed your test? Are we too belligerent? If we are, you could help us."

He wanted to shout at her to be silent, but it was too late. She had gone too far; she would know, willed she or not. When he spoke, it was with the shamed anger of one who knows he is doing wrong.

"Why should we help you! We would leave this planet entirely alone but for one thing."

She drew away. "What?"

He stepped backwards, toward the house. "The life envelope surrounding it. There's not enough time." He was speaking more to himself than he was to her. Then he turned his eyes full on her. "Within a hundred years, your sun will enter the first stages of novation."

She drew hard away from him now, a scream working in her eyes.

"You could help us, evacuate us to some other system. There must be something we are useful for. You can't let us die."

"Why not? We're not responsible. The universe is destroying you. It is just as if we never stumbled across you."

"But you *are* here! You can't pretend you're not!"

He stood silent, something dark churning inside him.

"I am not my own master. There are others. . . ."

"What are you doing here then?"

"We are—collecting, works of art, works of literature, to save them from the flames."

"You collect our art, but you leave us here to die? Don't you have any feelings, can't you love anything!"

"As you understand those words, no. I feel only a shade of what you feel, as far as I understand what you feel; but still, the emotions of my people are a thousand times as powerful as the emotions of our masters. My people have a sense of beauty that none of the other peoples of the galaxy possess, and so we are made the art collectors for the galaxy." He laughed sadly. "It's quite a thing to have a work of art selected by one of us, because then you know that it is truly art, and truly beautiful, even if you can't feel it yourself."

He looked at her, sadness, as much as he could feel of it, welling up behind his eyes. "We are the critics of the galaxy, and you primitives are the creators. Your vicarious immortality depends on us. You perish, but your works go on. Someday they will become tired of us, and we will leave nothing behind."

She was looking at him in horror. "Why did you need *me?*"

"Because I am a man, even though I'm from a faraway world, and you are beautiful. I appreciate beautiful things."

She backed hard away from him, pushing with all her force at the wooden fence. "You're a monster, that's all."

He held out his arms. "Please, I—"

"No! Stay away from me."

A liquid was flowing from her eyes, glittering like dew on her cheeks.

The ocean rumbled like a giant heart below.

Above, some night bird had lost its way and cried plaintively.

He took a step forward. "Please. You're safe. You have a hundred years, at least. You may be able to save yourselves."

"Get away from me!" She spun around to run and threw herself against the fence, startled by its sudden hardness pressing against her. The old wood, exposed for years to hot days and cold nights and the rotting salt air, cracked. Slowly a section of it began to fall outwards.

He grabbed one of her hands in his, but with a look of disgust she tore it out of his grasp.

She didn't scream; all the way down, she didn't scream.

The moon caught the spinning glass as it fell like a clear drop of rain all the way down past the rough rocks of the cliff, down through the air to fall at last into the white waves of the ocean, dark, eternal. There was a small spray of water, and the waters of the deep closed over all.

He turned and stepped back into the house, noting above him the one star moved among all the others. It was almost time for pickup.

And below the cliffs, the waves burned with phosphorescence.

It had been a beautiful death.

Beautiful.

He stood again in the ship, the air still strong with ozone from the pickup chamber.

He wanted to do something important, but he didn't know what it was.

Behind him, men were moving the last of his equipment from the chamber to the storage holds, while others were moving the last of his recording crystals to the special room that would keep them safe from harm. He had done his own job well, recording all works of art and literature that he had found to be beautiful in the area assigned to him. He hoped the others, in this ship and in others around the planet, had done as well.

His executive officer walked toward him slowly. "You are the last, sir. We're ready to move to the rendezvous point."

"Let's go then."

There was a slight tingling as the drive was applied, and he turned to his console with an emptiness aching inside him.

On the screen he saw the blazing sun, far behind now and slowly falling behind even more. Someday it would expand in a process not completely understood and claim the debt owed it by its first four daughters.

And another planet that had produced beauty would be lost.

He knew now that he wanted his eyes to bleed with tears as the girl's had done before she had gone to her beautiful end, but his people had forgotten how twenty-five-thousand years ago.

There was a roaring that was swelling out and filling the universe to its deepest core. At first he thought that it was the memory of an ocean that his people had lost long ago, but then he realized that it was his own blood rushing through his own veins, dark, eternal.

THE LAST FLIGHT
OF DR. AIN

James Tiptree, Jr.

*Writing about your own story reminds me of those tremendous
floats you see in small-town Labor Day parades. You have this
moving island of flowers with people on it being Indian Braves
or Green Bay Packers or Astronauts-Landing-on-the-Moon (Rais-
ing-the-Flag-at-Iwo-Jima has happily gone out of fashion) and
great-looking girls being great-looking girls. That's the story. Under each float is an old truck chassis driven by a guy in sweaty
jeans who is also working the tapedeck and passing cherry bombs
to the Indians. That's the author. Now Harry wants me to crawl
out and say hello. Well, I love saying hello. But my feeling is that
the story is the game. Who really needs me and my carburetor
troubles up there blowing kisses with Miss Harvest Home?*

*Still, Harry is one of those for whom I'd row quite a ways in a
leaky boat, and you can always stop reading this and turn to the
tale. So . . .*

*Remember way back in 1967 B.E.? Before Ecology, that was;
we were worrying about The Bomb then. In those days I did my
screaming to myself; it sounded pretty silly saying, I love Earth.
Earth? Rocks, weeds, dirt? Oh, come on. A friend lectured me:
People have to relate to people; you can't relate to a planet.*

*Sorry, you can. But you'd better not. Because—as we're all find-
ing out—to love our Earth is to hurt forever. Earth was very beautiful with her sweet airs and clear waters, her intimacies and*

grandeurs and divine freakinesses and the mobile art works that were her creatures. She was just right for us. She made us human. And we are killing her.

Not because we're wicked, any more than a spirochete is wicked. (At this point maybe I'd better say that I do relate to some people, too.) Nor is modern Western technology the sole culprit. We're the current destructo champs, but man was always pretty good at ecocide. Innocent goatherds turned north Africa into desert; did you know that people used to take pigs to be fattened on the acorns of the majestic oak forests where the Sahara blows now? War and fire finished off the flora of the Hebrides before gunpowder. And sheer numbers of people scratching a living devastated much of India and China into the lunar landscape it is today. It's just us, man collectively, doing what comes naturally. A runaway product of the planet Earth, we have become a disease of Earth.

And of course it's speeded up unbelievably. Virgin lakes I knew only ten years ago in Canada are shore-to-shore beer cans now. Here's a few of the things we've lost in the four decades I've been observing (I thought they'd last forever, see?); Learning to swim in the pure water of—gasp—Lake Michigan in front of Chicago . . . Ten thousand canvasback ducks whistling down the wind of the peaks behind Santa Fé . . . The great bay of San Francisco before the bridges shackled it and the garbage poured in . . . Key West, a sleepy fishing village lush with tropical wildlife (and old John Dewey's doorknob head shining in the cantina) before the Navy and Disney heard of it . . . Timber wolves singing where shopping centers are now in Wisconsin . . . The magic trolley-ride to Glen Echo, in ten minutes from the heart of D.C. you were clicking along silently (and fumelessly) with flowers and songbirds coming in the window . . . A very nice life, only a few years back.

And it's the same all over, you know. I spent part of my childhood in Africa and it hurts to remember the beauty of the Ruwenzoris—the Mountains of the Moon—before the planes and

*the guns and the landrovers and Hemingway and the rest of the
white man's crap rolled in. And even I can't believe I rode a pony
in peaceful woodlands in a place now called Vietnam . . .*

*All gone. Gone under the concrete and plastic and bombs and
oil and people and garbage unending, growing and spreading
daily.*

Can you stand one more?

*I'm writing this in the moonlight on a coconut plantation on
the "wild" shore of Yucatan. The jungle was homesteaded in
1936 and worked by a few Maya families. Miles of nothing but
white coral beach, the Caribbean making slow music on the reef,
shadows of palm-fronds wreathing over the sand. The moon is
brighter than my lantern. A pelican crosses the moon, looking
like a wooden bird from some mad giant's cuckoo clock. Paradise . . .*

Ah oui.

*The fish the pelican is hunting are tainted with chlorinated
hydrocarbons now; her eggs are thin-shelled, may not hatch. The
same for the flamingoes and roseate spoonbills and noble frigate-
birds on the lagoon behind me. They are also scared up daily
by Maya powerboats. On the shore, each wave as it breaks leaves
myriad globules of tar from ships over the horizon, leaves also a
dish-pan ring of plastic bottles, broken zoris, light bulbs and dis-
membered dolls. (I wonder about those dolls. Do crazed tourists
gather at midnight for strange rites at the rail?) The trash is not
just ugly; each globule of tar smothers and poisons one more
small sphere of the sea's life—and the oceans, we know now, are
fragile and finite. The plastics too break down, releasing poly-
chlorinated biphenyls to be absorbed by organisms. An average
of 3,500 little bits of plastic per square kilometer was measured
last year—in the Sargasso Sea. And we've all heard about the
miles of floating human offal Heyerdahl met in mid-Atlantic. The
refuse isn't all microscopic either; last month a forty-five-foot
shrimp boat, apparently abandoned for insurance, broke up on
the reef. The day of the marine junkyard is at hand.*

*But the point is that the human beings who are doing all this
are not malicious or aberrant. They are doing what we have always done. It's right and natural in human terms to flush a toilet
or an oilbilge, to throw away a broken light bulb or a broken
boat, to zap an insect attacking your food or your child. Even
the trawlers who are fishing with nets five miles long—killing
everything in huge swathes of the Florida seas—are doing the
human food-getting thing.*

*How can we stop? How can we possibly change ourselves
enough and in time?*

*I fear we can't—and there's where my real nightmare begins.
Because if we do kill everything else on Earth, we probably won't
die. At least, not right away. We will, I terribly fear . . . adapt.*

*You've seen the pictures of Calcutta and Bangladesh. Calcutta
isn't a musical comedy; it's a symbol of a steady state humanity
can reach, 'way down the entropic slide. I was there as a kid too.
I remember stepping over and around the endless bodies, living
and dead, inhabiting the pavement about one to a square yard
as far as I could see to the horizon. Starving dwarf-children rov-
ing around racks of bones that were mothers trying to nurse more
babies, toothless mouths and unbearable eyes turning on me from
rag-heaps that were people—people—a million people born
there and going to die there, unable to help themselves or even
to protest, world without end forever. Surviving . . .*

*That's what we do, you know. We don't change our behaviour,
we adapt to the results of it. Even to extremis where the human
being is stripped down to a machine for keeping the genes alive,
waiting for rescue. But if we pass the point of irreversible damage to our biosphere, our Earth, there will be no rescue. The
beauty that is going is only another name for the health of Earth
and her children, the condition of our humanity. As our Earth
dies under us, what will we do? Change ourselves in time? Die?*

*Neither. When the last housefly and the last crabgrass plant
have died in the world's last zoo, when the oceans are dead and
the land is paved over, we'll go on. Our marvellous vitality will*

carry us down, shoulder-to-buttock, gasping our own poisons and scrabbing for algae soup as the conveyor belt creaks by. Don't worry: We'll survive.

Excuse me while I put out my garbage.

OK, Harry?

—James Tiptree, Jr.

Dr. Ain was recognized on the Omaha-Chicago flight. A biologist colleague from Pasadena came out of the toilet and saw Ain in an aisle seat. Five years before, this man had been jealous of Ain's huge grants. Now he nodded coldly and was surprised at the intensity of Ain's response. He almost turned back to speak, but he felt too tired; like nearly everyone, he was fighting the flu.

The stewardess handing out coats after they landed remembered Ain too: A tall thin nondescript man with rusty hair. He held up the line staring at her; since he already had his raincoat with him she decided it was some kooky kind of pass and waved him on.

She saw Ain shamble off into the airport smog, apparently alone. Despite the big Civil Defense signs, O'Hare was late getting underground. No one noticed the woman.

The wounded, dying woman.

Ain was not identified en route to New York, but a 2:40 jet carried an "Ames" on the checklist, which was thought to be a misspelling of Ain. It was. The plane had circled for an hour while Ain watched the smoky seaboard monotonously tilt, straighten, and tilt again.

The woman was weaker now. She coughed, picking weakly at the scabs on her face half-hidden behind her long hair. Her hair, Ain saw, that mahogany mane which had been so splendid, was drabbed and thin. He looked to seaward, willing himself to think of cold, clean breakers. On the horizon he saw a vast black rug: somewhere a tanker had opened its vents. The woman coughed again. Ain closed his eyes. The smog closed in.

He was picked up next while checking in for the BOAC flight to Glasgow. Kennedy-Underground was a boiling stew of people, the air system unequal to the hot September afternoon. The check-in line swayed and sweated, staring dully at the newscast. SAVE THE LAST GREEN MANSIONS—a conservation group was protesting the defoliation and drainage of the Amazon basin. Several people recalled the beautifully colored shots of the new clean bomb. The line squeezed together to let a band of uniformed men go by. They were wearing buttons inscribed: WHO'S AFRAID?

That was when a woman noticed Ain. He was holding a newssheet and she heard it rattling in his hand. Her family hadn't caught the flu, so she looked at him sharply. Sure enough, his forehead was sweaty. She herded her kids to the side away from Ain.

He was using *Instac* throat spray, she remembered. She didn't think much of *Instac;* her family used *Kleer*. While she was looking at him, Ain suddenly turned his head and stared into her face, with the spray still floating down. Such inconsiderateness! She turned her back. She didn't recall him talking to any woman, but she perked up her ears when the clerk read off Ain's destination. Moscow!

The clerk recalled that too, with disapproval. Ain checked in alone, he reported. No woman had been ticketed for Moscow, but it would have been easy enough to split up her tickets. (By that time they were sure she was with him.)

Ain's flight went via Iceland with an hour's delay at Kevlavik.

Ain walked over to the airport park, gratefully breathing the sea-filled air. Every few breaths he shuddered. Under the whine of bull-dozers the sea could be heard running its huge paws up and down the keyboard of the land. The little park had a grove of yellowed birches and wheat ears foraged by the path. Next month they would be in North Africa, Ain thought. Two thousand miles of tiny wing-beats. He threw them some crumbs from a packet in his pocket.

The woman seemed stronger here. She was panting in the sea wind, her large eyes fixed on Ain. Above her the birches were as gold as those where he had first seen her, the day his life began . . . Squatting under a stump to watch a shrewmouse he had been, when he caught the falling ripple of green and recognized the shocking naked girl-flesh—creamy, pink-tipped—coming toward him among the golden bracken. Young Ain held his breath, his nose in the sweet moss and his heart going *crash!—crash!* And then he was staring at the outrageous fall of that hair down her narrow back, watching it dance around her heart-shaped buttocks, while the shrewmouse ran over his paralyzed hand. The lake was utterly still, dusty silver under the misty sky, and she made no more than a muskrat's ripple to rock the floating golden leaves . . . The silence closed back: the trees burning like torches where the naked girl had walked the wild wood, reflected in Ain's shining eyes . . . For a time he believed he had seen an Oread.

Ain was last on board for the Glasgow leg. The stewardess recalled dimly that he seemed restless. She could not identify the woman. There were a lot of women on board—and babies. Her passenger list had had several errors.

At Glasgow airport a waiter remembered that a man like Ain had called for Scottish oatmeal, and eaten two bowls, although of course it wasn't really oatmeal. A young mother with a pram saw him tossing crumbs to the birds.

When he checked in at the BOAC desk, he was hailed by a Glasgow professor who was going to the same conference at Moscow. This man had been one of Ain's teachers. (It was now known that Ain had done his postgraduate work in Europe.) They chatted all the way across the North Sea.

"I wondered about that," the professor said later. "Why have you come 'round about? I asked him. He told me the direct flights were booked up." (This was found to be untrue: Ain had apparently avoided the Moscow jet hoping to escape attention.)

The professor spoke with relish of Ain's work.

"Brilliant? Oh, aye. And stubborn, too, very very stubborn. It was as though a concept—often the simplest relation, mind you—would stop him in his tracks, and fascinate him. He would hunt all 'round it instead of going on to the next thing as a more docile mind would. Truthfully, I wondered at first if he could be just a bit thick. But you recall who it was said that the capacity for wonder at matters of common acceptance occurs in the superior mind? And, of course, so it proved when he shook us all up over that enzyme conversion business. A pity your government took him away from his line, there . . . No, he said nothing of this, I say it to you, young man. We spoke in fact largely of my work. I was surprised to find he'd kept up. He asked me what my *sentiments* about it were, which surprised me again. Now, understand, I'd not seen the man for five years, but he seemed—well, perhaps just tired, as who is not? I'm sure he was glad to have a change; he jumped out for a legstretch wherever we came down. At Oslo, even Bonn . . . Oh yes, he did feed the birds, but that was nothing new for Ain . . . His social life when I knew him? Radical causes? Young man, I've said what I've said because of who it was that introduced you, but I'll have you know it is an impertinence in you to think ill of Charles Ain, or that he could do a harmful deed. Good evening."

The professor said nothing of the woman in Ain's life.

Nor could he have, although Ain had been intimately with her in the university time. He had let no one see how he was obsessed with her, with the miracle, the wealth of her body, her inexhaustibility. They met at his every spare moment, sometimes in public, pretending to be casual strangers under his friends' noses, pointing out a pleasing view to each other, with grave formality. And later, in their privacies—what doubled intensity of love! He revelled in her, possessed her, allowed her no secrets. His dreams were of her sweet springs and shadowed places and her white rounded glory in the moonlight—finding always more, always new dimensions of his joy.

The danger of her frailty was far off then in the rush of birdsong and the springing leverets of the meadow. On dark days she might cough a bit, but so did he. In those years he had had no thought to the urgent study of the disease.

At the Moscow conference nearly everyone noticed Ain at some point or another, which was to be expected in view of his professional stature. It was a small high-calibre meeting. Ain was late in; a day's reports were over, and his was to be on the third and last.

Many people spoke with Ain, and several sat with him at meals. No one was surprised that he spoke little; he was a retiring man except on a few memorable occasions of hot argument. He did strike some of his friends as a bit tired and jerky.

An Indian molecular engineer who saw him with the throat spray kidded him about bringing over Asian flu. A Swedish colleague recalled that Ain had been called away to the transatlantic phone at lunch; and when he returned Ain volunteered the information that something had turned up missing in his home lab. There was another joke, and Ain said cheerfully, "Oh yes, quite active."

At that point one of the Chicom biologists swung into his daily propaganda chore about bacteriological warfare and accused Ain of manufacturing biotic weapons. Ain took the wind out of his sails by saying: "You're perfectly right." By tacit consent, there was very little talk about military applications, industrial dusting, or subjects of that type. And nobody recalled seeing Ain with any woman other than old Madame Vialche, who could scarcely have subverted anyone from her wheelchair.

Ain's own speech was bad, even for him. He always had a poor public voice, but his ideas were usually expressed with the lucidity so typical of the first-rate mind. This time he seemed muddled, with little new to say. His audience excused this as the muffling effects of security. Ain then got into a tangled point about the course of evolution in which he seemed to be trying to show that something was very wrong indeed. When he wound up with a reference to Hudson's bell bird "singing for a later race," several listeners wondered if he could be drunk.

The big security break came right at the end, when he suddenly began to describe the methods he had used to mutate and redesign a leukemia virus. He explained the procedure with admirable clarity in four sentences and paused. Then he said other sentences about the effects of the mutated strain. It was maximal only on the higher primates, he said; recovery rate among the lower mammals and other orders was close to 90 percent. As to vectors, he went on, any warm-blooded animal served. In addition, the virus retained viability in most environmental media and performed very well airborne. Contagion rate was extremely high. Almost off-hand, Ain added that no test primate or accidentally exposed human had survived beyond the twenty-second day.

These words fell into a silence broken only by the running feet of the Egyptian delegate making for the door. Then a gilt chair went over as an American bolted after him.

Ain seemed unaware that his audience was in a state of unbelieving paralysis. It had all come so fast: a man who had been blowing his nose was staring popeyed around his handkerchief. Another who had been lighting a pipe grunted as his fingers singed. Two men chatting by the door missed his words entirely and their laughter chimed into a dead silence in which echoed Ain's words: "—really no point in attempting."

Later they found he had been explaining that the virus utilized the body's own immunomechanisms, and so defense was by definition hopeless.

That was all. Ain looked around vaguely for questions and then started down the aisle. By the time he got to the door, people were swarming after him. He wheeled about and said rather crossly, "Yes, of course it is very wrong. I told you that. We are all wrong. Now it's over."

An hour later they found he had gone, having apparently reserved a Sinair flight to Karachi. The security men caught up with him at Hong Kong. By then he seemed really very ill, and went with them peacefully. They started back to the States via Hawaii.

His captors were civilized types; they saw he was gentle and treated him accordingly. He had no weapons or drugs on him. They took him out handcuffed for a stroll at Osaka . . . let him feed his crumbs to the birds, and they listened with interest to his account of the migration routs of the common brown sandpiper. He was very hoarse. At that point, he was wanted only for the security thing. There was no question of a woman at all.

He dozed most of the way to the islands, but when they came in sight he pressed to the window and began to mutter, the security man behind him got the first inkling that there was a woman in it and turned on his recorder.

". . . blue, blue and green until you see the wounds. Oh my girl! Oh beautiful, you won't die. I won't let you die. I tell you girl, it's over . . . Lustrous eyes, look at me, let me see you now alive! Oh great queen, my sweet body, my girl, have I saved you? . . . Oh terrible to know, and noble—Chaos' child green-robed in blue, and golden light . . . The thrown and spinning ball of life alone in space . . . Have I saved you?"

On the last leg, he was obviously feverish.

"She may have tricked me, you know," he said confidentially to the government man. "You have to be prepared for that, of course. I know her!" He chuckled confidentially. "She's no small thing. But wring your heart out—"

Coming over San Francisco, he was merry. "Don't you know the otters will go back in there? I'm certain of it. That fill won't last; there'll be a bay there again."

They got him on a stretcher at Hamilton Air Base, and he went unconscious shortly after takeoff. Before he collapsed, he'd insisted on throwing the last of his birdseed on the field.

"Birds are, of course, warmblooded," he confided to the agent who was handcuffing him to the stretcher. Then Ain smiled gently and lapsed into inertness. He stayed that way almost all the remaining ten days of his life. By then, of course, no one really cared. Both the government men had died quite early, after they finished analyzing the birdseed and throat-spray. The woman at Kennedy was only just then feeling sickish.

The tape-recorder they put by his bed functioned right on through, but if anybody had been around to replay it they would have found little but babbling. "Gaea Gloriatrix!" he crooned. At times he was grandiose and tormented. "Our life, your death!" he yelled. "Our death would have been your death too, no need for that, no need . . ."

At other times he was accusing. "What did you do about the dinosaurs?" he demanded. "How did you fix *them?* Did they annoy you? Cold. Queen, you're too cold! You came close to it this time, my girl," he raved. And then he wept and caressed the bedclothes and was maudlin.

Only at the end, lying in his filth and thirst, still chained where they had forgotten him, he was suddenly coherent. In the light clear voice of a lover planning a summer picnic he asked the recorder happily:

"Have you ever thought about *bears?* They have so much . . . funny they never came along further. By any chance were you saving them, girl?" And he chuckled in his ruined throat. And later, died.

ULLWARD'S RETREAT

Jack Vance

"*Ullward's Retreat*" *is in certain ways a precursor to a novelette I've just finished*—The Insufferable Red-headed Daughter of Commander Tynott O.T.E., *in case anyone is interested. The two stories are essentially dissimilar, except for an idea which appears in "Ullward's Retreat" somewhat glancingly, but which propels* The Red-headed Daughter.

I am intensely reluctant to analyze my own work publicly, and I won't categorically identify this common thread, although maybe I'll hint at it once or twice.

"*Ullward's Retreat*" *is the frivolous treatment of a serious subject: the overcrowding of Earth. I don't propose "Ullward's Retreat" as a preview of times to come. Earth is here grotesquely overcrowded and probably intolerable. Furthermore the story presupposes economic institutions and social attitudes much like those of the present, a situation which under the circumstances is hardly likely. Why don't I postulate a society no less altered than the environment? Because* (1) *the ideas contained in "Ullward's Retreat" are adequate to ballast a story of such a length; to make every aspect of the story meticulously consistent would require altogether too much didactic exposition, hence dullness; and* (2) *the superimposition of strange circumstances upon familiar institutions creates an amusing absurdity, like dressing the cat in doll's clothes and a baseball cap, to which young John recently subjected his cat Patterfoot.*

All this by way of digression. Another matter, while it occurs to me and which is relevant to the above: in a recent article the perceptive and intelligent Joanna Russ mentioned that, in dealing with societies of the future, writers often presuppose man-woman relationships similar or identical to those of today. Miss Russ asserts that different arrangements are inevitable and that writers should allow for evolution here as they do in other aspects of society. Well they should, if possible and feasible. Science fiction writers don't necessarily deny the possibility of change; more often they ignore the matter so as not to slow the pace of their stories. Again, and tangentially, current trends are undoubtedly phases of a cycle. Time extends a long time ahead, and nothing persists: male dominance, female dominance, equality or mutual detestation. Maybe ordinary old-fashioned marriage will prove the most utilitarian and viable condition after all. In any event I suspect that women will continue to be constricted by their biological functions despite any amount of earnest altruism: unless babies are forever to be cultivated in glass tanks.

All this, of course, has little bearing upon "Ullward's Retreat," except that I feel impelled to explain why, in circumstances so different from those of today, the customary social relationships appear to exist unchanged.

I find that I haven't so much as touched upon the common thread linking "Ullward's Retreat" and The Insufferable Red-headed Daughter. Has it occurred to any of you out there that a cognoscente's expertise in regard to music and books and drama might well be a socially acceptable vice leading to pacifism, debility, and extinction? Please don't write me yes or no; merely brood about the matter in private. I don't want to answer 200,000 furious letters.

—Jack Vance

Bruham Ullward had invited three friends to lunch at his ranch: Ted and Ravelin Seehoe, and their adolescent daughter Iugenae. After an eye-bulging feast, Ullward offered around a tray of the digestive pastilles which had won him his wealth.

"A wonderful meal," said Ted Seehoe reverently. "Too much, really. I'll need one of these. The algae was absolutely marvelous."

Ullward made a smiling easy gesture. "It's the genuine stuff."

Ravelin Seehoe, a fresh-faced, rather positive young woman of eighty or ninety, reached for a pastille. "A shame there's not more of it. The synthetic we get is hardly recognizable as algae."

"It's a problem," Ullward admitted. "I clubbed up with some friends; we bought a little mat in the Ross Sea and grow all our own."

"Think of that," exclaimed Ravelin. "Isn't it frightfully expensive?"

Ullward pursed his lips whimsically. "The good things in life come high. Luckily, I'm able to afford a bit extra."

"What I keep telling Ted—" began Ravelin, then stopped as Ted turned her a keen warning glance.

Ullward bridged the rift. "Money isn't everything. I have a flat of algae, my ranch; you have your daughter—and I'm sure you wouldn't trade."

Ravelin regarded Iugenae critically. "I'm not so sure."

Ted patted Iugenae's hand. "When do you have your own child, Lamster Ullward?" (*Lamster: contraction of Landmaster —the polite form of address in current use.*)

"Still some time yet. I'm thirty-seven billion down the list."

"A pity," said Ravelin Seehoe brightly, "when you could give a child so many advantages."

"Some day, some day, before I'm too old."

"A shame," said Ravelin, "but it has to be. Another fifty billion people and we'd have no privacy whatever!" She looked admiringly around the room, which was used for the sole purpose of preparing food and dining.

Ullward put his hands on the arms of his chair, hitched forward a little. "Perhaps you'd like to look around the ranch?" He spoke in a casual voice, glancing from one to the other.

Iugenae clapped her hands; Ravelin beamed. "If it wouldn't be too much trouble!" "Oh, we'd love to, Lamster Ullward!" cried Iugenae.

"I've always wanted to see your ranch," said Ted. "I've heard so much about it."

"It's an opportunity for Iugenae I wouldn't want her to miss," said Ravelin. She shook her finger at Iugenae. "Remember, Miss Puss, notice everything very carefully—and don't *touch!*"

"May I take pictures, Mother?"

"You'll have to ask Lamster Ullward."

"Of course, of course," said Ullward. "Why in the world not?" He rose to his feet—a man of more than middle stature, more than middle pudginess, with straight sandy hair, round blue eyes, a prominent beak of a nose. Almost three hundred years old, he guarded his health with great zeal, and looked little more than two hundred.

He stepped to the door, checked the time, touched a dial on the wall. "Are you ready?"

"Yes, we're quite ready," said Ravelin.

Ullward snapped back the wall, to reveal a view over a sylvan glade. A fine oak tree shaded a pond growing with rushes. A path led through a field toward a wooded valley a mile in the distance.

"Magnificent," said Ted. "Simply magnificent!"

They stepped outdoors into the sunlight. Iugenae flung her arms out, twirled, danced in a circle. "Look! I'm all alone! I'm out here all by myself!"

"Iugenae!" called Ravelin sharply. "Be careful! Stay on the path! That's real grass and you mustn't damage it."

Iugenae ran ahead to the pond. "Mother!" she called back. "Look at these funny little jumpy things! And look at the flowers!"

"The animals are frogs," said Ullward. "They have a very interesting life-history. You see the little fishlike things in the water?"

"Aren't they funny! Mother, do come here!"

"Those are called tadpoles and they will presently become frogs, indistinguishable from the ones you see."

Ravelin and Ted advanced with more dignity, but were as interested as Iugenae in the frogs.

"Smell the fresh air," Ted told Ravelin. "You'd think you were back in the early times."

"It's absolutely exquisite," said Ravelin. She looked around her. "One has the feeling of being able to wander on and on and on."

"Come around over here," called Ullward from beyond the pool. "This is the rock garden."

In awe, the guests stared at the ledge of rock, stained with red and yellow lichen, tufted with green moss. Ferns grew from a crevice; there were several fragile clusters of white flowers.

"Smell the flowers, if you wish," Ullward told Iugenae. "But please don't touch them; they stain rather easily."

Iugenae sniffed. "Mmmm!"

"Are they real?" asked Ted.

"The moss, yes. That clump of ferns and these little succulents are real. The flowers were designed for me by a horticulturist and are exact replicas of certain ancient species. We've actually improved on the odor."

"Wonderful, wonderful," said Ted.

"Now come this way—no, don't look back; I want you to get the total effect . . ." An expression of vexation crossed his face.

"What's the trouble?" asked Ted.

"It's a damned nuisance," said Ullward. "Hear that sound?"

Ted became aware of a faint rolling rumble, deep and almost unheard. "Yes. Sounds like some sort of factory."

"It is. On the floor below. A rug-works. One of the looms creates this terrible row. I've complained, but they pay no attention . . . Oh, well, ignore it. Now stand over here—and look around!"

His friends gasped in rapture. The view from this angle was a rustic bungalow in an Alpine valley, the door being the opening into Ullward's dining room.

"What an illusion of distance!" exclaimed Ravelin. "A person would almost think he was alone."

"A beautiful piece of work," said Ted. "I'd swear I was looking into ten miles—at least five miles—of distance."

"I've got a lot of space here," said Ullward proudly. "Almost three-quarters of an acre. Would you like to see it by moonlight?"

"Oh, could we?"

Ullward went to a concealed switch-panel; the sun seemed to race across the sky. A fervent glow of sunset lit the valley; the sky burned peacock blue, gold, green, then came twilight—and the rising full moon came up behind the hill.

"This is absolutely marvelous," said Ravelin softly. "How can you bring yourself to leave it?"

"It's hard," admitted Ullward. "But I've got to look after business too. More money, more space."

He turned a knob; the moon floated across the sky, sank. Stars appeared, forming the age-old patterns. Ullward pointed out the constellations and the first-magnitude stars by name, using a penciltorch for a pointer. Then the sky flushed with lavender and lemon yellow and the sun appeared once more. Unseen ducts sent a current of cool air through the glade.

"Right now I'm negotiating for an area behind this wall here." He tapped at the depicted mountainside, an illusion given reality and three-dimensionality by laminations inside the pane. "It's quite a large area—over a hundred square feet. The owner wants a fortune, naturally."

"I'm surprised he wants to sell," said Ted. "A hundred square feet means real privacy."

"There's been a death in the family," explained Ullward. "The owner's four-great-grandfather passed on and the space is temporarily surplus."

Ted nodded. "I hope you're able to get it."

"I hope so too. I've got rather flamboyant ambitions—eventually I hope to own the entire quarterblock—but it takes time. People don't like to sell their space and everyone is anxious to buy."

"Not we," said Ravelin cheerfully. "We have our little home. We're snug and cozy and we're putting money aside for investment."

"Wise," agreed Ullward. "A great many people are space-poor. Then when a chance to make real money comes up, they're undercapitalized. Until I scored with the digestive pastilles, I lived in a single rented locker. I was cramped—but I don't regret it today."

They returned through the glade toward Ullward's house, stopping at the oak tree. "This is my special pride," said Ullward. "A genuine oak tree!"

"Genuine?" asked Ted in astonishment. "I assumed it was simulation."

"So many people do," said Ullward. "No, it's genuine."

"Take a picture of the tree, Iugenae, please. But don't touch it. You might damage the bark."

"Perfectly all right to touch the bark," assured Ullward.

He looked up into the branches, then scanned the ground. He stooped, picked up a fallen leaf. "This grew on the tree," he said. "Now, Iugenae, I want you to come with me." He went to the rock garden, pulled a simulated rock aside, to reveal a cabinet with washbasin. "Watch carefully." He showed her the leaf. "Notice? It's dry and brittle and brown."

"Yes, Lamster Ullward." Iugenae craned her neck.

"First I dip it in this solution." He took a beaker full of dark liquid from a shelf. "So. That restores the green color. We wash off the excess, then dry it. Now we rub this next fluid carefully into the surface. Notice, it's flexible and strong now. One more solution—a plastic coating—and there we are, a true oak leaf, perfectly genuine. It's yours."

"Oh, Lamster Ullward! Thank you ever so much!" She ran off to show her father and mother, who were standing by the pool, luxuriating in the feeling of space, watching the frogs. "See what Lamster Ullward gave me!"

"You be very careful with it," said Ravelin. "When we get home, we'll find a nice little frame and you can hang it in your locker."

The simulated sun hung in the western sky. Ullward led the group to a sundial. "An antique, countless years old. Pure marble, carved by hand. It works too—entirely functional. Notice. Three-fifteen by the shadow on the dial . . ." He peered at his belt-watch, squinted at the sun. "Excuse me one moment." He ran to the control board, made an adjustment. The sun lurched ten degrees across the sky. Ullward returned, checked the sundial. "That's better. Notice. Three-fifty by the sundial, three-fifty by my watch. Isn't that something now?"

"It's wonderful," said Ravelin earnestly.

"It's the loveliest thing I've ever seen," chirped Iugenae.

Ravelin looked around the ranch, sighed wistfully. "We hate to leave, but I think we must be returning home."

"It's been a wonderful day, Lamster Ullward," said Ted. "A wonderful lunch, and we enjoyed seeing your ranch."

"You'll have to come out again," invited Ullward. "I always enjoy company."

He led them into the dining room, through the living room-bedroom to the door. The Seehoe family took a last look across the spacious interior, pulled on their mantles, stepped into their run-shoes, made their farewells. Ullward slid back the door. The Seehoes looked out, waited till a gap appeared in the traffic. They waved good-by, pulled the hoods over their heads, stepped out into the corridor.

The run-shoes spun them toward their home, selecting the appropriate turnings, sliding automatically into the correct lift and drop-pits. Deflection fields twisted them through the throngs. Like the Seehoes, everyone wore mantle and hood of filmy reflective stuff to safeguard privacy. The illusion-pane along the ceiling of the corridor presented a view of towers dwindling up into a cheerful blue sky, as if the pedestrian were moving along one of the windy upper passages.

The Seehoes approached their home. Two hundred yards away, they angled over to the wall. If the flow of traffic carried them past, they would be forced to circle the block and make another attempt to enter. Their door slid open as they spun near; they ducked into the opening, swinging around on a metal grab-bar.

They removed their mantles and run-shoes, sliding skillfully past each other. Iugenae pivoted into the bathroom and there was room for both Ted and Ravelin to sit down. The house was rather small for the three of them; they could well have used another twelve square feet, but rather than pay exorbitant rent, they preferred to save the money with an eye toward Iugenae's future.

Ted sighed in satisfaction, stretching his legs luxuriously under Ravelin's chair. "Ullward's ranch notwithstanding, it's nice to be home."

Iugenae backed out of the bathroom.

Ravelin looked up. "It's time for your pill, dear."

Iugenae screwed up her face. "Oh, Mama! Why do I have to take pills? I feel perfectly well."

"They're good for you, dear."

Iugenae sullenly took a pill from the dispenser. "Runy says you make us take pills to keep us from growing up."

Ted and Ravelin exchanged glances.

"Just take your pill," said Ravelin, "and never mind what Runy says."

"But how is it that I'm 38 and Ermara Burk's only 32 and she's got a figure and I'm like a slat?"

"No arguments, dear. Take your pill."

Ted jumped to his feet. "Here, Babykin, sit down."

Iugenae protested, but Ted held up his hand. "I'll sit in the niche. I've got a few calls that I have to make."

He sidled past Ravelin, seated himself in the niche in front of the communication screen. The illusion-pane behind him was custom-built—Ravelin, in fact, had designed it herself. It simulated a merry little bandit's den, the walls draped in red and yellow silk, a bowl of fruit on the rustic table, a guitar on the bench, a copper teakettle simmering on the countertop stove. The pane had been rather expensive, but when anyone communicated with the Seehoes, it was the first thing they saw, and here the house-proud Ravelin had refused to stint.

Before Ted could make his call, the signal light flashed. He answered; the screen opened to display his friend Loren Aigle, apparently sitting in an airy arched rotunda, against a background of fleecy clouds—an illusion which Ravelin had instantly recognized as an inexpensive stock effect.

Loren and Elme, his wife, were anxious to hear of the Seehoes' visit to the Ullward ranch. Ted described the afternoon in detail. "Space, space and more space! Isolation pure and simple! Absolute privacy! You can hardly imagine it! A fortune in illusion-panes."

"Nice," said Loren Aigle. "I'll tell you one you'll find hard to believe. Today I registered a whole planet to a man." Loren worked in the Certification Bureau of the Extraterrestrial Properties Agency.

Ted was puzzled and uncomprehending. "A whole planet? How so?"

Loren explained. "He's a freelance spaceman. Still a few left."

"But what's he planning to do with an entire planet?"

"Live there, he claims."

"Alone?"

Loren nodded. "I had quite a chat with him. Earth is all very well, he says, but he prefers the privacy of his own planet. Can you imagine that?"

"Frankly, no! I can't imagine the fourth dimension either. What a marvel, though!"

The conversation ended and the screen faded. Ted swung around to his wife. "Did you hear that?"

Ravelin nodded; she had heard but not heeded. She was reading the menu supplied by the catering firm to which they subscribed. "We won't want anything heavy after that lunch. They've got simulated synthetic algae again."

Ted grunted. "It's never as good as the genuine synthetic."

"But it's cheaper and we've all had an enormous lunch."

"Don't worry about me, Mom!" sang Iugenae. "I'm going out with Runy."

"Oh, you are, are you? And where are you going, may I ask?"

"A ride around the world. We're catching the seven o'clock shuttle, so I've got to hurry."

"Come right home afterward," said Ravelin severely. "Don't go anywhere else."

"For heaven's sake, Mother, you'd think I was going to elope or something."

"Mind what I say, Miss Puss. I was a girl once myself. Have you taken your medicine?"

"Yes, I've taken my medicine."

Iugenae departed; Ted slipped back into the niche. "Who are you calling now?" asked Ravelin.

"Lamster Ullward. I want to thank him for going to so much trouble for us."

Ravelin agreed that an algae-and-margarine call was no more than polite.

Ted called, expressed his thanks, then—almost as an afterthought—chanced to mention the man who owned a planet.

"An entire planet?" inquired Ullward. "It must be inhabited."

"No, I understand not, Lamster Ullward. Think of it! Think of the privacy!"

"Privacy!" exclaimed Ullward bluffly. "My dear fellow, what do you call this?"

"Oh, naturally, Lamster Ullward—you have a real showplace."

"The planet must be very primitive," Ullward reflected. "An engaging idea, of course—if you like that kind of thing. Who is this man?"

"I don't know, Lamster Ullward. I could find out, if you like."

"No, no, don't bother. I'm not particularly interested. Just an idle thought." Ullward laughed his hearty laugh. "Poor man. Probably lives in a dome."

"That's possible, of course, Lamster Ullward. Well, thanks again, and good night."

The spaceman's name was Kennes Mail. He was short and thin, tough as synthetic herring, brown as toasted yeast. He had a close-cropped pad of gray hair, a keen, if ingenuous, blue gaze. He showed a courteous interest in Ullward's ranch, but Ullward thought his recurrent use of the word "clever" rather tactless.

As they returned to the house, Ullward paused to admire his oak tree.

"It's absolutely genuine, Lamster Mail! A living tree, survival of past ages! Do you have trees as fine as that on your planet?"

Kennes Mail smiled. "Lamster Ullward, that's just a shrub. Let's sit somewhere and I'll show you photographs."

Ullward had already mentioned his interest in acquiring extraterrestrial property; Mail, admitting that he needed money, had given him to understand that some sort of deal might be arranged. They sat at a table; Mail opened his case. Ullward switched on the wallscreen.

"First I'll show you a map," said Mail. He selected a rod, dropped it into the table socket. On the wall appeared a world projection: oceans, an enormous equatorial land-mass named Gaea; the smaller sub-continents Atalanta, Persephone, Alcyone. A box of descriptive information read:

MAIL'S PLANET

Claim registered and endorsed at Extraterrestrial Properties Agency

Surface area:	.87 Earth normal
Gravity:	.93 Earth normal
Diurnal rotation:	22.15 Earth hours
Annual revolution:	2.97 Earth years
Atmosphere:	Invigorating
Climate:	Salubrious
Noxious conditions and influences:	None
Population:	1

Mail pointed to a spot on the eastern shore of Gaea. "I live here. Just got a rough camp at present. I need money to do a bit better for myself. I'm willing to lease off one of the smaller continents, or, if you prefer, a section of Gaea, say from Murky Mountains west to the ocean."

Ullward, with a cheerful smile, shook his head. "No sections for me, Lamster Mail. I want to buy the world outright. You set your price; if it's within reason, I'll write a check."

Mail glanced at him sidewise.

"You haven't even seen the photographs."

"True." In a businesslike voice, Ullward said, "By all means, the photographs."

Mail touched the projection button. Landscapes of an unfamiliar wild beauty appeared on the screen. There were mountain crags and roaring rivers, snow-powdered forests, ocean dawns and prairie sunsets, green hillsides, meadows spattered with blossoms, beaches white as milk.

"Very pleasant," said Ullward. "Quite nice." He pulled out his checkbook. "What's your price?"

Mail chuckled and shook his head. "I won't sell. I'm willing to lease off a section—providing my price is met and my rules are agreed to."

Ullward sat with compressed lips. He gave his head a quick little jerk. Mail started to rise to his feet.

"No, no," said Ullward hastily. "I was merely thinking . . . Let's look at the map again."

Mail returned the map to the screen. Ullward made careful inspection of the various continents, inquired as to physiography, climate, flora and fauna.

Finally he made his decision. "I'll lease Gaea."

"No, Lamster Ullward!" declared Mail. "I'm reserving this entire area—from Murky Mountains and the Calliope River east. This western section is open. It's maybe a little smaller than Atalanta or Persephone, but the climate is warmer."

"There aren't any mountains on the western section," Ullward protested. "Only these insignificant Rock Castle Crags."

"They're not so insignificant," said Mail. "You've also got the Purple Bird Hills, and down here in the south is Mount Cairasco —a live volcano. What more do you need?"

Ullward glanced across his ranch. "I'm in the habit of thinking big."

"West Gaea is a pretty big chunk of property."

"Very well," said Ullward. "What are your terms?"

"So far as money goes, I'm not greedy," Mail said. "For a twenty-year lease: two hundred thousand a year, the first five years in advance."

Ullward made a startled protest. "Great guns, Lamster Mail! That's almost half my income!"

Mail shrugged. "I'm not trying to get rich. I want to build a lodge for myself. It costs money. If you can't afford it, I'll have to speak to someone who can."

Ullward said in a nettled voice, "I can afford it, certainly—but my entire ranch here cost less than a million."

"Well, either you want it or you don't," said Mail. "I'll tell you my rules, then you can make up your mind."

"What rules?" demanded Ullward, his face growing red.

"They're simple and their only purpose is to maintain privacy for both of us. First, you have to stay on your own property. No excursions hither and yon on my property. Second, no subleasing. Third, no residents except yourself, your family and your servants. I don't want any artists' colony springing up, nor any wild noisy resort atmosphere. Naturally you're entitled to bring out your guests, but they've got to keep to your property just like yourself."

He looked sidewise at Ullward's glum face. "I'm not trying to be tough, Lamster Ullward. Good fences make good neighbors, and it's better that we have the understanding now than hard words and beam-gun evictions later."

"Let me see the photographs again," said Ullward. "Show me West Gaea."

He looked, heaved a deep sigh. "Very well. I agree."

The construction crew had departed. Ullward was alone on West Gaea. He walked around the new lodge, taking deep breaths of pure quiet air, thrilling to the absolute solitude and privacy. The lodge had cost a fortune, but how many other people of Earth owned—leased, rather—anything to compare with this?

He walked out on the front terrace, gazed proudly across miles —genuine unsimulated miles—of landscape. For his home site, he had selected a shelf in the foothills of the Ullward Range (as he had renamed the Purple Bird Hills). In front spread a great golden savannah dotted with blue-green trees; behind rose a tall gray cliff.

A stream rushed down a cleft in the rock, leaping, splashing, cooling the air, finally flowing into a beautiful clear pool, beside which Ullward had erected a cabana of red, green and brown plastic. At the base of the cliff and in crevices grew clumps of spiky blue cactus, lush green bushes covered with red trumpet-flowers, a thick-leafed white plant holding up a stalk clustered with white bubbles.

Solitude! The real thing! No thumping of factories, no roar of traffic two feet from one's bed. One arm outstretched, the other pressed to his chest, Ullward performed a stately little jig of triumph on the terrace. Had he been able, he might have turned a cartwheel. When a person has complete privacy, absolutely nothing is forbidden!

Ullward took a final turn up and down the terrace, made a last appreciative survey of the horizon. The sun was sinking through banks of fire-fringed clouds. Marvelous depth of color, a tonal brilliance to be matched only in the very best illusion-panes!

He entered the lodge, made a selection from the nutrition locker. After a leisurely meal, he returned to the lounge. He stood thinking for a moment, then went out upon the terrace, strolled up and down. Wonderful! The night was full of stars, hanging like blurred white lamps, almost as he had always imagined them.

After ten minutes of admiring the stars, he returned into the lodge. Now what? The wall-screen, with its assortment of recorded programs. Snug and comfortable, Ullward watched the performance of a recent musical comedy.

Real luxury, he told himself. Pity he couldn't invite his friends out to spend the evening. Unfortunately impossible, considering the inconvenient duration of the trip between Mail's Planet and Earth. However—only three days until the arrival of his first guest. She was Elf Intry, a young woman who had been more than friendly with Ullward on Earth. When Elf arrived, Ullward would broach a subject which he had been mulling over for several months—indeed, ever since he had first learned of Mail's Planet.

Elf Intry arrived early in the afternoon, coming down to Mail's Planet in a capsule discharged from the weekly Outer Ring Express packet. A woman of normally good disposition, she greeted Ullward in a seethe of indignation. "Just who is that brute around the other side of the planet? I thought you had absolute privacy here!"

"That's just old Mail," said Ullward evasively. "What's wrong?"

"The fool on the packet set me the wrong coordinates and the capsule came down on a beach. I noticed a house and then I saw a naked man jumping rope behind some bushes. I thought it was you, of course. I went over and said 'Boo!' You should have *heard* the language he used!" She shook her head. "I don't see why you allow such a boor on your planet."

The buzzer on the communication screen sounded. "That's Mail now," said Ullward. "You wait here. I'll tell him how to speak to *my* guests!"

He presently returned to the terrace. Elf came over to him, kissed his nose. "Ully, you're pale with rage! I hope you didn't lose your temper."

"No," said Ullward. "We merely—well, we had an understanding. Come along, look over the property."

He took Elf around to the back, pointing out the swimming pool, the waterfall, the mass of rock above. "You won't see that effect on any illusion-panel! That's genuine rock!"

"Lovely, Ully. Very nice. The color might be just a trifle darker, though. Rock doesn't look like that."

"No?" Ullward inspected the cliff more critically. "Well, I can't do anything about it. How about the privacy?"

"Wonderful! It's so quiet, it's almost eerie!"

"Eerie?" Ullward looked around the landscape. "It hadn't occurred to me."

"You're not sensitive to these things, Ully. Still, it's very nice, if you can tolerate that unpleasant creature Mail so close."

"Close?" protested Ullward. "He's on the other side of the continent!"

"True," said Elf. "It's all relative, I suppose. How long do you expect to stay out here?"

"That depends. Come along inside. I want to talk with you."

He seated her in a comfortable chair, brought her a globe of Gluco-Fructoid Nectar. For himself, he mixed ethyl alcohol, water, a few drops of Haig's Oldtime Esters.

"Elf, where do you stand in the reproduction list?"

She raised her fine eyebrows, shook her head. "So far down, I've lost count. Fifty or sixty billion."

"I'm down thirty-seven billion. It's one reason I bought this place. Waiting list, piffle! Nobody stops Bruham Ullward's breeding on his own planet!"

Elf pursed her lips, shook her head sadly. "It won't work, Ully."

"And why not?"

"You can't take the children back to Earth. The list would keep them out."

"True, but think of living here, surrounded by children. All the children you wanted! And utter privacy to boot! What more could you ask for?"

Elf sighed. "You fabricate a beautiful illusion-pane, Ully. But I think not. I love the privacy and solitude—but I thought there'd be more people to be private from."

The Outer Ring Express packet came past four days later. Elf kissed Ullward good-by. "It's simply exquisite here, Ully. The solitude is so magnificent, it gives me gooseflesh. I've had a wonderful visit." She climbed into the capsule. "See you on Earth."

"Just a minute," said Ullward suddenly. "I want you to post a letter or two for me."

"Hurry. I've only got twenty minutes."

Ullward was back in ten minutes. "Invitations," he told her breathlessly. "Friends."

"Right." She kissed his nose. "Good-by, Ully." She slammed the port; the capsule rushed away, whirling up to meet the packet.

The new guests arrived three weeks later: Frobisher Worbeck,

Liornetta Stobart, Harris and Hyla Cabe, Ted and Ravelin and Iugenae Seehoe, Juvenal Aquister and his son Runy.

Ullward, brown from long days of lazing in the sun, greeted them with great enthusiasm. "Welcome to my little retreat! Wonderful to see you all! Frobisher, you pinkcheeked rascal! And Iugenae! Prettier than ever! Be careful, Ravelin—I've got my eye on your daughter! But Runy's here, guess I'm out of the picture! Liornetta, damned glad you could make it! And Ted! Great to see you, old chap! This is all your doing, you know! Harris, Hyla, Juvenal—come on up! We'll have a drink, a drink, a drink!"

Running from one to the other, patting arms, herding the slow-moving Frobisher Worbeck, he conducted his guests up the slope to the terrace. Here they turned to survey the panorama. Ullward listened to their remarks, mouth pursed against a grin of gratification.

"Magnificent!"

"Grand!"

"Absolutely genuine!"

"The sky is so far away, it frightens me!"

"The sunlight's so pure!"

"The genuine thing's always best, isn't it?"

Runy said a trifle wistfully, "I thought you were on a beach, Lamster Ullward."

"Beach? This is mountain country, Runy. Land of the wide open spaces! Look out over that plain!"

Liornetta Stobart patted Runy's shoulder. "Not every planet has beaches, Runy. The secret of happiness is to be content with what one has."

Ullward laughed gayly. "Oh, I've got beaches, never fear for that! There's a fine beach—ha, ha—five hundred miles due west. Every step Ullward domain!"

"Can we go?" asked Iugenae excitedly. "Can we go, Lamster Ullward?"

"We certainly can! That shed down the slope is headquarters for the Ullward Airlines. We'll fly to the beach, swim in Ullward Ocean! But now refreshment! After that crowded capsule, your throats must be like paper!"

"It wasn't too crowded," said Ravelin Seehoe. "There were only nine of us." She looked critically up at the cliff. "If that were an illusion-pane, I'd consider it grotesque."

"My dear Ravelin!" cried Ullward. "It's impressive! Magnificent!"

"All of that," agreed Frobisher Worbeck, a tall sturdy man, whitehaired, red-jowled, with a blue benevolent gaze. "And now, Bruham, what about those drinks?"

"Of course! Ted, I know you of old. Will you tend bar? Here's the alcohol, here's water, here are the esters. Now, you two," Ullward called to Runy and Iugenae. "How about some nice cold soda pop?"

"What kind is there?" asked Runy.

"All kinds, all flavors. This is Ullward's Retreat! We've got methylamyl glutamine, cycloprodacterol phosphate, metathiobromine-4-glycocitrose . . ."

Runy and Iugenae expressed their preferences; Ullward brought the globes, then hurried to arrange tables and chairs for the adults. Presently everyone was comfortable and relaxed.

Iugenae whispered to Ravelin, who smiled and nodded indulgently. "Lamster Ullward, you remember the beautiful oak leaf you gave Iugenae?"

"Of course I do."

"It's still as fresh and green as ever. I wonder if Iugenae might have a leaf or two from some of these other trees?"

"My dear Ravelin!" Ullward roared with laughter. "She can have an entire tree!"

"Oh, Mother! Can—"

"Iugenae, don't be ridiculous!" snapped Ted. "How could we get it home? Where would we plant the thing? In the bathroom?"

Ravelin said, "You and Runy find some nice leaves, but don't wander too far."

"No, Mother." She beckoned to Runy. "Come along, dope. Bring a basket."

The others of the party gazed out over the plain. "A beautiful view, Ullward," said Frobisher Worbeck. "How far does your property extend?"

"Five hundred miles west to the ocean, six hundred miles east to the mountains, eleven hundred miles north and two hundred miles south."

Worbeck shook his head solemnly. "Nice. A pity you couldn't get the whole planet. Then you'd have real privacy!"

"I tried, of course," said Ullward. "The owner refused to consider the idea."

"A pity."

Ullward brought out a map. "However, as you see, I have a fine volcano, a number of excellent rivers, a mountain range, and down here on the delta of Cinnamon River an absolutely miasmic swamp."

Ravelin pointed to the ocean. "Why, it's Lonesome Ocean! I thought the name was Ullward Ocean."

Ullward laughed uncomfortably. "Just a figure of speech—so to speak. My rights extend ten miles. More than enough for swimming purposes."

"No freedom of the seas here, eh, Lamster Ullward?" laughed Harris Cabe.

"Not exactly," confessed Ullward.

"A pity," said Frobisher Worbeck.

Hyla Cabe pointed to the map. "Look at these wonderful mountain ranges! The Magnificent Mountains! And over here—the Elysian Gardens! I'd love to see them, Lamster Ullward."

Ullward shook his head in embarrassment. "Impossible, I'm afraid. They're not on my property. I haven't even seen them myself."

His guests stared at him in astonishment. "But surely—"

"It's an atom-welded contract with Lamster Mail," Ullward explained. "He stays on his property, I stay on mine. In this way, our privacy is secure."

"Look," Hyla Cabe said aside to Ravelin. "The Unimaginable Caverns! Doesn't it make you simply wild not to be able to see them?"

Acquister said hurriedly, "It's a pleasure to sit here and just breathe this wonderful fresh air. No noise, no crowds, no bustle or hurry."

The party drank and chatted and basked in the sunshine until late afternoon. Enlisting the aid of Ravelin Seehoe and Hyla Cabe, Ullward set out a simple meal of yeast pellets, processed protein, thick slices of algae crunch.

"No animal flesh, cooked vegetation?" questioned Worbeck curiously.

"Tried them the first day," said Ullward. "Revolting. Sick for a week."

After dinner, the guests watched a comic melodrama on the wallscreen. Then Ullward showed them to their various cubicles, and after a few minutes of badinage and calling back and forth, the lodge became quiet.

Next day, Ullward ordered his guests into their bathing suits. "We're off to the beach, we'll gambol on the sand, we'll frolic in the surf of Lonesome Ullward Ocean!"

The guests piled happily into the air-car. Ullward counted heads. "All aboard! We're off!"

They rose and flew west, first low over the plain, then high into the air, to obtain a panoramic view of the Rock Castle Crags.

"The tallest peak—there to the north—is almost ten thousand feet high. Notice how it juts up, just imagine the mass! Solid rock! How'd you like that dropped on your toe, Runy? Not so good, eh? In a moment, we'll see a precipice over a thousand feet straight up and down. There—now! Isn't that remarkable?"

"Certainly impressive," agreed Ted.

"What those Magnificent Mountains must be like!" said Harris Cabe with a wry laugh.

"How tall are they, Lamster Ullward?" inquired Liornetta Stobart.

"What? Which?"

"The Magnificent Mountains."

"I don't know for sure. Thirty or forty thousand feet, I suppose."

"What a marvelous sight they must be!" said Frobisher Worbeck. "Probably make these look like foothills."

"These are beautiful too," Hyla Cabe put in hastily.

"Oh, naturally," said Frobisher Worbeck. "A damned fine sight! You're a lucky man, Bruham!"

Ullward laughed shortly, turned the air-car west. They flew across a rolling forested plain and presently Lonesome Ocean gleamed in the distance. Ullward slanted down, landed the air-car on the beach, and the party alighted.

The day was warm, the sun hot. A fresh wind blew in from the ocean. The surf broke upon the sand in massive roaring billows.

The party stood appraising the scene. Ullward swung his arms. "Well, who's for it? Don't wait to be invited! We've got the whole ocean to ourselves!"

Ravelin said, "It's so rough! Look how that water crashes down!"

Liornetta Stobart turned away with a shake of her head. "Illusion-pane surf is always so gentle. This could lift you right up and give you a good shaking!"

"I expected nothing quite so vehement," Harris Cabe admitted.

Ravelin beckoned to Iugenae. "You keep well away, Miss Puss. I don't want you swept out to sea. You'd find it Lonesome Ocean indeed!"

Runy approached the water, waded gingerly into a sheet of retreating foam. A comber thrashed down at him and he danced quickly back up the shore.

"The water's cold," he reported.

Ullward poised himself. "Well, here goes! I'll show you how it's done!" He trotted forward, stopped short, then flung himself into the face of a great white comber.

The party on the beach watched.

"Where is he?" asked Hyla Cabe.

Iugenae pointed. "I saw part of him out there. A leg, or an arm."

"There he is!" cried Ted. "Woof! Another one's caught him. I suppose some people might consider it sport . . ."

Ullward staggered to his feet, lurched through the retreating wash to shore. "Hah! Great! Invigorating! Ted! Harris! Juvenal! Take a go at it!"

Harris shook his head. "I don't think I'll try it today, Bruham."

"The next time for me too," said Juvenal Aquister. "Perhaps it won't be so rough."

"But don't let us stop you!" urged Ted. "You swim as long as you like. We'll wait here for you."

"Oh, I've had enough for now," said Ullward. "Excuse me while I change."

When Ullward returned, he found his guests seated in the air-car. "Hello! Everyone ready to go?"

"It's hot in the sun," explained Liornetta, "and we thought we'd enjoy the view better from inside."

"When you look through the glass, it's almost like an illusion-pane," said Iugenae.

"Oh, I see. Well, perhaps you're ready to visit other parts of the Ullward domain?"

The proposal met with approval; Ullward took the air-car into the air. "We can fly north over the pine woods, south over Mount Cairasco, which unfortunately isn't erupting just now."

"Anywhere you like, Lamster Ullward," said Frobisher Worbeck. "No doubt it's all beautiful."

Ullward considered the varied attractions of his leasehold. "Well, first to the Cinnamon Swamp."

For two hours they flew, over the swamp, across the smoking crater of Mount Cairasco, east to the edge of Murky Mountains, along Calliope River to its source in Goldenleaf Lake. Ullward pointed out noteworthy views, interesting aspects. Behind him, the murmurs of admiration dwindled and finally died.

"Had enough?" Ullward called back gayly. "Can't see half a continent in one day! Shall we save some for tomorrow?"

There was a moment's stillness. Then Liornetta Stobart said, "Lamster Ullward, we're simply dying for a peek at the Magnificent Mountains. I wonder—do you think we could slip over for a quick look? I'm sure Lamster Mail wouldn't really mind."

Ullward shook his head with a rather stiff smile. "He's made me agree to a very definite set of rules. I've already had one brush with him."

"How could he possibly find out?" asked Juvenal Aquister.

"He probably wouldn't find out," said Ullward, "but—"

"It's a damned shame for him to lock you off into this drab little peninsula!" Frobisher Worbeck said indignantly.

"Please, Lamster Ullward," Iugenae wheedled.

"Oh, very well," Ullward said recklessly.

He turned the air-car east. The Murky Mountains passed below. The party peered from the windows, exclaiming at the marvels of the forbidden landscape.

"How far are the Magnificent Mountains?" asked Ted.

"Not far. Another thousand miles."

"Why are you hugging the ground?" asked Frobisher Worbeck. "Up in the air, man! Let's see the countryside!"

Ullward hesitated. Mail was probably asleep. And, in the last analysis, he really had no right to forbid an innocent little—

"Lamster Ullward," called Runy, "there's an air-car right behind us."

The air-car drew up level. Kennes Mail's blue eyes met Ullward's across the gap. He motioned Ullward down.

Ullward compressed his mouth, swung the air-car down. From
behind him came murmurs of sympathy and outrage.

Below was a dark pine forest; Ullward set down in a pretty
little glade. Mail landed nearby, jumped to the ground, signaled
to Ullward. The two men walked to the side. The guests murmured together and shook their heads.

Ullward presently returned to the air-car. "Everybody please
get in," he said crisply.

They rose into the air and flew west. "What did the chap have
to say for himself?" queried Worbeck.

Ullward chewed at his lips. "Not too much. Wanted to know
if I'd lost the way. I told him one or two things. Reached an understanding . . ." His voice dwindled, then rose in a burst of
cheerfulness. "We'll have a party back at the lodge. What do
we care for Mail and his confounded mountains?"

"That's the spirit, Bruham!" cried Frobisher Worbeck.

Both Ted and Ullward tended bar during the evening. Either
one or the other mingled rather more alcohol to rather less esters
into the drinks than standard practice recommended. As a result,
the party became quite loud and gay. Ullward damned Mail's
interfering habits; Worbeck explored six thousand years of
common law in an effort to prove Mail a domineering tyrant;
the women giggled; Iugenae and Runy watched cynically, then
presently went off to attend to their own affairs.

In the morning, the group slept late. Ullward finally tottered
out on the terrace, to be joined one at a time by the others. Runy
and Iugenae were missing.

"Young rascals," groaned Worbeck. "If they're lost, they'll have
to find their own way back. No search parties for me."

At noon, Runy and Iugenae returned in Ullward's air-car.

"Good heavens," shrieked Ravelin. "Iugenae, come here this instant! Where have you been?"

Juvenal Aquister surveyed Runy sternly. "Have you lost your mind, taking Lamster Ullward's air-car without his permission?"

"I asked him last night," Runy declared indignantly. "He said yes, take anything except the volcano because that's where he slept when his feet got cold, and the swamp because that's where he dropped his empty containers."

"Regardless," said Juvenal in disgust, "you should have had better sense. Where have you been?"

Runy fidgeted. Iugenae said, "Well, we went south for a while, then turned and went east—I think it was east. We thought if we flew low, Lamster Mail wouldn't see us. So we flew low, through the mountains, and pretty soon we came to an ocean. We went along the beach and came to a house. We landed to see who lived there, but nobody was home."

Ullward stifled a groan.

"What would anyone want with a pen of birds?" asked Runy.

"Birds? What birds? Where?"

"At the house. There was a pen with a lot of big birds, but they kind of got loose while we were looking at them and all flew away."

"Anyway," Iugenae continued briskly, "we decided it was Lamster Mail's house, so we wrote a note, telling what everybody thinks of him and pinned it to his door."

Ullward rubbed his forehead. "Is that all?"

"Well, practically all." Iugenae became diffident. She looked at Runy and the two of them giggled nervously.

"There's more?" yelled Ullward. "What, in heaven's name?"

"Nothing very much," said Iugenae, following a crack in the terrace with her toe. "We put a booby-trap over the door—just a bucket of water. Then we came home."

The screen buzzer sounded from inside the lodge. Everybody looked at Ullward. Ullward heaved a deep sigh, rose to his feet, went inside.

* * *

That very afternoon, the Outer Ring Express packet was due to pass the junction point. Frobisher Worbeck felt sudden and acute qualms of conscience for the neglect his business suffered while he dawdled away hours in the idle enjoyment.

"But my dear old chap!" exclaimed Ullward. "Relaxation is good for you!"

True, agreed Frobisher Worbeck, if one could make himself oblivious to the possibility of fiasco through the carelessness of underlings. Much as he deplored the necessity, in spite of his inclination to loiter for weeks, he felt impelled to leave—and not a minute later than that very afternoon.

Others of the group likewise remembered important business which they had to see to, and those remaining felt it would be a shame and an imposition to send up the capsule half-empty and likewise decided to return.

Ullward's arguments met unyielding walls of obstinacy. Rather glumly, he went down to the capsule to bid his guests farewell. As they climbed through the port, they expressed their parting thanks:

"Bruham, it's been absolutely marvelous!"

"You'll never know how we've enjoyed this outing, Lamster Ullward!"

"The air, the space, the privacy—I'll never forget!"

"It was the most, to say the least."

The port thumped into its socket. Ullward stood back, waving rather uncertainly.

Ted Seehoe reached to press the Active button. Ullward sprang forward, pounded on the port.

"Wait!" he bellowed. "A few things I've got to attend to! I'm coming with you!"

"Come in, come in," said Ullward heartily, opening the door to three of his friends: Coble and his wife Heulia Sansom, and Coble's young, pretty cousin Landine. "Glad to see you!"

"And we're glad to come! We've heard so much of your wonderful ranch, we've been on pins and needles all day!"

"Oh, come now! It's not so marvelous as all that!"

"Not to you, perhaps—you live here!"

Ullward smiled. "Well, I must say I live here and still like it. Would you like to have lunch, or perhaps you'd prefer to walk around for a few minutes? I've just finished making a few changes, but I'm happy to say everything is in order."

"Can we just take a look?"

"Of course. Come over here. Stand just so. Now—are you ready?"

"Ready."

Ullward snapped the wall back.

"Ooh!" breathed Landine. "Isn't it beautiful!"

"The space, the open feeling!"

"Look, a tree! What a wonderful simulation!"

"That's no simulation," said Ullward. "That's a genuine tree!"

"Lamster Ullward, are you telling the truth?"

"I certainly am. I never tell lies to a lovely young lady. Come along, over this way."

"Lamster Ullward, that cliff is so convincing, it frightens me."

Ullward grinned. "It's a good job." He signaled a halt. "Now —turn around."

The group turned. They looked out across a great golden savannah, dotted with groves of blue-green trees. A rustic lodge commanded the view, the door being the opening into Ullward's living room.

The group stood in silent admiration. Then Heulia sighed. "Space. Pure space."

"I'd swear I was looking miles," said Coble.

Ullward smiled, a trifle wistfully. "Glad you like my little retreat. Now what about lunch? Genuine algae!"

THE MAN WHO LOVED
THE FAIOLI

Roger Zelazny

When Harry Harrison asked me what shorter piece of mine I might like to see in an Authors' Choice collection, "The Man Who Loved the Faioli" came immediately to scratch at the doors of my mind. I am quite fond of it, and there is a story behind the story.

This particular tale came into existence in a reverse-sequence sort of way, just the opposite from what the people who read it in its original magazine appearance probably thought had occurred. What happened was that Fred Pohl, who was then editing Galaxy, purchased a piece of artwork to use as a cover for the magazine: a bleak setting, a valley full of bones with multi-armed robots tromping through it like tired Sicilian grape-crushers, a prominent dark blue sun hanging in an eerie sky. He showed it to me and asked whether I might write him a story to go behind it. I agreed, although I had no idea at the time as to what I was going to do with it.

I propped the painting on a table in my living room, where I could not fail to see it each time I passed through. A couple days went by and nothing recommended itself. It even accompanied me through a memorable New Year's celebration, where I tested whether a systematic derangement of the senses in its presence would serve to throw the switch on the story machine in my head. The following day I thought a lot about graveyards.

It was not until that evening, while listening to the song, "We'll Sing in the Sunshine," that something clicked. It was the line, ". . . . But though I'll never love you, I'll stay with you one year" that did whatever was done. The graveyard world, the characters, the entire situation were suddenly all together—in short, the whole story. I sat down and wrote it in a matter of hours; Fred bought it and it subsequently appeared as planned.

I suppose I could stop right there and satisfy the anecdote-minded, or those who enjoy knowing how these things sometimes come about. But there is a little more to it.

Just the other day I received a copy of the French Galaxie, with a fresh cover illustrating—yes—"L'Homme Qui Aimait une Faioli." It showed a female form with a cameo profile, wrapped in pastel wings which extended on before her, sparkling hair drifting out behind.

I paused a moment to think about both of the illustrations and the story itself.

Most writers will, I believe, agree that there is generally a gap between the way they see the goings-on in their tales and the way an illustrator does them up, the essence necessarily preceding the existence with an unavoidable slippage between. It is often quite distressing. With the cover coming first for "The Man Who Loved the Faioli," however, it was one of the few instances where I felt things to be perfectly meshed—while as much as I enjoyed the French illustration as an illustration, it did not give me the same feeling of verisimilitude.

Thus was it brought home to me how an artist, given a story to read and illustrate, must feel when he has finished his work. For him, it would seem, the story and the artwork should always mesh more completely than they do for the writer. He draws and paints what he sees and feels in the story, just as I wrote what I came to see and feel in the first illustration.

So, from the two covers—before and after—did this story grant me a Janus-like view of a notion's progress, emerging from and returning to artwork, along with the only nonsexual explanation

I have ever come across as to why illustrators tend to look more satisfied than writers.

As for the story itself, now standing before you bereft of either study, it doesn't really matter that it began in an unusual fashion, that I once sat regarding the Valley of Bones and muttering, "Are those really Zoromes coming my way? Yes. No. Yes. Damn!" The story is itself, whole and entire, and I like it in, of, by and for itself, which is why I chose it for this volume.

And unlike my cat and many things that I have written, I know where this one came from. Sort of.

—Roger Zelazny

It is the story of John Auden and the Faioli, and no one knows it better than I. Listen—

It happened on that evening, as he strolled (for there was no reason not to stroll) in his favorite places in the whole world, that he saw the Faioli near the Canyon of the Dead, seated on a rock, her wings of light flickering, flickering, flickering and then gone, until it appeared that a human girl was sitting there, dressed all in white and weeping, with long black tresses coiled about her waist.

He approached her through the terrible light from the dying, half-dead sun, in which human eyes could not distinguish distances nor grasp perspectives properly (though his could), and he laid his right hand upon her shoulder and spoke a word of greeting and of comfort.

It was as if he did not exist, however. She continued to weep, streaking with silver her cheeks the color of snow or a bone. Her almond eyes looked forward as though they saw through him, and her long fingernails dug into the flesh of her palms, though no blood was drawn.

Then he knew that it was true, the things that are said of the Faioli—that they see only the living and never the dead, and that they are formed into the loveliest women in the entire universe. Being dead himself, John Auden debated the consequences of becoming a living man once again, for a time.

The Faioli were known to come to a man the month before his death—those rare men who still died—and to live with such a man for that final month of his existence, rendering to him every pleasure that it is possible for a human being to know, so that on the day when the kiss of death is delivered, which sucks the remaining life from his body, that man accepts it—no, seeks it!—with desire and with grace. For such is the power of the Faioli among all creatures that there is nothing more to be desired after such knowledge.

John Auden considered his life and his death, the conditions of the world upon which he stood, the nature of his stewardship and his curse and the Faioli—who was the loveliest creature he had seen in all of his four hundred thousand days of existence —and he touched the place beneath his left armpit which activated the necessary mechanism to make him live again.

The creature stiffened beneath his touch, for suddenly it was flesh, his touch, and flesh, warm and woman-filled, that he was touching, now that the sensations of life had returned to him. He knew that his touch had become the touch of a man once more.

"I said 'hello, and don't cry,'" he said, and her voice was like the breezes he had forgotten through all the trees that he had forgotten, with their moisture and their odors and their colors all brought back to him thus:

"From where do you come, man? You were not here a moment ago."

"From the Canyon of the Dead," he said.

"Let me touch your face." And he did, and she did.

"It is strange that I did not feel you approach."

"This is a strange world," he replied.

"That is true," she said. "You are the only living thing upon it." And he said, "What is your name?"

She said, "Call me Sythia," and he did.

"My name is John," he told her, "John Auden."

"I have come to be with you, to give you comfort and pleasure," she said, and he knew that the ritual was beginning.

"Why were you weeping when I found you?" he asked.

"Because I thought there was nothing upon this world, and I was so tired from my travels," she told him. "Do you live near here?"

"Not far away," he answered. "Not far away at all."

"Will you take me there? To the place where you live?"

"Yes."

And she rose and followed him into the Canyon of the Dead, where he made his home.

They descended and they descended, and all about them were the remains of people who once had lived. She did not seem to see these things, however, but kept her eyes fixed upon John's face and her hand upon his arm.

"Why do you call this place the Canyon of the Dead?" she asked him.

"Because they are all about us here, the dead," he replied.

"I feel nothing."

"I know."

They crossed through the Valley of the Bones, where millions of the dead from many races and worlds lay stacked all about them, and she did not see these things. She had come to the graveyard of all the worlds, but she did not realize this thing. She had encountered its tender, its keeper, and she did not know what he was, he who staggered beside her like a man drunken.

John Auden took her to his home—not really the place where he lived, but it would be now—and there he activated ancient circuits within the building within the mountain. In response light leaped forth from the walls, light he had never needed before, but now required.

The door slid shut behind them, and the temperature built up to a normal warmth. Fresh air circulated. He took it into his lungs and expelled it, glorying in the forgotten sensation. His heart beat within his breast, a red warm thing that reminded him of the pain and of the pleasure. For the first time in ages, he prepared a meal and fetched a bottle of wine from one of the deep, sealed lockers. How many others could have borne what he had borne?

None, perhaps.

She dined with him, toying with the food, sampling a bit of everything, eating very little. He, on the other hand, glutted himself fantastically, and they drank of the wine and were happy.

"This place is so strange," she said. "Where do you sleep?"

"I used to sleep in there," he told her, indicating a room he had almost forgotten; and they entered and he showed it to her, and she beckoned him toward the bed and the pleasures of her body.

That night he loved her, many times, with a desperation that burnt away the alcohol and pushed all of his life forward with something like a hunger, but more.

The following day, when the dying sun had splashed the Valley of the Bones with its pale, moonlike light, he awakened and she drew his head to her breast, not having slept herself, and she asked him, "What is the thing that moves you, John Auden? You are not like one of the men who live and who die, but you take life almost like one of the Faioli, squeezing from it everything that you can and pacing it at a tempo that bespeaks a sense of time no man should know. What are you?"

"I am one who knows," he said. "I am one who knows that the days of a man are numbered and one who covets their dispositions as he feels them draw to a close."

"You are strange," said Sythia. "Have I pleased you?"

"More than anything else I have ever known," he said.

And she sighed, and he found her lips once again.

They breakfasted, and that day they walked in the Valley of the Bones. He could not distinguish distances nor grasp perspectives properly, and she could not see anything that had been living and now was dead. So, of course, as they sat there on a shelf of stone, his arm about her shoulders, he pointed out to her the rocket which had just come down from out of the sky, and she squinted after his gesture. He indicated the robots, which had begun unloading the remains of the dead of many worlds from the hold of the ship, and she cocked her head to one side and stared ahead, but she did not really see what he was talking about.

Even when one of the robots lumbered up to him and held out the board containing the receipts and the stylus, and as he signed the receipt for the bodies received, she did not see or understand what it was that was occurring.

In the days that followed, his life took upon it a dreamlike quality, filled with the pleasure of Sythia and shot through with certain inevitable streaks of pain. Often, she saw him wince, and she asked him concerning his expressions.

And always he would laugh and say, "Pleasure and pain are near to one another," or some thing such as that.

And as the days wore on, she came to prepare the meals and to rub his shoulders and mix his drinks and to recite to him certain pieces of poetry he had somehow once come to love.

A month. A month, he knew, and it would come to an end. The Faioli, whatever they were, paid for the life that they took

with the pleasures of the flesh. They always knew when a man's
death was near at hand. And in this sense, they always gave
more than they received. The life was fleeing anyway, and they
enhanced it before they took it, away with them, to nourish themselves most likely, price of the things that they'd given.

John Auden knew that no Faioli in the entire universe had
ever met a man such as himself.

Sythia was mother-of-pearl, and her body was alternately cold
and warm to his caresses, and her mouth was a tiny flame, ig-
niting wherever it touched, with its teeth like needles and its
tongue like the heart of a flower. And so he came to know the
thing called love for the Faioli called Sythia.

Nothing must really happen beyond the loving. He knew
that she wanted him, to use him ultimately, and he was perhaps
the only man in the universe able to gull one of her kind. His was
the perfect defense against life and against death. Now that
he was human and alive, he often wept when he considered it.

He had more than a month to live.

He had maybe three or four.

This month, therefore, was a price he'd willingly pay for what
it was that the Faioli offered.

Sythia racked his body and drained from it every drop of
pleasure contained within his tired nerve cells. She turned him
into a flame, an iceberg, a little boy, an old man. When they were
together, his feelings were such that he considered the *consola-
mentum* as a thing he might really accept at the end of the month,
which was drawing near. Why not? He knew she had filled his
mind with her presence, on purpose. But what more did existence
hold for him? This creature from beyond the stars had brought
him every single thing a man could desire. She had baptized him
with passion and confirmed him with the quietude which follows
after. Perhaps the final oblivion of her final kiss was best after all.

He seized her and drew her to him. She did not understand
him, but she responded.

He loved her for it, and this was almost his end.

There is a thing called disease that battens upon all living things, and he had known it beyond the scope of all living men. She could not understand, woman-thing who had known only life.

So he never tried to tell her, though with each day the taste of her kisses grew stronger and saltier, and each seemed to him a strengthening shadow, darker and darker, stranger and heavier, of that one thing which he now knew he desired most.

And the day would come. And come it did.

He held her and caressed her, and the calendars of all his days fell about them.

He knew, as he abandoned himself to her ploys and the glories of her mouth, her breasts, that he had been ensnared, as had all men who had known them, by the power of the Faioli. Their strength was their weakness. They were the ultimate in Woman. By their frailty they begat the desire to please. He wanted to merge himself with the pale landscape of her body, to pass within the circles of her eyes and never depart.

He had lost, he knew. For as the days had vanished about him, he had weakened. He was barely able to scrawl his name upon the receipts proffered him by the robot who had lumbered toward him, crushing ribcages and cracking skulls with each terrific step. Briefly, he envied the thing. Sexless, passionless, totally devoted to duty. Before he dismissed it, he asked it, "What would you do if you had desire and you met with a thing that gave you all the things you wished for in the world?"

"I would—try to—keep it," it said, red lights blinking about its dome, before it turned and lumbered off, across the Great Graveyard.

"Yes," said John Auden aloud, "but this thing cannot be done."

Sythia did not understand him, and on that thirty-first day they returned to that place where he had lived for a month, and he felt the fear of death, strong, so strong, come upon him.

She was more exquisite than ever before, but he feared this final encounter.

"I love you," he said finally, for it was a thing he had never said before, and she kissed him.

"I know," she told him, "and your time is almost at hand, to love me completely. Before the final act of love, my John Auden, tell me a thing: What is it that sets you apart? Why is it that you know so much more of things-that-are-not-life than mortal man should know? How was it that you approached me on that first night without my knowing it?"

"It is because I am already dead," he told her. "Can't you see it when you look into my eyes?"

"I do not understand," she said.

"Kiss me and forget it," he told her. "It is better this way."

But she was curious and asked him (using the familiar for the first time), "How then dost thou achieve this balance between life and that-which-is-not-life, this thing which keeps thee conscious yet unliving?"

"There are controls set within this body I happen, unfortunately, to occupy. To touch this place beneath my left armpit will cause my lungs to cease their breathing and my heart to stop its beating. It will set into effect an installed electro-chemical system, like those my robots (invisible to you, I know) possess. This is my life within death. I asked for it because I feared oblivion. I volunteered to be gravekeeper to the universe, because in this place there are none to look upon me and be repelled by my deathlike appearance. This is why I am what I am. Kiss me and end it."

But having taken the form of woman, or perhaps being woman all along, the Faioli who was called Sythia was curious, and she said, "This place?" and she touched the spot beneath his left armpit.

With this he vanished from her sight, and with this also, he knew once again the icy logic that stood apart from emotion.   E

Because of this, he did not touch upon the critical spot once again.

Instead, he watched her as she sought for him about the place where he once had lived.

She checked into every closet and adytum, and when she could not discover a living man, she sobbed once, horribly, as she had on that night when first he had seen her. Then the wings flickered, flickered, weakly flickered, back into existence upon her back, and her face dissolved and her body slowly melted. The tower of sparks that stood before him then vanished, and later on that crazy night during which he could distinguish distances and grasp perspectives once again he began looking for her.

And that is the story of John Auden, the only man who ever loved a Faioli and lived (if you could call it that) to tell of it. No one knows it better than I.

No cure has ever been found. And I know that he walks the Canyon of the Dead and considers the bones, sometimes stops by the rock where he met her, blinks after the moist things that are not there, wonders at the judgment that he gave.

It is that way, and the moral may be that life (and perhaps love also) is stronger than that which it contains, but never that which contains it. But only a Faioli could tell you for sure, and they never come here any more.